*To Mary Ann*

## Acknowledgments

I would like my readers to know the assistance I received during the creation of this novel.

First I'd like to express my appreciation to Meghan Clark and Bridget Clark, along with Austin DiMartino and Michael DiMartino for the time they spent with me, in Yellowstone National Park, researching the story. Their creative thoughts and companionship was greatly appreciated. Thanks for the character ideas and helping me put the story in motion. I'm also grateful for Richard Chiaramonte's ongoing tutelage and leadership as he shared with me his familiarity with the rugged beauty of the Yellowstone area.

I am particularly grateful to Barry Horne for his continued support and first-rate editorial skills.

The title of this novel was borrowed from a quote of William Faulkner's. "**The Past is Never Dead**, it isn't even past."

# 1

Oliver Clearmountain paused to mop his brow as the dust settled on his feet. He removed his sunglasses and wiped his face with his handkerchief. Although Montana claimed to be the big sky country, it was just as large in Wyoming. Soon the sun would slip out of the cloudless blue heaven and drop behind the Wind River Range of the Rockies, still the air hadn't cooled. He had spent the better part of the day searching for a band of destructive troublemakers. They were causing serious turmoil north of the Indian Reservation and locals had reported damage to personal property as well as missing livestock. One fellow reported his dog had been shot. Oliver figured if they were locals, they were holed up at the base of the Absaroka Range in the Shoshone National Forest. He wanted to find them before he had to turn this problem over to the police. He suspected they were youngsters from Lander or Thermopolis, maybe even from the Wind River Reservation. He didn't want to make a federal case out of what was probably bored teens flexing their summer muscles.

A day of hiking could leave a guy exhausted, but he knew his Jeep was right over the next ridge. He quickened his pace. He didn't want to have to negotiate the dreadful dirt roads between here and the highway to Pinedale after dark. He was still sweating, a good sign because he only had a few mouthfuls of water left in his bottle. A few hours of tracking in the wilderness area his ancestors once hunted was not a challenge for him. Oliver Clearmountain was a National Park Ranger. He was also Two Fox, a Shoshone chief, a title he inherited at birth. Oliver had left the tribal ways behind years ago when he went off to school, but the idea of needing to be rescued from his own mountains was unthinkable. Still, if he had planned to be gone this long he would have prepared better. As Oliver crested the ridge he was looking forward to getting home and figuring out this mystery.

"What the... Where's my Jeep?" Oliver exclaimed to no one but himself. He hastily double checked his surroundings and confirmed he was in the right spot. The Jeep wasn't. He left it at the base of the ridge because he didn't want to tear up the ground anymore than he already had. That and the fact it created more noise than he wanted on this particular trip.

He suddenly couldn't wait to call the police. The offenders had just made it personal. That was his Jeep they took. Well as soon as he made the last two payments it would be his. Calling the police would have to wait because his radio and cell phone were in the Jeep. He left the cell phone behind because he couldn't get a signal in this area. He never thought twice about leaving the keys in the ignition as that was common practice around here. He looked for tracks as he wondered what kind of an individual would steal a person's vehicle in this rugged country. It was then that he noticed a separate set of tire tracks. They were wide tracks. Whoever it was didn't need transportation as they had their own. There were two sets of footprints between where the vehicles had been parked. It looked like two people had exited their vehicle and one got in his Jeep and drove away. One of the prints in the sandy soil was made by Merrell Gemini's, the same type shoe he was wearing. He recognized the lug pattern and it suggested these were fairly new. The other appeared to be a Wellington type boot, the type you would wear around horses or motorcycles. The Wellington wearer must have been much heavier because the prints were deeper. Now he knew he was looking for at least two people.

Without transportation Oliver knew getting to Pinedale tonight was out of the question. It was forty miles as the crow flies and that crow would have to fly over the 13,000 foot Wind River Range. The walk to the town of Dubois was possible but he would have to rest first and then it would be too dark. That journey would have to wait until tomorrow. Oh well, he thought, a night outdoors would be a good reminder of the comforts of home. He was considerably more upset about his missing Jeep than he was about sleeping under the stars.

He walked west toward a stream, careful to avoid any natural animal trails. There was no reason to upset other creature's evening visit to the stream just because he was put out. After getting a drink and filling his water bottle he found a gnarly old tree that would more than sustain his 175 pounds. By wedging a few large sticks among the branches he created a seat that also supported his back. It actually moved in the breeze. He lifted himself into the tree and got comfortable in his swinging bed. Six feet off the ground he felt safe from nosey intruders. The clear sky assured him it wouldn't rain in the next few hours, so he looked forward to some much needed sleep.

    He thought about his trip the next day. With Franc Peak behind him Oliver knew if he walked west he would come to Horse Creek Road and then south to Dubois. Fortunately, the ridges ran Southwest in this part of the region so the journey wouldn't include a lot of difficult climbing. He rested in his tree lounge thinking about who would steal his Jeep and why?

# 2

    Oliver woke long before dawn. It had been an unusually dark night because of the new moon and the clouds that moved in. Fortunately for him they didn't bring rain although the region needed it badly. That was another reason he wanted to find the group of troublemakers. Their carelessness could start a fire. Yellowstone National Park averages 34 fires a year and the region was in high risk because of the unusually dry spring.
    Oliver waited for first light so he could see where he was going. He probably could walk these hills with his eyes closed, but it was safer to see where he was stepping. Finally, the sky in the east began to lighten. He knew the sun had broken over the eastern horizon but he was too deep in the ravine to see it.
    He eased himself out of this tree perch and landed quietly on the ground. A few minutes of stretching and he would begin his trek to Dubois. He estimated he had only gotten three hours sleep but apparently it was enough because he was rested and ready to go.
    He approached the stream and threw some water in his face. It was cold and felt refreshing. He topped off his water bottle and continued across the shallow flow. He expected to make Dubois before noon.
    As the sky got brighter he noticed tire tracks as he walked. They were heading in the same direction. He had traveled roughly a mile when he saw his Jeep parked two hundred yards ahead of him. He crouched and slipped into the brush. There wasn't any movement around the Jeep but he waited a few moments to see if he had been spotted. Satisfied no one had seen him, he slowly crept forward while traversing up the slope. Oliver smiled to himself because he could hear his grandfather saying, "When stalking, always do it from high ground, down wind." Now that he had a better view, he paused again to scan the area and make sure he was still alone. His jeep sat in the middle of a treeless gulch. It looked like a TV location where they were about to film a commercial for a four wheel drive vehicle. The entire area was as

quiet as an empty church. It appeared his Jeep had been abandoned by the thieves. That puzzled Oliver because he knew it had plenty of gas in it and was in very good working order. From this distance it appeared to be undamaged.

He waited a few minutes longer. His rough country trained eye looked for anything moving, but his Jeep appeared unaccompanied. He continued slowly down the slope, cautiously alert to any movement or signs that things had been disturbed. He didn't even have his hunting knife for defense. He had left it in the glove box of the Jeep. He wasn't planning to hurt anyone just for auto theft, because if he was forced to confront anyone or anything his quickness and knowledge of the surrounding area were his best defense. He reached the drivers side of the Jeep and saw that the keys were still in the ignition.

Now he was sure this was a group of teens having fun at his expense. He searched the immediate perimeter and discovered nothing but a few similar footprints. He assumed it was the thieves changing vehicles.

While examining the Jeep for clues, he noticed the back bench seat had a new stain. It figured, teens drinking cheap wine. His cell phone and hunting knife were missing. Other than that the Jeep was fine. It started on the first crank and Oliver was on his way. No sense going to Dubois now, he would head to Pinedale. He made up his mind during the ride home that he wouldn't report the missing Jeep incident to anyone. He didn't want to give his tormentors the satisfaction of the local paper headlines, "**Park Naturalist Clearmountain stranded in Absaroka Range.**"

Oliver had been living in Pinedale since he became a National Park Service Ranger four years ago. The first ten years after graduation he worked for the federal government and lived all over the globe, never putting down roots. The reason he left the Secret Service was his last assignment. He was responsible for advance security for Presidential travels. The accountability was intense. The job skills came natural to Oliver, but it was difficult to deal with the stress. The explosive urban population growth in major cities made the job of securing the Presidents safety in foreign countries unfeasible in his eyes. Even New York City now had 16.6 million souls. Tokyo had exploded to 28 million and counting while Buenos Aires was 12 million. With all the illegal aliens coming up from the south, Mexico City still had a head count of 18 million. The world's urban areas were bursting at the seams.

The wide open spaces promised to be Oliver's sanity sanctuary, so he quit that branch of the government and came home. Although he decided not to move back onto the reservation, the tribal council welcomed him back. He considered himself lucky to remain with the government, thus maintaining his pension plan. He just had to switch branches, from the Justice Department to the Department of the Interior. Now Oliver's responsibility was the western most part of R2, the Rocky Mountain Region. So the bottom line was that Oliver went from insuring the safety of the leader of the free world to insuring the future of our greatest resources, our National forest and grasslands.

One year after he returned to Wyoming, Oliver fell in love and got married. His wife, Betsy, was a teacher in the Pinedale school system. She taught history and current events.

Oliver Clearmountain and Betsy Brooks wanted the same thing at this point in their lives, peace and quiet. And like Oliver, Betsy had another life she'd left behind. After graduating from Rutgers University with a master degree in U.S. History, she decided to enjoy herself. For seven years Betsy was an Atlantic City showgirl with a teaching degree. At five foot nine inches she was only two inches shorter than Oliver. And with heels on they were the same height. Her stunning good looks and dancing ability and plenty of hard work allowed this leggy beauty a glamorous fun loving life style.

That is until the head of the local crime family started putting pressure on Betsy. Michael Bondinni, a.k.a. Mike Bond, became infatuated with her. She had no intention of become his *amante*. At first the attention and lavish gifts were fun. It quickly became serious as he made his intention known. Finally Betsy was left with no choice. One evening, fearing for her well being, she left Atlantic City without telling a soul. She simply got on a Greyhound bus and vanished into the night. She made sure to leave no debt behind and nothing that would lead to her whereabouts. She traveled first to Tennessee, then to Indiana. She worked as a waitress, office temporary, anything that would provide income without exposing her location. After more than two years of constantly looking over her shoulder for Mike Bond's henchmen she landed, with degree in hand, in Pinedale Wyoming. Only then was she comfortable in the fact she had eluded him. She was in her first year of teaching at Pinedale High School when Oliver came into her life. He was giving a seminar in the High School auditorium on forest conservation when Betsy first saw him. His dark features and chiseled good looks caught her attention when he took the stage. His lean body bounded to center stage, taking his place at the podium in a graceful fluid motion. His jet black hair was closely cropped, but not too short. His uniform was perfectly tailored giving him a military demeanor. His eyes were black and his gaze was intense, as if he was looking through things rather than at them. She never heard a word he said the entire lecture, the only thought in her head was I sure hope he's single because I'm going to marry that man. A year later, Oliver confesses that his attention that afternoon was focused on a body and it wasn't the student body.

# 3

Oliver pulled the Jeep alongside the house that he and Betsy built. It was just on the edge of town, yet remote enough to be the retreat they had both longed for. He walked through the side door into the kitchen and glanced at the wall clock. Oliver didn't wear a wrist watch. If he was outdoors he could tell what time it was if it really mattered unless it was cloudy and raining, and then he didn't care. His past life was so time conscious and deadline focused, that removing his wrist watch helped him leave those days behind. He only needed to know the time to see if Betsy was available. He wanted to call her cell phone which she turned on between classes. She would be concerned that he didn't come home last night, although he knew she wouldn't be worried. Oliver occasionally got stuck somewhere in the region overnight without a cell phone signal. Betsy used to joke, "Why should I worry? What can happen to my Superman?" She knew Oliver was the most self reliant man on the planet.

He had his head in the refrigerator when the phone rang, "Hello," Oliver said.

"Hi honey," came the reply. "Where're you been?"

"I was just getting something to eat and then I was going to call and tell you I was okay," Oliver said.

"Did ya get stuck in the mountains last night?" Betsy chuckled. She liked to tease him about the outdoors.

Oliver nodded with a smile. He knew Betsy was grinning on the other end of the phone. "Yeah, I'll tell you all about it when you get home."

"I called your cell phone earlier and Deputy Jimmy Hawk answered. What are the police doing with your phone?"

"I don't know. What did Jimmy say?"

"He was sparse with information. He said someone found it."

"Yeah, I lost it yesterday along with my Jeep. Someone moved it. I found the Jeep this morning, but my phone was missing."

"Are you sure you're okay?" She sounded concerned.

"I'm fine, Legs," he said, using his pet name for her while trying to keep the conversation light.

"Ok Chief," she laughed. "I'll be home by 3:45. I've got to get back to class, LYL," she said and hung up.

Oliver held the phone to his ear with his shoulder as he replied "Love you lots," but she was already gone.

He had been searching the refrigerator for something to eat during their brief conversation. He grabbed eggs, bacon and butter from the shelf and frozen waffles from the freezer. He'd already popped the waffles in the toaster and placed the pan on the stove before he hung up the phone. He was starving.

Oliver was rinsing his plate when the doorbell rang. He glanced out the kitchen window before he went to the door. He saw the sheriff's patrol car parked behind his Jeep.

"Yeah, I'll be there in a minute," he hollered. "I've got to take a nap first." He paused in the kitchen, near the door waiting for the expected reply.

"Open the door Clearmountain or I'll come through it and that will make a mess." It was Oliver's good friend, Sheriff Kevin Cahill.

Oliver knew this was not an idle threat. All six foot five 240 pounds of Kevin could come through that door with as little effort as he would expend opening it.

Oliver laughed as he opened the door, "Impatient as ever."

"We got to talk" Kevin said as he pushed pass Oliver and went into the house.

"Come on in."

Oliver noticed Deputy Jimmy Hawk standing in the driveway next to his Jeep. "You too," he said to Jimmy with a motion of the head.

"He'll stay where he is," barked Kevin as he turned around to face Oliver. Oliver knew Kevin well enough to sense he was upset.

"What's set you off today?" he inquired. "You want some coffee? I was just going to make some." Oliver closed the door and walked to the sink.

"This isn't a social visit," was the curt reply.

"I guessed as much," Oliver chuckled. "You're not very social."

Holding up a cell phone, Sheriff Cahill said, "Is this yours?"

Oliver gave Kevin a sarcastic look, "If it's the one Jimmy answered when my wife called, you know it is." Oliver was pouring water into the Mr. Coffee machine. "Now it's my turn. Where did you get it?"

"Hector Oacha had it."

"Where did he get it?"

"He didn't say."

Oliver held out his hand to take the phone, but Kevin slipped it in his pocket.

With his other hand he produced Oliver's hunting knife. "Is this yours?" Oliver nodded. "It's similar to the one I own. Where did you get it?"

"Hector had it."

"And he didn't say where he found it, right?"

"He couldn't," Kevin said. "But I'll tell you where I found it." Kevin stared at Oliver with a concerned face. "I found it sticking out of Hector's chest."

Oliver felt weak in the knees as if he had been punched in the gut. He leaned back against the kitchen counter for support. Kevin pulled out the chair from the table and settled his large frame into it. From under the table he kicked a chair out for Oliver to sit. "Start at the beginning," he said.

# 4

Oliver explained in detail what had taken place during the last twenty hours.

Kevin sat silent for the entire report. Because of Oliver's background, there wasn't any reason to ask questions. He didn't leave out anything.

When Oliver finished Kevin said, "So you don't have an alibi."

Oliver registered a puzzled look, "Do I need one?"

Kevin said, "Can you think of another suspect I might talk too?"

Oliver leaned back in the chair and exhaled exasperated. "Why would I kill Hector?"

"Why would Hector have your knife in his chest?"

"It's got to be the guys that took my Jeep," Oliver said. "But why would they want to incriminate me?"

"Look Oliver, I know you didn't do it, but you have to come down to the station and give an official statement and then we'll see what the DA has to say. Come on, you ride with me. I'll make Jimmy Hawk ride in the back seat." Kevin smiled as he rose from the chair and headed for the door.

Oliver quickly looked around as his mind raced. They are going to arrest me, he thought. But what choices do I have? I can't run.

"Don't think about running," Kevin said, without looking back at his friend. "I'd have to shoot you." He then turned around at the door and winked, letting Oliver know he knew what his friend was thinking.

"Get in the back seat Jimmy. You can watch the suspect better from there," Kevin said with authority as he went down the two steps to the driveway.

Jimmy whispered something to Kevin as Oliver was making sure the door was locked. Kevin just nodded and slipped into his car.

Jimmy Hawk was a young twenty-four year old full blooded Shoshone. He looked up to Oliver. In fact most young Shoshone used Oliver

Clearmountain as a role model. On the reservation he was a good example of what a young man could do if he applied himself.

"I noticed a stain on the back seat of the Jeep," Jimmy said as the car backed out of the driveway.

"So did I," Oliver responded. "I think whoever borrowed my Jeep spilled whatever they were drinking."

Jimmy nodded.

Oliver repeated his entire story again, this time into a recorder and in front of a stenographer. When he finished Jimmy brought him a cup of coffee.

"Sheriff Cahill said for you to stay here," Jimmy said as he placed the coffee in front of Oliver. "Black, right?" he said referring to the coffee.

"Yeah," Oliver nodded. "Did Kevin say how long he'd be?"

"Just a few minutes," Jimmy said over his shoulder as he and the stenographer left the room.

Oliver heard the door lock as it closed. He sipped his coffee and wondered who would involve him in this murder and why?

He had finished his coffee when Kevin returned.

"I called Betsy and told her you were here," Kevin said. He leaned on the table with both hands which put his face close to Oliver.

Oliver managed a slight grin. "When did you tell her I'd be home?" What he wanted to say was, *when are you going to release me?*

"I told her you weren't coming home," Kevin said. "We are going to book you for the murder of Hector Oacha."

Oliver's blood ran cold. "You can't...I mean why?"

"I just received a report from the crime lab," Kevin said as he eased himself into the chair across from Oliver. "That stain on the back seat in your Jeep is blood. I'm not going to wait to see if it belongs to Hector, because you and I both know it does." He leaned toward his friend. "What we've got to find out is who's framing you and why?"

Oliver hung his head and shook it, "I haven't a clue."

After a long moment of silence, Oliver raised his head. "Do I get a call? I think I'm going to need a lawyer."

Kevin smiled and nodded. "Don't waste it. I already called Gordon Cundiff. He'll be here in an hour."

# 5

For the first time all day Oliver felt relief when he saw Gordon Cundiff walk through the door. Gordon was Oliver and Betsy's lawyer. He had helped on the house closing, but real estate law wasn't his specialty. He was a defense attorney who had a decent practice in Jackson. Gordon was a Notre Dame graduate who lived and died on the football team's won and lost record. He had played football at Notre Dame and had earned a try out with Green Bay in the NFL but decided instead to go to law school, a decision he never regretted. He and his wife Marilyn were good friends of the Clearmountian's as well as Sheriff Cahill.

He shook Oliver's hand and smiled. "It's not as bad as it seems. I was on the phone all the way down here. We have some wiggle room. Now I know you don't want to hear what I'm going to say next, but tell me everything that happened."

Oliver groaned and turned back into the room to repeat, for what he hoped the last time, everything that had transpired in the last twenty four hours.

Gordon followed Oliver's every word while perusing the type written transcript. He glanced at his watch and said "I think we have enough daylight left. Let's get Kevin and the three of us go see if we can find those footprints you talked about.

Kevin made excellent time getting back into the mountains and with Oliver's directions, found the spot where the Jeep was stolen.

"They're right over there," Oliver pointed in front of Kevin's SUV.

Kevin took a digital camera out of his pocket and took some shots of the prints.

"I'll call the lab and see if they can get their butt's out here to make casts." He looked up into the sky, "I hope it doesn't rain tonight."

While Kevin was on the phone, Oliver showed Gordon where he had come from that afternoon and how the tire tracks led down the ravine.

Kevin popped his head out of the SUV and said, "They told me to cover them with something and use the yellow tape to mark the area." He walked to the rear of the vehicle and checked to see what he could use for a cover.

"What are these footprints going to prove other than there were people in the region?" Oliver said.

"Sheriff Cahill can now testify on your behalf," Gordon said. "He can say that he saw the prints and identified them with the tire tracks made by your Jeep."

He turned to Kevin who was covering the prints with boxes he found in the back of his Suv. "You got pictures of the prints in relationship to the tracks of Oliver's Jeep as well as the other vehicle's tracks didn't you?"

Kevin nodded and kept working, placing heavy rocks on the boxes to stabilize them. Oliver helped by taping off the area with the yellow police tape.

Kevin stood up, satisfied with his work, "Come-on, I'll buy you guy's a beer before I take Oliver to jail." Oliver's head snapped up and he saw Kevin and Gordon smiling. "Since I'm a prisoner, I suppose you're going to expense it."

On the way back to town Oliver, who was sitting in the back seat said, "I don't know if you two noticed but the footprints up there were made by the same type of shoe I'm wearing."

Kevin and Gordon just looked at each other and moaned. Gordon said, "It never gets easier."

It was Oliver's turn to laugh, "But I can show you the difference. The tracks were made by new shoes and mine are nearly worn out."

They drove in silence for a while and then Oliver said, "Has Hector's family been notified?"

"Yes, this morning," said Kevin. "His brothers were very upset and wanted to know who did it." Kevin looked over his shoulder into the back seat. "They were sharpening their scalping knives."

## THE PAST IS NEVER DEAD

"Knock it off, Bigfoot," Oliver said.

True to his word, Kevin stopped at the Outlaw Saloon in Dubois. This was not the type of café you would read reviews about. In fact not much good was said about it other than the beer was cold. Oliver had never felt threatened or intimidated in his life, but the fact that Kevin was the Sheriff made it a little more pleasant entering the saloon. The interior was dark by design but not bad once your eyes adjusted. Any additional lighting would have exposed the dilapidated condition of the floor and furnishing. Gordon looked out of place in his pinstriped Hickey Freeman suit. Oliver was the grubbiest of the three, still in the sweat marked clothes he'd slept in.

The majority of attendees had ridden motorcycles to the Saloon. The bikes were lined up outside just like the horses of yesteryear. The main difference between this crowd and the people who might have occupied this saloon one hundred and thirty years ago was the clothes. Drawing a comparison between generations Oliver was sure both crowds wore leather and he was certain this group had as many weapons, just not hanging on their hips. The men in here wore leather vests with their beefy arms exposed. Oliver knew it was only his ancestors that went bare-chested back then.

Kevin spoke as they sat down at a table, "This is a HAHO!"

"Easy," Gordon said. "I'm sure they don't like to be laughed at."

Oliver whispered to Gordon, "HAHO means Hells Angel's Hang Out."

Oliver was an expert at sizing up a situation fast and he saw trouble brewing.

There were six inebriated bikers at the bar and three at the table near the back. One of the three at the table was female. Now Oliver knew the Hell's Angel's National club was a fine organization which did wonders at Christmas with its annual toy collection for the needy. This group, however, was the type that gives bikers a bad rap.

"I'll buy the beer," Gordon said, as he went to the bar and ordered three cold long neck Coors. The well worn and scratched glasses were a distasteful, seldom used option.

Oliver watched those at the bar whisper to one another and grin. They were up to something.

Gordon returned to the table and gave Kevin and Oliver their beer. Gordon sat with his back to the front door and the bar to his right. Kevin had his back to the wall facing the bar and Oliver sat facing Gordon and the front door with the bar on his left.

Soon one biker pushed away from the bar and started toward the rear of the saloon. "Got to take a piss," he announced. As he staggered past the table he stumbled and fell into the table sending everything that was on it crashing to the floor.

He turned to Gordon and screamed, "You tripped me!"

Oliver was out of his chair in a flash, "You tripped over your own feet," he said calmly, "and I think it was intentional."

The biker turned to Oliver in a belligerent manner and slurred, "What do you mean, intentional?"

"Intentional, meaning deliberate, like this," Oliver said as his arm came straight up from his waist and hit the biker flush on the jaw with the heel of his open hand. You could hear the jawbone crack as he sunk to the floor, first on his butt and then flat on his back, out cold.

Another came charging for Oliver from the bar. "You'll pay for that," he announced. Gordon, who was still seated, stuck his foot out. This time the trip was intentional. Oliver caught him by the vest with both hands, preventing him from falling. He then headed the surprised biker with a sharp blow delivered with his forehead on the bridge of the man's nose. Blood rushed from his broken nose as he fell to his knees screaming. Two more started to leave the bar when Oliver heard Kevin's gun cock.

"I've seen enough assault and battery to convince me that the next assailant needs to be shot," Kevin said as he kicked the table away from in front of him. Oliver knew he did it for effect. The noise served its purpose because now everyone in the place was looking at Kevin and his Colt 45. He remained seated, but was very much in control. "You boys pay up and leave, and don't forget to take your friend. This one," pointing his Colt at the unconscious one on the floor, "will need your assistance." Then Kevin looked to the bartender. "We'll need three more beers and charge your departing customers for them."

Oliver righted the table and sat down. Kevin turned to him and said, "Now what were we talking about?"

*THE PAST IS NEVER DEAD*

Kevin glanced to his left and noticed the three bikers at the back table. He pointed at them with his finger and then with the same hand gave the thumb out hitchhiking motion toward the front door, indicating they should leave. They quietly filed out.

# 6

They left the Outlaw Saloon after their second beer. Gordon was downright giddy. He said he hadn't had this much fun since South Bend during his college days. Kevin's satisfied look was underlined by an evil grin. The drive back to Pinedale was silent. Finally Oliver couldn't keep it in. "Alright, Alright," he said. "This is bull. Kevin, you stopped there on purpose because you're bored and you knew you could stir up some trouble. Gordon, you enjoyed the opportunity to revert back to your tough guy days, and I'm the one going to jail. What's wrong with this picture?"

"You enjoyed it. Admit it," Kevin said never taking his eyes off the road, "and furthermore you're not going to jail for fighting. You're going to jail because you're an antisocial, degenerate who sleeps in the woods alone, when you have an absolutely gorgeous wife at home, who adores you." He turned to Gordon, "I'd look at an insanity plea if I was defending him."

When they arrived back at the station, Oliver was placed in a holding cell. Kevin and Gordon's moods had turned sober again. Gordon told him to sit tight. He was going to talk with the DA and a judge if necessary. He believed with Oliver's service record and good standing in the community something could be arranged.

This gave Oliver time to think for the first time today. He sat back in his quiet cell and pondered who would want to set him up like this? The first person who popped into his mind was Sharad Ramadoos. It was just before he left the service. India was on a Tier Two watch list because they had charged China with transferring missiles to Pakistan. The President's visit was to try to defuse the tension.

Two days before the President was to visit New Delhi, Oliver had stumbled across an indebt bondage ring that trafficked in women and children for commercial sexual exploitation. It wasn't Oliver's charter to get involved, but at the last minute circumstances threatened the President's safety. Oliver had to shoot a thug and his involvement exposed Sharad Ramadoos entire operation. Sharad felt he'd lost face in his country and now he swore he would kill Oliver. Now, as Oliver reflected he remembered the rage and loathing Ramadoos expressed with his furious pledge.

Come to think of it, Ramadoos wasn't the only one who swore to kill Oliver. There had been the threat by Tyrell Jackson. He was thug that Oliver had put away, for threatening our National Safety, by building a dirty bomb. He had sworn he was going to kill the President because he was Satan. He might be crazy enough to track Oliver across the country. Or Jonathan Yokatory couldn't be discounted. He was a real nasty depraved evil doer. His intent was to overthrow the country. And as Oliver remembered, his followers had their headquarters in Colorado. He leaned back on his cot exhausted when he realized he had plenty of enemies who pledged to do him harm.

When he opened his eyes, Betsy was standing in front of his cell. She had changed from her very proper school attire to her second skin Levi's, so called by Oliver because they couldn't get any tighter. She had the bottoms tucked into her Arizona sunrise Justin cowboy boots. On her head she had her knock around black cowgirl hat with the flame band, tilted as only Betsy could wear it. Her open denim shirt covered a low cut tee shirt. *God she is beautiful,* Oliver thought.

"Why don't you look that good when I'm not locked up?" Oliver offered with a grin.

"Forbidden fruit syndrome," she smiled. "Everything you can't have looks good. When Kevin called to say you wouldn't be home again tonight, I thought I better see for myself the trouble you've gotten into this time."

"They think I killed Hector Oacha," Oliver said.

"Kevin said he knows you didn't do it, but the evidence made him hold you." Betsy moved up to the bars and offered a kiss. Her breast jammed through in an alluring manner. And the bars pressed snugly to each cheek exaggerating her puckered lips.

"Stop it Betsy," Oliver said, as he reached through the bars and grabbed her hips. "You're killing me." He kissed her and turned away. "This is torture, being locked up and away from you for another night."

"Relax lover." Betsy cooed. "Gordon got you sprung."

"How?" Oliver said, as he snapped around to face her.

"I'll explain when we get home," she said revealing the keys she'd been holding behind her back.

Oliver looked toward the door and saw Kevin leaning against the doorframe grinning. He nodded his head, confirming what Betsy had said.

"You know Cahill you're a sick perverted excuse for a human." Oliver said. "You enjoyed this little show didn't you?"

"Like you said, I am human." Kevin slipped his hat down over his eyes and turned and walked out of sight.

On the short ride home Betsy explained what happened. The District Attorney and the Judge agreed there was no reason to hold Oliver based on circumstantial evidence. His character spoke for itself and Kevin testified there had indeed been prints around his Jeep lending credence to Oliver's story. His fingerprints weren't on the knife. In fact it had been wiped clean. This fact alone aroused the judge's suspicion. In fact he said, "If I was going to kill someone with my own knife and leave it in the body, the last thing I would think of would be to wipe the prints off." Kevin reminded them of the courts request that Oliver, stick around.

The Jeep came to a skidding stop in the gravel driveway. Oliver couldn't get Betsy in the house fast enough. Betsy ran into the bedroom ahead of Oliver, taking off her shirt and laughing. She threw herself on the bed, shouting, "Run for your lives, Indian uprising."

# 7

Betsy awoke with the alarm buzzing in her ear. The alarm clock was on her side of the bed because Oliver didn't need an alarm clock. He would just set his mind too what time he needed to awake and he would. Betsy rolled over and looked at the love of her life. Oliver was lying on his back with his arms behind his head, gazing at the ceiling.

"Another day, another dollar," Betsy groaned, still not completely awake.

"Million days, a millionaire," Oliver replied, still staring at the ceiling.

Betsy propped herself up on her elbow and placed her hand on him, "A penny for your thoughts," she said, rubbing his hairless chest.

"Huh, and you on your way to becoming a millionaire," he grinned. He paused and then, still looking at the ceiling, said, "First I'm going to call the Regional Foresters office and tell C.W what's going on and that I'm taking a few days off. Then I think I should go over to Fort Washakie and talk to Hector's elders and arrange a meeting with the General Council."

"How long will you be gone?" Betsy said.

"It's only 50 miles over the range, but since I can't fly with the eagles, it's a 150 mile drive. Just one overnight I hope," he said, still focusing on the ceiling.

"Well I've got to get to school," she said as she rolled over and popped out of bed. "Oh" she exclaimed as she suddenly realized she was naked as a Jay bird.

Oliver turned his head and admired her innocent predicament.

"What's your first class, Sex Ed?" he grinned.

Oliver left the house the same time as Betsy. He had let her shower first because it didn't take him as long to get ready. She had her mug full of coffee and he had his overnight bag and a plastic bag full of Kashi, the dry breakfast cereal he like to munch on.

They walked out together and Betsy kissed him on the cheek and jumped into her bright red Ford 150 4x4, tooted the horn and spun what little gravel was left in the driveway. Oliver could see her laughing as she power turned in the doublewide driveway instead of backing out. Spewing stones, she headed out.

Oliver stood in the dust cloud, staring after her thinking, *not only is she a knock out, that woman can drive.* He hated when she tore up the driveway, but she made him laugh with her antics. He was also glad they didn't have any close neighbors that might see their supposedly mature High School teacher acting like one of her students. He backed his Jeep Wrangler out of the driveway in a grown-up manner and started his three an a half hour trip to Fort Washakie which was named after the great Chief Washakie.

Oliver had packed his only connection with his old life, his Berretta 92 FS Brigadier. It was a .40 caliber work of art. All Districts Rangers ware issued Sig Sauer's and that was Oliver's official weapon, but he kept his Berretta as his personal backup. Rangers wear many hats. They are responsible for the preservation and protection of the National Parks as well as law and regulation enforcement, protection of property and search and rescue. There is also a firefighter division in the Forrest Ranger.

The reservation was 2.2 million acres that was shared by 3500 Shoshone and 7,000 Arapaho. One hundred and fifty years ago they were warring tribes. Chief Washakie once fought a Crow warrior on Crowheart Butte to settle what tribe would control the valley. Legend has it the Chief cut out and ate the defeated warrior's heart, honoring his bravery. Chief Washakie was the leader who established peace among the tribes. Today they coexist in what the Shoshone still call Warm Valley. The rest of the nation refers to it as the Wind River Reservation.

At its largest the Shoshone nation never exceeded 8000 people. Oliver's people had sometimes been referred to as the Snake Indians because of the proximity of the Snake River. They were a proud and peaceful tribe who adapted the way of the Plains Indian when they were introduced to horses. They then became great Buffalo Hunters improving their diet from nuts, berries and rabbit to buffalo meat. Their clothing also improved. They were among the best horse thieves in the region according to the Crow, Arapaho, and Lakota. Any tribe that had horses missing blamed the Shoshone.

It was 11:30AM when Oliver pulled into Fort Washakie. He had spoken to Hectors uncle on the way down and they had arranged to meet at the General Council Lodge.

Oliver hadn't bothered to snap the top back on his Jeep. He was win blown as he steeped out of the Jeep, smoothed his hair, adjusted his sunglasses, and put on his hat. Today, because of where he was, he wore his uniform. Hector's uncle was standing on the porch waiting for him.

Glancing at the position of the sun, Oliver said "Good morning Willie."

Willie Oacha nodded and turned and walked inside. Oliver followed him. There was an empty conference room that Willie had arranged for them to use. Oliver followed Willie into the room.

Willie sat down at the table and pointed to the chair across from him.

"How is the family taking the loss of Hector?" Oliver said as he slipped into the chair.

Willie shook his head, "Bad."

Oliver folded his hands in front of him, "Do they have any idea what happened?"

Willie nodded, "You killed him!"

Oliver's head jerked back as if avoiding a punch. "What?"

"You tell me what happened." Willie showed no expression.

"Willie, I didn't kill Hector," Oliver replied, somewhat surprised with the accusation.

"Why was your knife in his chest?" Willie remained passive. His hands on the table in front of him palms down. His voice was controlled and monotone.

Oliver removed his sunglasses. He paused to look deep into Willie's eyes, "Because, whoever murdered Hector, took it from my Jeep." Oliver stated.

"Why would someone steal your Jeep and then murder Hector?"

"Maybe Hector tried to stop them?" Oliver said. He was getting tired of being cross examined. Before Willie could ask another question Oliver said, "Who was Hector kicking around with these days?"

"Nobody special," Willie said. "He was looking for a job." His eyes left Oliver for the first time as he gave a fleeting look to the door. Oliver quickly looked over his shoulder. Slumped against the door frame was Hectors older brother Lusk. His stance said attitude.

"Sit down," Oliver pointed to a chair. "I'd like to talk to you. Where is the youngest?"

Lusk didn't move from the door, "I couldn't let Jackie in here. He wants to smash your face in. He's waiting outside, so I wouldn't be in a hurry to leave if I was you."

Oliver grinned and nodded. He knew there would be a problem when he left. Jackie was the younger of the Oacha boys and definitely the wildest. He was only seventeen, but he had been arrested more than his two older brothers combined.

Oliver turned in his chair and directed his question to Lusk.

"When was the last time you saw Hector?"

"You mean alive?" Lusk snarled, "Because I just came from the funeral parlor. I had to identify the body."

This line of questioning wasn't getting Oliver anywhere. It was obvious that Oacha's weren't going to co-operate. Oliver slid his chair back and got to his feet. "I'm meeting with the council here at 3:00PM. You two are invited." He walked to the door and very politely said "Excuse me." Lusk slowly unfolded his arms and stood sideways allowing just enough room for Oliver to slip past. He walked toward the door of the Lodge wondering what Jack had in store for him. He paused on the porch at the top of the steps. Jack was nowhere in sight.

Oliver drove back to Lander to get a room at the Silver Spur Motel. It would be 30 miles closer to home when he left tomorrow and gave him time to plan what he wanted to get done at the council meeting. He was also going to have some lunch, maybe a good piece of pizza at Tony's. Oliver checked in and went to his room just to put his overnight bag down and make sure the air conditioning was on. He opened his bag to put his toiletries out on the bathroom shelf. His heart jumped, his Beretta was missing, holster and all, which meant the thief had a .40 caliber semi-automatic pistol with thirty rounds of ammunition. He slumped on the edge of the bed. He had to call Kevin and report it before, like his knife, it kills someone.

# 8

Oliver was not very amused on the ride back to the council meeting. He was so livid he didn't even remember what the pizza tasted like. In all his years in the Secret Service he never had his weapon taken from him. Plus he didn't need the lecture Kevin had given him about being responsible. He was sure there was smoke coming out of his ears as he pulled back into Fort Washakie.

It was exactly three o'clock according to the lobby clock as he entered the meeting room. There were ten people milling around talking. Six of them were the council members and he recognized the four members of the Oacha family in the far corner. Hector's father Larry, Uncle Willie and the two brothers Lusk and Jackie.

Oliver walked directly to Larry out of respect. He extended his hand and said, "I'm sincerely sorry for your loss."

Larry nodded, "Thank you."

He then whispered softly in Larry's ear, "Excuse me for what I'm about to do."

A puzzled look crossed Larry's face, but Oliver had already grabbed Jackie's left wrist and pushed hard on his right shoulder. The surprise move caused Jackie to turn to his right and Oliver twisted his left arm behind his back. He drove Jackie to the wall with his shoulder. Holding Jackie's body to the wall and his arm high on his back, Oliver's free hand grabbed the back of Jackie's pants and removed his Berretta, holster and all.

Holding the gun aloft he declared "This belongs to me."

He spoke firmly in Jackie's ear. "Make a move and I'll break your shoulder. Do you understand?"

The surprised Jackie nodded nervously and groaned when Oliver applied more pressure.

Oliver turned to Lusk, "Take your brother outside. He has committed a federal offense, and out of respect to your father and deceased brother I won't press charges if he stays out of my way."

Jackie started to protest, "I...."

"Shut up," Oliver demanded. "If I want any of your shit I'll unscrew your head and dip it out." He pushed Jackie toward his brother. "GO!"

The brothers disappeared quickly out the door.

Oliver fastened the clip-on holster in the small of his back. He turned to the council members and said, "I'm sorry for the disturbance. It was not my intention to bring disgrace to one of the tribe. I hope the young man has learned his lesson." He removed his sunglasses and put them in his breast pocket. "Now if you would be so kind to take your seats I'll present my case and try to explain how I think you can help us solve the murder of a fine young man."

Everyone sat down without a word. Oliver found himself standing at the head of a large conference table. Eight of the twelve chairs were full with a solemn and attentive audience.

"We need your help," Oliver started. "I believe someone Hector was involved with stole my Jeep. When Hector tried to stop them he was killed in the struggle. Where I think you can help is to ask around and let me know who Hector's mates were. Who had he been seen with recently. I'm looking for at least two, maybe three people."

"Do you know what they look like?" a council member asked.

"I don't know if they are male or female," Oliver responded.

Another member said, "How do we know they exist at all?"

That question pained Oliver. One man spoke what everyone was thinking; he was lying to the council.

The member continued, "We heard you spent the night in jail because they think you killed Hector."

"You information is incorrect. I didn't spend the night in jail. I was only held because my knife was used." Oliver didn't offer the fact that Hector's blood was found in his Jeep.

"Why would you kill a young Indian?" another voice asked.

"I didn't," Oliver barked quickly, defending himself.

Suddenly, Chief Tigree stood. The room fell silent. Tigree Clearmountain was Oliver's uncle, but Oliver wasn't expecting glad tidings. The Chief slowly looked around the room making eye contact with everyone. It was only then that he spoke. "Sit," he said looking directly at Oliver. Oliver slid into the chair at the end of the table.

"I will not allow arguing and false charges brought up in this room. The first and only priority in this room is to solve the murder of one of our young men, Hector Oacha." The Chief stated with a commanding voice. "And that will not be accomplished today. We will proceed in a tribal manner. First, Oliver you must leave. You have done yourself a disservice coming here to plead you case."

"I haven't come here to..."

"Silence." The chief stared at Oliver. "Your authority doesn't work here. You accuse Young Jackie Oacha of a federal offense? Your mere presence is a tribal offense to some members of this council.

Oliver closed his eyes as the words cut at his heart.

Chief Tigree continued. "You have made it clear what world you live in, don't try to contaminate ours with your laws. We will find the killer. The incident took place on our land. Our laws will apply." The Chief had his eyes fixed on Oliver as did everyone else in the room.

Oliver felt alone and hurt. They thought he had come down here to use them. This had definitely not gone as Oliver had planned. He looked around the room for an understanding friendly face, there were none. The silence was painful and becoming uncomfortable as long as everyone stared at Oliver. At least in the outdoors there would be a hole to crawl into.

Finally, Chief Tigree said, "We're waiting for you to leave."

Oliver scooted back his chair and rose. He felt like a school boy being sent to the principles office. He walked to the door trying to hold his head up. It took all his will-power not to say something. A mere goodbye wouldn't be prudent at this point. He felt ridiculous, but he understood that saying anything at this moment would be considered not only a weakness in his character, but disrespectful.

By the time he reached the top of the porch steps his disposition had changed from submissive to seething. He was mad at the council for not understanding but most of all at himself for forgetting the customs and philosophy of the Shoshone. He had made it seem as if he thought they weren't capable of helping themselves. How stupid of him. He jumped into the jeep and slammed the door. The tires spun the moment the engine fired. His embarrassment surfaced in his impatience to leave Fort Washakie. He thought of driving back tonight but the truth was he was too upset to trust himself on the highway. He was already exceeding the limit on the road to Landers.

After he called Betsy to tell her he was not coming home, he tossed and turned all night. He finally left the Silver Spur Motel at 4:30AM.

# 9

Oliver was quite upset with his performance at the Meeting Lodge. It was apparent he had been away too long and had forgotten what works on the reservation and what doesn't. The Shoshones are a proud people and resist anyone who they think is using them. It was a shame he hadn't handled the whole thing better. They would have been a big help. This investigation was going to be out of his hands very soon unless he came up with something. The forest service wouldn't want him tied up investigating a murder, especially if he's a suspect.

He was planning to stop at the sheriff's office to see if Kevin's hard work might have removed him from the primary candidate list of suspects. He called Kevin to tell him he had his weapon back and that he had made a mess of things at Fort Washakie. When he asked Kevin if he had any new leads he responded with, "We'll talk when you get here.

Kevin shouted his welcome as soon as Oliver hit the door. He was out of sight in his office but he had positioned a wide angle mirror in the corner of the ceiling opposite the front door. He could see who was coming and going without leaving his desk, let alone his office. Oliver also knew he had a warning chime that alerted him when the door was opened.

Oliver glanced at Jimmy Hawk who was sitting at a desk in the outer office. Jimmy smiled and nodded toward Kevin's office.

"Well how much have you accomplished towards my freedom today?" Oliver asked as he slumped down in a chair.

"We're on the scent."

"Explain yourself.

"Hector had been drugged before he was stabbed, according to the ME," Kevin put his boots up on his desk. "Also Secret Agent Man, did you notice anything about the tracks?" Kevin asked smiling.

"Do you mean the footprints or tire tracks?"

"Both," Kevin said smugly.

Oliver shook his head while he tried to recall his first impression of the tire tracks "The tire tracks were large, maybe a truck tire. And the footprints were made by a hiking shoe and a boot. The boot wearer was much heavier."

"Close, but close only counts in horseshoes, hand grenades and slow dancing," Kevin smiled.

"Okay, help me out, Wyatt Earp" Oliver replied.

"How about a motorcycle?" Kevin raised his eyebrows, mimicking surprise.

"Motorcycle tires are smaller."

"Not the rear tire on one of those custom built choppers," Kevin informed Oliver. "The tread pattern indicates it was a bike" he concluded.

Oliver closed his eyes and his chin hit his chest. "The Outlaw Saloon," he exclaimed in discovery.

"That's not all. The hiking shoe could have been a female. That's why the boot looked so much larger."

"The three at the rear table," Oliver announced with excitement. "That's why they didn't make a move during the trouble. They weren't with the six at the bar." Oliver was now nodding his head in recognition of Kevin's discovery. "Do we have any idea who they were?"

Kevin was pleased with himself until this point and now the smile started too slide off his face. "Word has it they have been hanging around for a few days asking questions about people"

"What people?" Oliver inquired.

"Oliver Clearmountain and Betsy Brooks," Kevin said. The smile had disappeared.

Oliver leaned forward, his eyes focused on Kevin. He paused, and then with his elbows on the desk he clasped his hands and rested his chin on them. His years of training had taught him not to react until you have all the facts. "What kind of questions?" His mind was racing. Was Betsy safe?

As if he read Oliver's mind Kevin said, "Betsy's safe. The moment I found out I had a deputy watch your house. We also followed her to school this morning." Kevin gave Oliver a reassuring wink. "Just doing my job." He took his feet off the desk and grabbed a piece of paper, "According to my deputy's report, as to the questions they were asking, they wanted to know how long you've been married? Where did you work and where did you live? They said they knew an Oliver Clearmountain from back East and were wondering if you were the same guy."

"Yeah, there's a lot of Oliver Clearmountains running around the country." Oliver stated, his tone dripping with sarcasm.

"Whatever," Kevin said, "that's what we've got and here's where we're going. We're checking the shoe store to see if anybody recently purchased a pair of Merrell Gemini hiking shoes. We're talking to all motorcycle dealers and mechanics to see if our suspects had any repairs done on their bikes. We're also checking all the campgrounds and motels in the area. Can you think of anything else?"

"You're doing fine. Keep looking for them and I'll start looking for motive. I've got to check on the whereabouts of a few people. I'm going to call some friends in D.C. and see if I can track down some people that would like to see me suffering or dead."

"I can't imagine there would be people like that. Someone who doesn't like you," Kevin held his hand over his mouth in mock surprise.

Oliver got to his feet. "Funny!" he said, gesturing to the door. "Can I use that empty desk out there to make a few phone calls?"

"Be my guest," Kevin extended his arm to the door, "My department is funded by the taxpayers and I assume that's you."

# 10

Oliver was occupied at the spare desk the rest of the morning, occasionally taking time to notice the workings of the Sheriff's office. It was a very busy place, more so than he had imagined. His wasn't the only unsolved crime in the county. He was working his list when, suddenly he was aware of Kevin looming over the desk.

"You buying lunch?" he asked.

"Come to think of it I am hungry," Oliver said as he sat back. "Where we going?"

"That depends on who's buying," Kevin said as he walked out the front door.

They were seated at the rear booth at Mo's Restaurant. This was Kevin's spot because he could see the entire restaurant from his seat. Big Mo was taking their order personally.

Kevin looked up at the large man poised at the table. He had a large white apron tied around his chest. It covered his entire front. He stood with his feet firmly planted and his hands on his hips as if to challenge them to a fight.

"What's good today?"

"Me," Big Mo said, without any change in his facial expression. He was equal to Kevin in height, perhaps thirty pounds heavier. A pound for each year he had on the Sheriff. He turned to Oliver and said,"Why aren't you out in the mountains eating bark or something?"

Oliver smiled, "It's nice to see you again, Mo."

Kevin put the menu down, "Why is it everything you serve here comes in a basket? Chicken –in-a basket, Hamburger and fries-in-a basket, Fish and Chips-in-a basket."

Maintaining his stoic expression Mo said, "I don't like to do dishes. Now are you going to order or criticize the place?"

## THE PAST IS NEVER DEAD

"Bring us two of your famous Fish and Chips," Oliver said. "Also an orange soda and a root beer."

Mo grunted and started to walk away when Oliver said," Oh yeah, and bring me a Soup-in-a basket also." He winked at Kevin and they both chuckled.

"Wise ass Cowboys and Indians, that's all I get in here anymore," Mo mumbled as he walked behind the counter.

Big Mo was a wonderful soul. He was a plotting loner, in love with the past. On the wall at every booth was the old Jukebox selector. No song past 1962 was on the index. Mo lived in the rear of the restaurant. His car was a 1957 Chevy convertible in the summer and a rebuilt World War II Jeep for the winter. Even his clothes represented the sixties. What hair he had left was combed into a DA. The pictures and posters on the wall reflected the days gone by.

Kevin shook his head, "Big Mo will never change. He's a dinosaur, but he sure can cook."

Oliver was looking through the Jukebox selections when Kevin asked, "Did your calls to D.C. accomplish anything?"

"Yes and no," Oliver shrugged his shoulders. "Sharad Ramadoos is still in India. He's a broken man. I don't think he has the wherewithal to hire anyone. Tyrell Jackson died in the prison hospital from a brain aneurysm. However, Jonathan Yokatory is out of prison and we're not quite sure where he is, although he's suspected to be in Colorado. But he's third on my list of suspects. If he wanted me dead he'd do it himself. He wouldn't hire motorcycle types. Beside he would kill me, not try to frame me."

Kevin was staring intently at Oliver, listening to every fact. "So you aren't any closer to finding a suspect. What about on the reservation? Is there anyone you can think of who would want you framed for murder?"

"As of yesterday, I'd say all of them," Oliver shook his head sadly. "I'm not very popular there right now."

Kevin pushed away his basket that once contained two delicious lightly fried fillets of sole. It now contained a crushed up paper napkin and the crumbs of a few French fries. "I hope your morning was more productive."

Kevin shook his head, "Nothing yet, but we've only begun. You want to take a ride up to the Outlaw Saloon? I want to question the bartender myself."

Big Mo walked over and placed a basket in front of Kevin, with the check in it. He gave Oliver a wink. "Do you know why I wait on you myself?" he asked Kevin.

Kevin looked up, surprised by the question.

"Because you're such a lousy tipper I can't get any of my help to wait on you, you cheap bastard." Big Mo stated with authority.

Kevin looked at the fourteen dollar check in the basket and tossed in a twenty. "Keep the change," he proclaimed.

Mo's lips curled into a slight grin, he winked at Oliver and said, "It works every time." Mo picked up the basket and walked back behind the counter singing "Oh the shark babe has such teeth dear, and he shows them, pearly white…."

# 11

Kevin walked into the Saloon first. Oliver was right behind him with his hand on Kevin's shoulder as if he was a blind man being led. The truth was his eyes had been closed for the last thirty seconds. The Outlaw Saloon was so dark inside that it took a person's eyes a moment to adjust from the bright sunlight. Oliver wanted to see the moment he entered the building, so by having his eyes closed they were preconditioned to the dark.

He immediately saw two groups of people at the bar. Four bikers near the front and further down two guys who looked like working cowhands.

Only one of the bikers looked at them. Oliver quickly established these were not the same groups that were here two day ago. None of their faces were banged up. He also noted there were no females in the building.

Kevin walked up to the short end of the bar and motioned for the bartender to join him. Oliver stayed back giving the Sheriff and the bartender privacy.

"I don't want any trouble, Sheriff" the bartender said as he put his elbow on the bar in front of Kevin.

"I just need some answers," Kevin said as he noticed the four at the bar finish their beers and pick up their loose change as if to leave.

Turning toward them he said, "Why don't you boys stick around. I'll have some questions for you also."

Oliver stepped between them and the door and gestured to the chairs and tables along the wall. "Why don't you fellas have a seat? The Sheriff will be with you shortly."

The tension that suddenly filled the saloon was like static electricity. The absence of sound was unsettling, as if time stopped, until unhurriedly one of the bikers moved to a chair. The other three followed.

Oliver exhaled and smiled and in his most casual manner tried to release the tension. "This is just SOP. The Sheriff is looking for some folks and he'll need to know if you might have seen them" He put his foot on the chair at the door trying not to look antagonistic. "It won't take long, guys."

The first guy to sit down said, "Who's he looking for?"

"He'll tell you all about it." Oliver said, conscious of the fact that anything said to him would be just hearsay and not worthy testimony because he hadn't identified himself as a Federal Law Enforcement Officer.

What looked to Oliver to be the troublemaker of the four was checking out his uniform, "Hey Smokey, what are you a forest ranger or a boy scout?"

Oliver laughed, "I'm just one of the good guys."

"Listen, we know our rights," said another. "I'm a lawyer. We're on our way to Sturgis"

"The Harley-Davison rally isn't till August," Oliver smiled. "You're a little early."

"We're not going to the rally. We're just going to ride the country in the Black Hills," the alleged lawyer said.

"You'll enjoy it," Oliver said, "It's a great place for biking".

The two in the rear of the saloon were watching the entire episode with interest. Finally one of them said, "Mr. Clearmountain, do we have to stay too?"

Obviously, one or both of the cowboys knew who Oliver was. He held up his hand in a casual way. "Just stay there a few minutes. This won't be long. Go around the bar and get two beers on me." Oliver didn't recognize the cowboys.

"I'll get them," the bartender said, as Kevin dismissed him and came over to the seated bikers.

"Ya'all heading up to Sturgis?" Kevin questioned.

They nodded their head in unison.

"I'm looking for three people, two males and one female. The guys are dressed in black tee shirts and jeans. The female wore a Dixie flag do rag on her head and was wearing a white tank top. One guy was hatless the other had on a beat up black straw hat."

"Do you know how many motorcycles we passed on the way here from California?" the spokesman said.

"That's not my interest," Kevin said. "Do you recall seeing my suspects?"

The bikers all shook their heads. "Listen here, Sheriff, we're businessmen from San Francisco, we don't..."

"I don't care who or what you are. If I was interested, I would have asked," Kevin interrupted as he passed out business cards with his address and phone number. "If you see the people I described, you give me a call, understand?"

They looked at each other and again nodded their heads in unison.

"Okay boys, you can go," Kevin announced, "but I suggest you walk around our town for an hour and do some shopping, because if you put your butts in the seat of those bikes I'll DUI all of you."

Oliver walked to the rear of the dark saloon to see the two cowboys. He now recognized one as a recent graduate of Betsy's school. "Ethan isn't it?" Oliver inquired.

"Yes sir, Mr. Clearmountain," the young man replied.

"You heard Sheriff Cahill's description of the three he's looking for. Give us a call if you see them. Now Ethan, you and your friend hightail it out of here and don't come back until you're old enough to drink."

The young cowboys didn't question Oliver. They headed straight for the door.

"Get me back to your office," Oliver said. "I gotta get home. Betsy will be there by now."

As they walked to the patrol car Oliver said, "Did you learn anything new from the bartender?"

Kevin just shook his head. "Same old story my deputies got. They were interested in you and Betsy. They wanted to know where you both worked, where you lived and how long you've been here. They said they were old friends."

"Yeah right," Oliver said as he slipped into the passenger seat.

# 12

Oliver's mind was drifting as he drove home. Was someone trying to frame him or was Hector killed trying to stop somebody from taking his Jeep? What was a high school kid doing up there alone? Was he part of the kids who were causing trouble in the region? Or maybe Hector stumbled across someone waiting to ambush him? None of this was making any sense. He almost missed the turn onto the road to his house. Boy that motorcycle is loud he thought as it passed him. "What?" he screamed out loud as he slammed on the brakes and looked into his rearview mirror. *That was a broad driving that bike and she had on a Dixie do rag.* He turned the wheel to pursue her, but then a scary thought struck. *That bike was coming from the direction of my house.* Now he only had one thought in mind and that was Betsy's safety. He slammed the accelerator to the floor and straightened the wheel. He only released the pedal from the metal as he approached his house. He slid into the driveway almost hitting Betsy's truck as his tires struggled for traction in the loose gravel. He bounded to the side door barely touching the ground. He screamed her name as he ran into the kitchen, "BETSY!"

"WHAT?" Was the equally loud response from behind him? Betsy had been in the laundry room off the kitchen when he burst through the door. He had startled her with his suddenness.

"Are you alright?" he said, rushing to her and embracing her.

"I'm not sure," she smiled, "You scared the life out of me," she said returning the hug. "You just missed my friend Lee," she said, as she backed away from Oliver smiling.

"The broad on the bike?" Oliver was confused. "You know her?"

"Yeah, the broad, as you called her, and I used to dance together back in Atlantic City." Betsy was now folding clothes on the kitchen table.

Oliver sat down at the table, reached out and took Betsy's hands. "Sit," he said. "We've got to talk."

She smiled, "Would you like some coffee? I just made some for Lee."

Oliver nodded, "Start from the beginning."

"Lee and I used to work together at the Borgata," Betsy said casually and then paused, "You've heard all this before."

He nodded, "Yeah, Yeah, what I want to know was how she knew you lived here?"

"That's the funny part," Betsy said, grinning. "She said she thought she saw me driving through town a few days ago. But I was gone before she could follow me. She said she had been asking around but it wasn't easy finding me because she was asking for Bet Brooks. That's what she used to call me." Betsy sipped her coffee. "It was only last night when she found out I was married to Oliver Clearmountain."

"Did she say she was traveling alone?" Oliver inquired.

"No, she said she was traveling with her boyfriend and another guy." Betsy paused. "Boy, has she changed. She's turned into a biker babe. She said love makes you do strange things."

"What do you know about her?" Oliver continued.

"Not much." Betsy shook her head. "We were friends for awhile, but only because we worked together. We were never really close. She was kind of unique. Along with being beautiful and smart she was feisty. I never thought she would turn out like this. When I knew her she wanted only the finest things life had to offer. She didn't even like cars, only limousines. I never thought I'd see her ass on a bike." Betsy made herself laugh. "Lee could be considered by some a snob, a gold digger, looking for the best of everything."

"So she was just driving through Pinedale in the middle of nowhere and sees you after all these years." Oliver's speech dripped with cynicism.

"It's only been four."

Oliver pushed back in the chair and stretched his legs out. He sighed, "It doesn't smell right." Suddenly, Oliver sat up, "By any chance did you notice what kind of shoes she was wearing?"

"As a matter of fact I did," Betsy said proudly. "She was wearing the same shoes that you wear, those Merrill Geminis. I thought they were unusual for motorcycle riding. Too soft I would think. What's with all the questions?"

"It was shoes like that that made the prints around my stolen Jeep."

Oliver pulled his cell phone out of his pocket and dialed Kevin.

"Yes, she was in my house," he said as he brought Kevin into the loop on the latest incident.

"They must still be staying in the area," Kevin replied. "Did she tell Betsy anything about where they were staying or might be going?"

"Nope," Oliver said. "They just had coffee and chatter for about half an hour and then Lee said she had to be going and left as suddenly as she arrived. Oh, by the way, Betsy said her name was Lee Fitzpatrick and at one time she talked of being a stock trader." Oliver chuckled. "I think she undershot her goal."

Oliver and Betsy talked at the table for quite some time. He explained his concern for her.

Betsy listened intently but Oliver wasn't sure she comprehended the threat her friend represented.

That evening Betsy said, "Let's go out to eat. I don't feel like cooking."

Oliver groaned, "I haven't had a home cooked meal in days."

"So what's another day," Betsy said. She was already up and heading for the door. "Come on, I'll let you drive my truck."

"Oh, the excitement, I can hardly contain myself," mocked Oliver as he followed her out the door.

One thing Oliver admired about Betsy was the fact he never had to wait for her to get ready. She wasn't like most women he knew who had to put make-up on and comb their hair before they could go anywhere.

# 13

Sitting in a booth at Mo's Restaurant, Oliver said, "I've already eaten here once today."

"So," Betsy smiled that cute little girl smile she was so capable of, "Don't order the same thing and make believe it's another day."

The waitress said, "What can I get you folks?"

"What's the special tonight?" Betsy asked.

"Beef stew."

Oliver looked at the waitress, "Is Mo's old dog still alive?"

The waitress wrinkled her brow in a puzzled manner. "Old Blue? Sure he's out back, why?"

"Just checking, Okay then, I'll have the stew," Oliver said. "But don't put it in a basket."

"Stop it Oliver," Betsy demanded.

The waitress took Betsy's order and walked away shaking her head.

As they were eating their dessert and drinking their coffee Big Mo came over and pulled up a chair. "If you can put up with him, I guess it's a small price for me to pay to enjoy your company," he grumbled. "Do you mind if I sit a spell with you?"

"I'd consider it an honor, Mo" Betsy replied.

He ignored Oliver completely. Such was Mo's humor. "There were some people in here the other day asking about you. I didn't like them so I told them I didn't know you."

Betsy nodded knowingly. That's the way he was. If Big Mo didn't like you he didn't talk to you.

Oliver sat up straight and said. "Bikers, two guys and a girl?"

"Yep," Mo nodded, "they looked like they were part of Marlon Brando's wild bunch. Do you remember that movie, The Wild One?"

"It was before my time," Oliver said, "but I caught it on television." Mo loved everything in the past and often Oliver didn't know what he was referring too.

"Did they say where they were staying?" Oliver felt he knew the answer, Strangers don't normally volunteer where they are staying.

"Nope," replied Mo, shaking his head, "But I know."

Oliver almost spit out his coffee in surprise. "You know where they're staying?" he gasped.

"Yep, I was driving south of here, about dusk the other night and I saw them turn up the dirt logging road. You know the one just below the Welsh place?" Big Mo said.

"Welsh place?" Oliver was slowly trying to picture in his mind's eye which ranch it was…Oh you mean Jane Welsh?" he announced as it suddenly came to him where the ranch was located.

"Jane the pain," Mo mumbled, "the self-righteous protester who hides behind religion."

"Easy Mo," Betsy grinned. "She's just very vocal about her opinion. She's a nice lady."

Mo dismissed Betsy's remark with a grunt, "I think they're camping out behind her place. In the past, she's let people stay there if they praise the Lord."

Betsy smirked to Oliver, "It doesn't sound like the Lee Fitzgerald I knew."

Oliver pulled out his cell phone. "I've got to tell Kevin."

"Why, are they wanted dead or alive?" Mo joked.

Oliver shook his head as he waited for the phone to be answered.

"I hate those things," Mo said to Betsy, pointing to the cell phone. "They make everyone think they're important and in reality they're just plain rude. One minute he's talking to me," he said nodding to Oliver, "and now he ignores me to talk to someone who's not even here. It's just plain rude I tell you," Big Mo rose from the chair and walked away shaking his head.

Oliver gave Betsy a questioned shrug that said what's wrong with him.

He made an appointment to meet Kevin at 6:00 o'clock in the morning in front of Jane Welsh's place. When he hung up, Betsy said, "Big Mo is right and you owe him an apology."

"For what?" Oliver stuffed the last piece of a brownie into his mouth.

After Betsy explained, Oliver paid the check at the counter. He saw Mo talking to some people at another table. He started toward him to apologize. When Mo realized his intentions, he quickly said something to the person at the table and picked up their cell phone that was lying on the table. Holding it to his ear he waved Oliver off as if he was too busy to talk to him.

In the parking lot Betsy laughed as she walked slowly to her truck holding Oliver's arm, "He'll get over it, I hope you've learned your lesson about cell phones," she said. "Modern technology has infringed on old fashioned etiquette and common courtesy."

"It seems like I've been insensitive to a lot of old fashioned customs and considerations the last two days," Oliver confessed. "Now Big Mo and Uncle Tigree are both upset with me."

# 14

It was 5:45 AM when Oliver pulled his Jeep up along side Kevin's Ford Explorer., "Do you think we should wake Jane up?" Kevin said. "I don't want her shooting us if she sees us prowling around on her property."

"Call her on your cell, it might be safer," Oliver offered.

Kevin dialed her number, "Yes Ms. Welsh, this is Sheriff Cahill. I'm sorry to be calling you so early but I wanted to tell you we were going to be on your back property in a short while and I didn't want to cause you concern."

"Yes ma'am, I know there are people sleeping back there. We want to talk to them," Kevin rolled his eyes at Oliver.

"No ma'am, I don't need a warrant to set foot on your property." Kevin was starting to lose it. He listened awhile longer to what must have been a lecture and then he just hung up without saying anything. He turned to Oliver and said, "She's still talking."

"Let's go," Oliver said, as he pulled in behind the Sheriff's Explorer letting him enter the road first. It was about a half a mile up the road where Jane Welsh had cleared the ground for a fire pit and an overhead shelter on a cement slab. It was the size of a normal garage except there were no sides. She let people stay up there for five dollars a day. Sometimes she would even give them a few muffins or cupcakes, when she baked a batch for her church. There wasn't any running water or toilet facility. It was just an out of the way place to sleep under the stars without being hassled. Kevin knew it was used mostly by bikers.

The road was just a little wider than a car. Halfway up the road they saw two motorcycles pulling out of the clearing. Kevin hit his siren once. A single, loud, shrill blast filled the morning air. It was obvious both riders were startled. The bike with two people accelerated at once, heading right at Kevin's SUV. It was doing forty on that narrow dirt road when it flew by Kevin and Oliver. Oliver could see fear in the female rider's eyes as she hung on. The other biker saw that Kevin and Oliver had now filled the road with their two vehicles, turned up the mountain road and headed toward the tree line. Kevin pulled into the clearing. Oliver goosed his Jeep past the clearing and followed the motorcycle. He could see Kevin on the radio as he flew by him. In his rear view mirror he saw Kevin exit the clearing in pursuit of the first bike.

Oliver knew this logging road ended in the next hundred yards. He didn't know how long the rider in front of him could keep the bike upright, but he did know his Jeep wasn't going to go much further than the fast approaching tree line. Oliver had lost sight of the rider over a small hill. When he cleared the knoll, the biker was nowhere to be seen. It was obvious to Oliver he had turned into the trees. He traversed the tree line for fifty yards and then stopped the Jeep turned it off and got out quickly to listen.

Silence. No birds were signaling the coming morning or frogs and crickets clinging to the lingering night. It was eerie quiet.

Oliver smiled because he knew the biker was now on foot. He was sure the guy would realize he couldn't go any further with his bike, so he would leave it and head up hill. Oliver saw where the long grass was laid down by the bike wheels and knew the biker couldn't be fifty yards ahead of him. He gave the area a wide birth and headed up hill running. His thought was to get in front of the man that was in unfamiliar terrain and then just wait for him to climb up to meet him. He covered four hundred yards, and then slowed; his lungs were burning in the thin mountain air. He found a large outcropping of boulders and sat behind them to catch his breath. It wasn't long before he heard the crashing of a tired plodding man cursing as he climbed the mountain. Oliver didn't have to look because the noise was coming right at him.

The gasping man stopped right in front of the rocks where Oliver was sitting. He turned and looked down to where he had just come. His hands were on his knees and he was wheezing. He was gasping and couldn't catch his breath. He had his back to Oliver.

Oliver stood up and was now less than five yards away from the man.

"Those cigarettes will kill ya." Oliver said in an authoritative voice.

"Jesus…" the man was so surprised his feet slid out from under him and he fell on his backside.

Oliver looked down into the prone man's eyes, "What took you so long?"

"Aw, Christ," the biker gasp. He was too tired to talk let alone run.

"Sit up" Oliver said.

When the biker didn't move Oliver nudged him in the head with his foot.

"Come on, sit up," Oliver smiled nicely. Then the demeanor in his voice changed instantly "or I'll kick your friggin head in," he barked.

The biker sat up and Oliver fastened a nylon tie handcuff on his wrists. "When ever you're ready," Oliver said. "Your mother is probably worried about you," he joked.

"Are you a cop?" he managed to get out in one breath. "I didn't do anything," he struggle for the next breath.

"Why did you run?"

He looked up at Oliver with one eye closed because sweat was running in it. "Warrants"

"What are they for, stupidity?" Oliver grabbed his arm and hauled him to his feet, then gently pushed him down the hill.

# 15

When he got to the station Oliver turned his prisoner over to Jimmy Hawk. Jimmy put him in a holding cell.

"Where's Kevin?"

"He'll be along shortly," Jimmy said. "The two he was chasing dumped their bike out on 191. He's making sure they are being guarded in the hospital.

'They're alive?" Oliver asked.

Jimmy nodded, "Banged up, but alive is what Kevin said."

"Hey Jimmy," Oliver remembered, "You better send a deputy up behind Jane Welsh's place. He'll need a truck. That guy's bike," his head nodded toward the holding cell, "is lying in the woods. Tell them to just follow the tracks, they'll find it."

Jimmy acknowledged and got on the police radio.

Oliver saw Kevin's Explorer pull up in the lot.

Kevin came bursting through the front door and signaled Oliver to follow him into his office. Kevin went directly for his coffee machine, "Jimmy said you got your guy."

Oliver nodded, "He's in your holding cell. How did you do?"

"I lost one" Kevin made eye contact with Oliver. "The girl didn't make it."

"How about the guy?" Oliver wanted to know.

"Doc said he'll make it, but it will be awhile before we can talk to him." Kevin said as he sipped his black coffee. "Hell Oliver, that bike slid a hundred yards." Kevin shook his head is amazement. "So all we have is the guy in the cell."

"Let's go talk to him," Oliver said.

Kevin and Oliver looked through the bars at the guy sitting on the wall cot. "It's time to talk," Kevin said.

Oliver and Kevin were standing right in front of the cell.

"Talk about what?" the biker gestured to Oliver, "this maniac that chased me through the woods?"

"Open the cell," Oliver said to Kevin.

The biker stood up and backed into the far wall. "If you think you're going to get tough, you'll have a fight on your hands."

Kevin swung the cell door open and Oliver stepped to the threshold, "If I was going to get tough, you would be laying in the woods where I found you." He gestured to the guy, "Come on we're going outside.'

Kevin didn't know what Oliver had in mind, but he knew this wasn't his first time interrogating a prisoner. Oliver walked out the back door. The prisoner followed, and Kevin brought up the rear. Once they were outside Oliver put his arm around the nervous biker and said, "Look around at the beautiful mountains, suck in the fresh air. Because unless you start answering our questions, hell will freeze over before you see freedom again."

"I don't know anything…"

"Okay Sheriff," Oliver said, "let's lock him in the basement and take a week to process the paper work."

Kevin smiled, "I don't know if we can do it that fast."

"Wait, wait," the biker said. "What do you want to know?"

Now that didn't hurt, did it?" Oliver said, "Sit down on the bench." He reached into Kevin's breast pocket and took out one of Kevin's choice cigars. "Would you like a cigar?"

The man sat down in disbelief at the sudden kindness he was being shown. He warily took the cigar from Oliver. "You got a match?"

"I'm sure the sheriff has one, as soon as you tell me why you stole my Jeep." Oliver smiled.

"Listen, I don't know the whole story," he started, "It was Lee and Nick's deal. They said some guy they met in Denver paid them to harass you. He gave them a thousand dollars and promised five times that much if they would kidnap your wife and bring her to Denver. They weren't sure they wanted to get involved in kidnapping so while they were making up their minds they decided to scare you. They wanted to see just how hard it would be to swipe her."

"So what happened when you took my Jeep?" Oliver said, making sure he didn't say anything about Hector.

"I don't know. I wasn't there. My bike was misfiring," he continued. "Bad plugs and by the time I got it fixed they were coming down with a Jeep. Lee was driving and Nick was following on his bike." Kevin struck a match and held it up for the biker. He paused to puff on the cigar. The biker blew some smoke in the air. He was starting to enjoy his freedom and realized if he kept talking he might get out of this mess.

"Go on," Kevin said.

"Well I noticed a body in the back of the Jeep. Nick said this dumb Indian surprised them when they were fixin to steal the Jeep. The Indian said he knew who it belonged to. Lee told him to relax, it was just a joke they were pulling on someone. Nick offered him some marijuana and the Indian smoked his brains out. I guess he was used to smoking rag weed because they said the California Gold they gave him knocked him on his ass. He was out of it in ten minutes, damn near unconscious Lee said."

"So is that when they left the Jeep?" Oliver prompted.

The biker paused as he examined the cigar. "That's when the strangest thing happened. Nick was worried that the Indian could identify us. Suddenly, in one quick motion Lee stuck a knife in his chest, "Now he can't" she said showing no emotion.

"Hell, I don't even know where the knife came from, it all happened so fast." The biker shook his head. "Nick just stared at her and she grinned back at him with a crazy look and they both started laughing."

Oliver glared at the biker, he wasn't laughing.

# 16

Oliver was sitting on the edge of the chair, his elbows on his knees. Kevin was in his usual position with his feet on his desk, leaning back in his chair.

"It's Jonathan Yokatory," Oliver said.

"Who the hell is Jonathan Yokatory?" Kevin asked.

"He's an extremist who wants to destroy America and start all over again." Oliver was staring at the floor. "He's under the impression that white trash are the only people who should remain alive. He feels that Blacks, Orientals, anybody that doesn't burn and blister in the sun qualify for euthanasia." Oliver glanced up to see if Kevin got his little joke.

"Oh," Kevin said nodding his head. "So he doesn't like Indians."

Oliver wrapped up with Kevin before lunch. He drove directly to the High School in hopes of catching Betsy on her lunch break. He was sitting in the facility lounge when Betsy walked in.

She looked up and smiled, "Hi honey, did you come by to have lunch with me?" Oliver frequently would stop by for lunch when he was in the area.

Oliver nodded, "What's on the hot lunch menu today?"

"I'm not sure," Betsy said, holding up a bag. "I'm brown bagging it today."

Betsy sat down on the chair next to Oliver and took out a sandwich and said, "Do you want a bite?"

"When we went to pick up Lee Fitzpatrick and her friends for questioning this morning, her boyfriend decided to make a run for it on his bike. They crashed and Lee was killed." Oliver said, putting his hand on Betsy's arm.

Betsy closed her eyes tight when she heard the news. For a moment she was quiet. Then she said, "Was it quick?"

"I don't know. She was pronounced dead at the hospital, but I don't know if she ever regained consciousness."

Betsy looked at Oliver. "What is this whole thing about? Why did they run from Kevin? It wasn't just by chance she suddenly showed up in town, was it?"

"I don't know, Betsy, but I'm going to find out, "Oliver promised.

"Is it about me, something from back east, should I be worried?" Betsy had put her sandwich down and was now fiddling with the paper towel from the bag.

"There is nothing about your past that should concern us. No, it's about me," Oliver said. 'I think it's a crazy from my life in the Secret Service. A worthless piece of bile named Jonathan Yokatory. We think he's in Colorado. He can't hurt us honey, we'll find him soon enough." He smiled and patted her arm.

Oliver's little lie was so Betsy wouldn't concern herself. Oh he knew he'd catch Yokatory, he just didn't know how soon.

"How would Lee figure in with him?" Betsy wondered. "Don't tell me that's just a coincidence."

"There's no other explanation," Oliver said. He took a chocolate chip cookie from her lunch bag but Betsy slapped it out of his hand before he could get it in his mouth. "Have lunch first," she pointed in the direction of the cafeteria, "Then I'll give you a cookie."

Oliver looked at his beautiful wife. He respected her strength, and knew how hard she would fight to keep their life normal

Oliver called his uncle, Chief Tigree, and asked if he could meet with him. Tigree told him he would meet him in Atlantic City. He thought it was better if they met off the reservation. The Atlantic City that Tigree meant was a small mining community just beyond South Pass. It lay along the Beaver River and was connected to route 28 by dirt roads. Oliver wasn't sure how the town became know as Atlantic City. He suspected it was named after the mine. It was two thousand miles from the Atlantic Ocean with a population of 39, but there was a café.

As Oliver drove he reflected on the fact that he was no longer welcome on the reservation. He guessed he could be thankful Tigree took his call and was willing to meet with him. Maybe blood really was thicker than water.

Tigree was in his truck when Oliver pulled up along side of him. He looked over through his passenger window nodded and said, "Uncle".

Tigree response was similarly short, "Nephew," he replied.

Oliver came around to the driver's side, "Are we going in?"

"No," said Tigree. "Go get us something to drink. We'll meet here in my truck."

Oliver tried to lighten the moment, "Don't want to be seen with me, huh?"

Tigree's deadpan reply was, "I'll have a coke."

Oliver got back in the truck with two cokes. He handed one to Tigree, and he received no small talk in return. There was a very uncomfortable moment. Oliver took a long pull on his coke.

He finally said, "I have information on Hector's murder."

Tigree nodded for him continue.

"Apparently, he came across the people stealing my Jeep," Oliver said, and then he bent the truth as he continued. "He tried to stop them and they killed him." There wasn't any reason to explain he had befriended them and then smoked himself comatose with marijuana.

"I will tell his people he died a hero" Tigree said. "They need some good news."

Oliver's nod spoke volumes. It signified that he understood and agreed with what the chief was doing.

Tigree looked strong into Oliver's eyes. "Two Fox", he said, using Oliver's Indian name, "Hector was one of the five boys' you have been looking for. I have the other four. They are all from the reservation and will be subjected to Shoshone law. Let me know of any property damages that need to be reimbursed. "

The relief flowed over Oliver. By using his Indian name, Tigree had forgiven Oliver for his past blunder.

"I will," Oliver said. "I don't think it will amount to much. Maybe you can look into replacing the dog that was killed."

Tigree's grunt meant that he would. "Go, we are through here, but a word of advice. Visit your home every few moons and bring your wife. Show our elders you are proud of your people."

"I will, Uncle," he said, and slipped out of the truck. He left a package of Twinkies on the seat. Leaving a gift after a favorable meeting was a Shoshone custom. Besides they were Tigree's favorites.

# 17

That evening Oliver and Betsy were enjoying their coffee after a wonderful chicken dinner they had prepared together. One of the pleasant things they did in concert was cook. They tried to do it a couple of times a week. It was precious time together and they had become quite accomplished at it. They often spoke about opening a restaurant later in life, although they realized the dangerous downside of having to cook everyday and make a profit. Cooking together at this point of their life was a pleasant hobby.

Oliver was facing the side door so he saw Kevin just before he knocked. Oliver signaled him in, "It's unlocked," he said.

He walked up behind Betsy and kissed her on the neck, "Hi beautiful," he said.

"Mmm," Betsy moaned, "That will get you free coffee." She went to the cabinet, retrieved a mug and poured him a cup.

"Business or pleasure?" Oliver asked.

Kevin sat down. "Well, that was pleasurable," Kevin said smiling at Betsy as she put the mug on the table, "but I'm here on business. I thought you would like to know we have testimony from both bikers. You're in the clear. Of course they are both blaming the dead girl for the murder."

Betsy shuddered and shook her head in disbelief.

Kevin continued, but now directing his conversation to Betsy "I have no reason to doubt them since they haven't had a chance to conspire. The story they tell is too similar, I have to believe them."

He continued observing Betsy. "Don't you think Lee Fitzpatrick was capable of murder?"

Betsy looked at both men with a bewildered look, "I guess, I didn't know her very well."

Kevin continued, "As far as the kidnapping part of the story, I'll…"

## THE PAST IS NEVER DEAD

"Kidnapping?" Betsy said, looking at Oliver, "you didn't say anything about kidnapping!"

"Oops," Kevin said and picked up his mug as if he could hide behind it.

Oliver gave a disgusted glance to Kevin then smiled at Betsy. "One of the bikers told Kevin they were offered money from Jonathan Yokatory if they would kidnap my wife. The decided they weren't going to do it."

"Why kidnap me?" Betsy said.

"To hurt me," Oliver replied. "That's how sick this jerk is, and it's why I'm going down to Denver and find the punk."

Betsy had a surprised look on her face, "And just when were you going to tell me about it?"

"I was just about to discuss it with you over our coffee when Matt Dillon rode into our kitchen acting like the town crier." Oliver nodded his head at Kevin who was still hiding behind the coffee mug. Trying to diffuse the situation, he continued. "First I wanted to tell you about my meeting with Chief Tigree. He has forgiven my indiscretions and I'm welcome back on the reservation." He smiled at Betsy.

"Why are you so sure?" Betsy asked. "What did he say exactly?"

"It not so much what he said although he did invite both of us down as soon as we can make it," he smiled at Betsy. "But more importantly he accepted my gift."

Betsy looked puzzled for a moment and then started laughing, "You didn't," She giggled. "You gave him a Twinkie as a peace offering!"

Oliver nodded trying to contain himself, "Yep."

Betsy was relieved because she saw how happy Oliver was. She knew how important saving face was with the Shoshones, especially her Shoshone.

Kevin spoke up, "How are you going to find Yokatory? Colorado is a big state."

"My guys in DC gave me his PO Box in Fort Collins. That's how they have been keeping an eye on him. Someone picks up the mail everyday. It won't take me long to find him."

Kevin sipped his coffee and said, "And then what?"

"It shouldn't concern you," Oliver said, casting a stern look at Kevin. "It's out of your jurisdiction."

Betsy rested her face in her hands covering her eyes.

Knowing that Betsy couldn't see him, Kevin winked at Oliver. "Well I'll have a cell ready when you bring him back," Kevin said playing along with the charade. Both men knew Yokatory would be dead minutes after Oliver found him.

Betsy looked up. "Are you sure it's Yokatory that's doing this?"

"As sure as I can be," Oliver said. "He's the only one I can't account for." He studied the worried look on his wife's face. "Do you think it's someone from the casino trying to get you?"

Betsy shook her head unknowingly. "Mike Bond was pushing himself on me. I left town in the middle of the night because of that creep." Then she contradicted herself, "I didn't leave a clue behind. It can't be him."

"Love makes men do strange things," Kevin smiled.

Betsy snickered, "He wasn't in love. He was in lust. I'm sure he's forcing himself on some other young innocent kid who thinks he has her best interest at heart."

Oliver said, "If you believe that, then he isn't the guy."

Betsy paused with a pensive look and then nodded in agreement. "I guess you're right, but I still don't believe the fact that Lee Fitzpatrick just happened to show up here. That just sticks in my craw."

Oliver and Kevin looked at each other with a slight grin at Betsy's choice of words. She had come a long way from Atlantic City.

Kevin cleared his throat, "Hector's funeral is tomorrow."

"Yes, I know," Oliver acknowledged. "I'm going to attend and then continue on to Fort Collins."

Betsy got up from the table, "I'd better get the laundry done. You're going to need some clean clothes." She gave Oliver a peck on the cheek as she headed to the laundry room. Without looking back she said, "You're going to need a dress shirt and your suit pressed if you're going to a funeral."

Kevin banged the coffee mug on the table with a firm rap. "Do you have anything stronger than this, I'm officially off duty."

# 18

The funeral was a sobering affair. There isn't much comfort you can give parents who have to bury their children, Oliver thought, as he drove down Route 287 toward Fort Collins. He was relieved that he had been received so well by the elders. It seemed they were pleased he had taken the time to attend the services of a young fallen warrior. It never failed to impress him how stoic the Indian can be in times of distress. At times they appear to be indifferent to emotional pain or distress. Oliver knew this was trained self control of ones emotions.

The trip to Hector's funeral had, in a way, been a re-birth for Oliver. It caused him to reflect on his earlier life on the reservation. He recalled when his grandfather had given him his Indian name, Two Fox, he was twelve years old. His grandfather said, "My son, every person has a battle that goes on within them. It's the battle of two foxes. One is evil. It is angry, envious, jealous, and full of sorrow, regret, greed, arrogance, self-pity, guilt, lies, resentment, false pride and ego. The other one is good. It is joy, peace, love, hope, humility, kindness, truth, benevolence, generosity, compassion and faith."

Oliver looked at the old man in admiration and said, "Which fox wins the battle, grandfather?"

The old Shoshone simply replied, "The one YOU feed. Then you must learn from the fox, how to listen, but not been seen, be present, but no one notices."

Oliver pulled into a rest area and changed his clothes. His plans didn't include looking like a businessman. He arrived in Fort Collins just after two o'clock. He found the Post Office without much difficulty. He had given some thought to advising the Postmaster of his intentions to stake out PO Box 198. He eventually decided against it simply because the fewer people he involved the better. He was reasonably sure the outcome would be malevolent at best.

He stopped at a diner and got a hamburger and a cup of coffee, and then a coffee to go. He settled in to watching the post office for the balance of the day. He didn't follow everyone in to see their transaction. His experience would tell him at first glance just who might be a Yokatory follower.

Oliver didn't think he would be lucky enough to see anyone today, but the Post Office would be open a little longer and he didn't have anything else to do until he spotted the Yokatorian. He made sure he had a full tank of gas and was ready to roll, but the day ended uneventfully when the door of the Post Office was locked. He turned his thoughts on where to sleep.

Colorado State University's presence made for an abundance of coffee shops and restaurants as well as numerous Bed and Breakfast Inns. He picked one near Old Town and decided to get a good nights sleep and get to the Post Office early.

He hadn't waited an hour when a suspect walked up to Box 198 and emptied it. Oliver knew immediately he was a Jonathan Yokatory follower. He was wearing cargo style camouflaged pants, a tee shirt that had something written on it which Oliver couldn't read, and a black baseball cap that said CAT on it. He was around six feet tall, maybe six one. Oliver noticed he was wearing combat boots. He hurried to his Jeep and watched as the guy jumped into a beat up blue pickup truck. Oliver could tell from the dust and dents that it had seen a lot of back roads. Oliver waited a moment after the truck pulled away from the curb. He didn't want the guy to know he was being followed. What Oliver didn't notice was the second truck that followed him away from the curb.

In no time at all Oliver was in Poudre Canyon in the Northeast part of Roosevelt National Forest. It was rocks and pines and both were getting more plentiful as they traveled west. The truck turned off at a dirt road and quickly vanished over a rocky rise. Oliver crept slowly over the rise not knowing what was on the other side. As the hood of his Jeep settled back level to the road he saw the truck fifty yards in front of him. The driver of the truck was standing next to it pointing a rifle at Oliver's head. His first instinct was to throw the Jeep in reverse, as the wheels grabbed traction Oliver looked to see where he was going. At the top of the road not twenty feet behind him was another truck. He was trapped. He quickly put the Jeep in park and raised his hands in the air.

Looking straight ahead at the guy with the rifle he heard the one behind him say, "Get out of the Jeep and on your knees."

Oliver did as he was told, keeping his hands in plain sight the entire time. He knew what the next command would be.

"Keep your hands where I can see them," the one in front of him shouted.

These creeps had been trained in law enforcement.

Oliver could now read the tee-shirt of the one with the rifle as he walked up to him. It read 'GROW YOUR OWN DOPE—PLANT A BLOND. "Just where in the hell do you think you're going?"

"Now, I'm not too sure," Oliver said as he folded his hands behind his neck.

"Clasp you hands be…never mind," the one behind him said.

"You've done this before." The one in front of him said. "Do you make it a habit of being taken down?"

Another police term Oliver thought to himself, as he shook his head.

"Why were you following me?" he asked, as he put the rifle on the hood of Oliver's Jeep. He took out a cigarette and lit it.

Oliver knew the man behind him had a gun trained on his head or the one in front of him wouldn't be that careless.

"I wasn't following you at first," Oliver said. "We just happen to be going in the same direction. I got lost, so I was going to ask you for directions."

"Where is it you were headed?"

"I'm looking for someone," Oliver said, "but I'm not sure where he lives."

The voice from behind him said, "This is a big country, butt hole, how are you going to find your friend if you don't know where he lives?"

At this point Oliver had to take a chance. "Maybe you've heard of him, Jonathan Yokatory!" Oliver studied the face of the man in front of him for a reaction. It was obvious Oliver had identified these two correctly, when the guy's mouth fell open.

"How do you know Jonathan?"

"We're old friends," Oliver lied.

"What's your name?"

Oliver was now buying time, "Take me to him and he'll tell you my name."

The guy in front said to his friend behind Oliver, "Watch him." He walked back to his truck and pulled it off the road. Returning, he tossed his rifle to his friend and said, "Follow us." He jumped into the back of the Jeep and pointed a pistol at Oliver. "Drive," he said, beckoning Oliver into the driver seat with the pistol.

Oliver breathed a silent sigh of relief as he settled in behind the wheel. *If he wanted to know my name all he had to do was look in my wallet. I've survived phase one. But I'm clueless as to what to do next.*

# 19

The road wound between jagged rocks and ponderosa pines and each turn was steeper. The road almost disappeared and as Oliver was starting to pass two large boulders the man in the back said, "Stop."

He jumped out and walked to the thick brush between the boulders. With a push the bushes swung open as if on hinges. The opening was wide enough for the Jeep to pass. He observed as he passed that the hedges were actually potted plants woven through a swinging gate. Ingenious, he thought to himself, when suddenly he noticed he was in a rock canyon with numerous other people. A good size camp lay before him. Oliver counted six large military tents, the type with hard wood siding. His captor motioned him out of the Jeep. He was directed to a porta john, the kind you find on construction sites. It was obvious they wanted him to go in it, so he did. He noticed a lock on the outside as he entered. Although it was cleaner than most, it was also evident this was used as a holding cell rather than a latrine.

Oliver needed time to think. He knew he was dead the minute he met Yokatory face to face. This group wasn't interested in prisoners, besides, if he was right about Yokatory being behind the trouble in Pinedale, he was as good as dead. If he was mistaken about him and he wasn't the guy, he was still dead if Yokatory recognized him. This was a lose, lose situation and Oliver needed to do something pronto.

He was upset with himself for not noticing he'd been followed. That was a rookie mistake. He wondered, if they were dumb enough not to check his wallet maybe they hadn't checked the glove box on the Jeep and found his Berretta. He couldn't risk making a break for the Jeep only to find the glove box empty. He assumed there was a guard standing outside. He hadn't heard anyone lock the door after he entered. He could see a shadow of the guard through the vent on the side. He gently pushed the door, it opened slightly. Oliver was surprised it hadn't been locked. A loud noise erupted from the camp area. It sounded like a cheer. Oliver realized he might have a second of opportunity at this moment. He opened the door far enough to see the guard looking toward the camp. He silently slipped out and closed the door without making a noise. The guard's back was to him and his attention was focused on the camp. He quickly ducked behind the porta potty. In his haste he bumped it and the guard hastily turned his attention back on his duty.

"Keep it quiet in there," he demanded.

Olive put his mouth next to the outer slats of the rear vent and said, "Let me out of here. I haven't done anything wrong." He hoped it sounded like he was still inside.

"Shut up," the guard barked. And then Oliver heard the familiar click of a Yale lock being snapped shut. *He just locked the door. He thinks I'm still inside.* There was a garden hose coiled on the ground behind the structure. Oliver figured it was used to flush out the holding reservoir in the toilet. He wedged one end of the hose into the rear vent. Keeping the portable latrine between him and the guard, Oliver drifted slowly backwards through the long weeds into the bushes, uncoiling the hose as he went.

Oliver scanned the area. He couldn't get to his Jeep without being seen but he had to get out of the immediate area. Behind him the terrain sloped down ten feet.

Oliver put the end of the hose up to his mouth and said, "I want to see Jonathan."

The guard banged on the side of the structure with the butt of his weapon, "Shut up. They're deciding what to do with you. You don't want them to hurry," he laughed.

Oliver pulled on the hose and it snapped lose from the vent. He quickly gathered it in and hid it in the weeds. He slipped down the hill and made his way to the road. He was surrounded by high boulders but there was enough room to pass between them. His intention was to go for high ground away from the way he entered the area. He was sure searchers would look for him to escape the way he came in, so he turned further up the mountain keeping the entrance with the hidden gate to his back.

His plan was to wait until he was found missing. He figured they would mount a search party with every available able bodied person and go looking for him. He would then slip back into the camp and make a run for it with his Jeep. He was now three hundred yards above the camp on the hill opposite the entrance. He started to settle in when he was startled by movement in the brush behind him. A quick glance over his shoulder was all he needed to confirm his suspicions. A large, hungry looking, black bear, had just caught his scent and started directly toward him.

    Oliver didn't have time to think, he just reacted. He jumped from his hiding spot and started running back down the hill straight for the front gate. He could feel the bear in hot pursuit. He was now in a semi controlled fall down the slope. At any moment he felt he would go sprawling flat on his face. Finally the slope became more gradual. He gained control of his balance and ran as fast as he could for the gate. Suddenly, the gate opened and out rushed a dozen armed men. It was the search party setting out to find him. This might have been the shortest man hunt in history. They all looked surprised at the sight they saw. In unison they raised their guns and pointed in Oliver's direction. Oliver threw his arms up as he continued to run toward them. Twelve rifles fired at you all at once is a gut retching experience. Oliver could feel the concussion from the explosion and the bullets whizzing past him. He heard the thump of bullets hitting soft tissue. He knew the bear was close. But then he heard the crashing sound of a large mass rolling through the brush. He stopped twenty yards in front of the armed mob. Their cocked weapons were pointing at him. He took a quick look back and saw the black hairy mound of what was once a charging, snarling bear. It lay dead less than twenty feet behind him. He stood gasping for breath with his arms held up as high as he could reach.

# 20

Kevin put his feet up on his desk waiting for the school to answer the phone. He wanted to know if Betsy had heard from Oliver.

"Pinedale High School," said the pleasant female voice.

"This is Sheriff Cahill. I'd like to speak to Betsy Clearmountain," he said with as much authority he could muster. "If she is in class have her call me the first break she gets."

"She isn't here, Sheriff. Betsy took some personal time today. I believe she is home." The voice explained.

"Thank you," Kevin said. He clicked the phone off, but the receiver remained at his ear.

Kevin wondered why Betsy took time off, maybe Oliver is home already. He shook his head, dismissing that thought. He couldn't be back that quick.

He dialed the Clearmountain residence and let the phone ring until the answering machine notified him neither Oliver nor Betsy were home. It was Betsy's sweet voice that invited him to leave a message.

He hung up the phone, puzzled but not concerned. He sat at his desk pondering the reasons no one was home. He finally keyed the mike on his office two-way radio that sat on the credenza behind his desk. "Jimmy Hawk, Jimmy Hawk, come back," he shouted into the mike.

The radio crackled and buzzed and then he heard Jimmy, "What's up Sheriff? What do you need? Come back."

"Take a cruise past the Clearmountain place. See if the misses is home. Come back."

"Okay," Jimmy said. "What do I tell her if she's home? Come back"

"Just tell her to call me, Sheriff out," he said and threw the mike on the credenza.

It was almost an hour later when Jimmy walked into the Sheriff's office.

He looked confused. "No one is home at the Clearmountains. But the misses' truck is there," he said.

"Did you knock on the door?" Kevin inquired.

Jimmy gave him a cynical grin. "Now how would I know she's not home if I didn't knock on the door? I even walked around and peeked in the windows. No one is home." He declared.

Kevin rose quickly from his desk. "Oliver is out of state," he said walking to the door. "With her truck still there she couldn't go very far. Come on, we're going to take a closer look."

Oliver and Betsy's home looked peaceful and serene in the noon day sun. Kevin banged on the side door as Jimmy walked around the house peering in the windows to see if he could see any movement.

The radio in Kevin's SUV suddenly came alive. As always, Kevin had switched the external speaker on as he exited the vehicle. "Sheriff, Sheriff, this is Woody, I'm in pursuit of a traffic stop that decided to rabbit. Come back," Deputy Woody Page's voice echoed from the speaker under the front grille. Kevin jumped down off the steps, leaned into the SUV and grabbed the mike. "Well good for you, Page. What do you want from me? Come back." Kevin said.

"I thought you'd like to know Betsy Clearmountain is in the car, Come back." The deputy said.

"You're sure," Kevin demanded. "Come back."

"Yep," Page responded. "I walked up on them before they decided to bolt. It's her. Come back"

"Don't loose that car," Kevin screamed. "Treat this as a kidnapping. Use extreme force if necessary. I'll get you back-up. Where are you? Come back."

"I've notified the State boys, they're setting up a road block. I'm heading south on 191 about to pass 353 on my left. Damn," Woody screamed and then the radio went dead.

Kevin tooted the horn to get Jimmy Hawk's attention. The deputy came running.

"What's up, Sheriff?" Jimmy asked, as he slid into the passenger seat.

Kevin held up his hand asking for silence. He listened hard for Deputy Pages sign off. There was nothing.

Kevin turned the siren on and headed out to the highway. He flew through Pinedale with the siren screaming. "Dispatch, Dispatch. Come back."

"Yo Sheriff, come back," the dispatcher replied immediately.

"Get in touch with the State troopers. I want to know when that car hits their road block. Come back"

"Consider it done," the dispatcher said. "We've lost signal with Deputy Page. Come back."

"Keep trying, Sheriff out," Kevin threw the microphone on the seat. It bounced to the floor. Jimmy Hawk picked it up and clipped it to the dash.

Kevin knew his deputy had run into trouble, but his main concern was Betsy. He couldn't let that car get away. He had no idea what was going on, but he knew he had to find Betsy. If anything happened to her he couldn't imagine what Oliver would do.

He thought of calling Oliver's cell but what would he tell him? That his wife was in the process of being kidnapped and he didn't know where she was or who had taken her.

"Take it easy Sheriff," Jimmy said. "We can't help anybody if we're in a ditch."

Kevin glanced at the speedometer. He was going ninety on a two lane road just on the outskirts of town. He let up slightly on the accelerator.

Up ahead on the road, Kevin could see cars parked on the shoulder. As he approached the area he saw a deputy's car on its side in a ditch. He slammed on the brakes and had the transmission in park the second the SUV quit moving. He and Jimmy were running toward Deputy Page's car. Two men were tending to a prone body that was next to the smoking vehicle. There were a few other people standing around. One citizen was helping keep the traffic moving on the highway.

"How is he?" Kevin asked those attending Woody.

"I'm not hurt as bad as I will be when you get done with me," Deputy Page said looking up at Kevin. He was holding his left shoulder with his right hand. He grimaced, "I think my shoulder is broken."

# 21

Oliver sat on a stump in the center of the camp. There were fifteen men, all armed, in the immediate area. He was being questioned by one who was obviously in charge. He had Oliver's wallet in his hand.

"So how does a Forest Ranger know Jonathan Yokatory?"

"We go back to our youth, we went to school together," Oliver lied. He was racking his brain trying to remember Yokatory's portfolio, anything about where he was born, grew up, what schools he attended.

"So why do you want to see him now?" the questioner continued.

"Look, you have me at a disadvantage. You know who I am, but I don't know your name," Oliver was trying to take control of the conversation. "Am I going to get a chance to see Jonathan?" This was about as far in the corner as Oliver could paint himself. He was out of options. He was looking around to see who he should jump first. The fellow to his left was a likely candidate. He seemed to be fighting to stay awake. The shotgun was held loosely in the crook of his arm and he had a pistol strapped to his right hip. Oliver was sure he could take either weapon from him without much resistance. He might also be able to use the guy's body as a shield.

"I'm afraid that's going to be impossible," the leader said. "Jonathan Yokatory is dead."

Oliver's head snapped up to focus his attention to the speaker. "Dead, when?"

"Months ago, He died of cancer of the pancreas. The few of us that remain here are no longer followers of Jonathan's teaching. We're just trying to survive out of the mainstream of the crazy world. Live and let live is our new mission statement. We just want to be left alone. We're not driven by any religious morals of political ideology."

Oliver stared at the man, not wanting him to stop talking now, because his demeanor had changed. He was almost apologizing to Oliver.

"I'm sorry Jonathan died," Oliver lied. He decided to push his luck and stand up, "but I'm overjoyed with what you have to say. My purpose in coming here was to try one more time to convince Jonathan that his way of life was misguided." Oliver hung his head, trying to look despondent. *I've got to get my butt out of here.*

He's buried right over there," the man pointed to a clearing forty yards away, "If you'd like to pay your last respects."

Oliver nodded and starting walking toward the clearing. He couldn't believe his luck.

He stood at the grave site trying to look reverent, as if paying his last respects to an old friend. In reality he was planning how to get out of the camp. He sensed someone walking up to him as he stood with his head hung in a prayer like manner.

"Here's your cell phone," a camper said, handing Oliver his phone. "There's a call for you."

"Hello," Oliver turned his back to the camper as one does when seeking privacy with a phone call.

"Where the hell are you?" said Kevin. "I've been calling you all morning."

"Yokatory's camp," Oliver said.

"Can you leave?" Kevin sensed tension in Oliver's voice.

"I'm not sure. Ten minutes ago the answer was no, but now I'm not sure." He turned and looked at the camp. All eyes were on him.

Kevin picked his words carefully, "We have a situation back here that needs your attention. Betsy is missing."

Oliver felt the long distance blow in the gut. He actually flinched, the words Betsy is missing hurt so much. "Where is she?" He realized how dumb that question was before he finished saying it. His first rational thought was leaving the camp right now. "Call me back in five minutes," he said before Kevin could answer him. He turned and quickly walked back to the group that was staring at him.

"That was bad news, it's my wife. May I leave?" he asked the leader.

"Can you forget you were ever here?" The leader said.

"I'll swear I'll never mention this place to a soul," Oliver replied.

The leader nodded toward Oliver's Jeep. "Go, if you ever come back, you'll not leave the second time."

Oliver ran to his Jeep and jumped in. The fellow standing next to it, tossed him his Berretta and holster. "Nice weapon. I thought I was going to get to keep it," he said smiling.

Oliver was racing down Route 14 when his phone rang. It was Kevin "Are you free?"

"And heading home," Oliver said.

"Which way you coming home?" Kevin asked.

"287" Oliver responded.

"There will be a Wyoming State trooper at the border to escort you home. Blink your lights when you see him, then get on his rear bumper and try to catch him," Kevin said.

"What about Betsy?" Oliver asked.

"Focus on driving, we'll talk when you get here," Kevin told him and hung up before Oliver could ask anymore questions.

Oliver found it hard to focus on his driving. Negative thoughts raced through his mind. *I should have never left her alone. Who could have taken her and why, Yokatory was dead. Maybe Sharad Ramadoos isn't in India anymore. Could it be he's amassed some wealth and is coming after me? Maybe she went for a drive.*

When he crossed the Colorado/Wyoming state line he spotted the Wyoming Highway patrol's black Dodge Charger with the gold slash on the side. Sitting under the welcome sign. Oliver flashed his lights and floored it, pushing the Jeep to its limits. The 5.7 liter hemi powered Charger came past him like he was standing still and pulled in front of him. The trooper pumped his arm like truckers do when they are ready to roll. Oliver knew he had just caught the express to Pinedale.

# 22

It was still light out as Kevin briefed Oliver. Oliver's Jeep was parked in front of Kevin's SUV. They were on the side of route 191 at the 353 turn off.

"Woody lost control of his cruiser back up the road there," Kevin said as he motioned behind him. "He said they threw something out of the car and he swerved to avoid hitting it."

"Is he going to be okay?" Oliver asked.

"He's in better shape than his car," Kevin said. "The highway patrol had a moving roadblock coming north on 191. The suspect's car never reached the roadblock. So we searched up 353 and found their car just past Big Sandy. They're heading up into the Wind River range."

"So they're on foot?"

Kevin nodded, "As best we can tell. We have the area blocked off behind them, they can only go up. I don't think they're prepared for the elements. Woody said they were dressed in business suits"

"How long have they been hoofing it?"

"Five hours. We'll start a search in the morning. We'll get them Oliver. Woody said he didn't think they were from around here. The car is a rental. I believe they're city folk."

"I'm going in now," Oliver said. "There is 90 minutes of daylight left." He looked deep into Kevin's eyes and said, "Do try to stop me, it's my mountain."

Kevin tossed him a hand held radio. "Stay in touch we'll have air search up at first light. Good hunting."

Oliver drove to where the rental had been left. It was obvious they tried to drive it off road. They managed to get no more than 500 hundred yards off the paved road when their Ford bottomed out on the uneven terrain. Without traction, the car couldn't go any further.

## THE PAST IS NEVER DEAD

Oliver's Jeep had much better luck. Following their tracks wasn't much of a challenge. Four people plodding through the woods, three of them in unfamiliar surroundings leaving unintentional tracks, while the fourth person was leaving them on purpose. *Good girl Betsy,* Oliver thought, as he saw the once tall trodden down grass. He was moving very slowly in his Jeep but so far the tracks were easy to follow. He already knew he was gaining ground on them. He suspected they would stop moving after dark. He was sure they were too smart to start a camp fire, and he was also aware of the tricks the forest can play on someone's mind, especially someone unfamiliar with the wilderness at night. If they were under the canopy of the trees the night would get very black and unsettling. The alien hoot of the owl or mere scurrying about of nocturnal creatures could cause the mind to create images worthy of John Carpenter or Stephen King.

He continued following their tracks for the better part of an hour. He laughed quietly to himself as the Jeep crept along at three miles an hour. He had certainly put his vehicle through the test today. Chrysler would love to document his day as a testimony to their reliable Jeep, both on and off road. He had settled down and wasn't nearly as anxious as he had been, primarily because he was doing something and he felt he was making progress. For the first time he felt he would find Betsy safe.

The climbing was starting to become too steep and the terrain too cluttered even for the Jeep at this point. The large rocks and boulders dictated that he leave the Jeep and continue on foot. It was also getting very dark. He picked a relatively level spot to leave the Jeep. Now he had to make a decision. Should he spend some time resting in the comfort of the Jeep or should he press on into the night. He looked in the rear of the Jeep for the survival pack he always kept under the rear seat. It was gone. It must have been taken at the Yokatory camp. All he had with him was his 92 FS .40 cal. Beretta a pocketknife and his magnesium fire stick on his belt loop. He made the obvious, but not the most prudent decision to continue up the slope leaving the shelter of the Jeep behind.

As he walked up the mountain, Oliver was upset with himself for not checking the Jeep before he left Yokatory camp. He wondered what else they had stolen from him. He quickly checked the pistol to make sure it was loaded, it was. Finally, because of the darkness the trail became difficult to follow forcing him to stop pursuing his prey.

Oliver knew the evening temperatures would slip into the forties by morning and staying warm would be a concern. He decided to rest an hour at a time and then move further up the hill. He knew he would risk losing their trail but was comfortable he would find them again come daylight. The periodic movement would help keep him warm. His experience was that unless one made a concerted effort for comfort in the outdoors, erratic sleep was the best you could get. He was also very much aware restful sleep wouldn't come as long as Betsy was missing.

Oliver was startled awake from a shallow sleep by gun fire. First one report, then a pause, then two more. He nodded knowingly to himself, *nervous gun fire*. He knew the sequence of the gun fire signified the shooter was scared and they were shooting at sounds. An expert would fire in a different pattern. In fact a real expert wouldn't need the second two shots. He got to his feet, dusted off his butt and decided it was time to warm up. He started trekking toward the fading echoes. He was sure the shots weren't directed at Betsy. He knew enough of the criminal mind to know they wouldn't drag her three quarters up the Wind River Range just to shoot her. No, he knew they wanted her alive, what he didn't know was why they took her in the first place.

He rested one more time just before dawn. It was getting very cold so he planned to rest for only a half an hour. As he was sitting with his back against a tree, he thought her could hear voices in the distance. He'd rescue Betsy soon.

# 23

He must have been more tired than he thought because when he opened his eyes the sun was up. Oliver realized, once he got his bearings the kidnappers were heading into the Popo Agie Wilderness Area. This was a sub-alpine region of lakes, rivers and range grass. The area consisted of jagged peaks and deep narrow valleys and canyons. It was a popular climbers retreat. Betsy's captors had run out of room to run. Anyone ill equipped or lacking experience would be stranded in no time. They should be easy to spot from the air and Oliver expected to hear the Sheriff's copter shortly.

Because of the Wilderness act of 1964 this was a restricted area. Access was allowed only with passes. All civilian motorized equipment was prohibited. Oliver was secure in the fact he could pick a peak with a good view and watch them be apprehended. . Betsy's group would be very obvious when the shadows shortened. He was sure the authorities would find them, maybe even before Kevin's chopper did.

Oliver scanned the terrain below him. It was difficult because of the rising sun. He held his hand to his forehead shading the sun and squinted to see if he could spot them. He wished he had his binoculars because he thought he saw them on a flat plain area. It looked like four people sitting on the ground. They must have given up because they were out in the wide open. The sheriff's copter would see them even if the spotter was blind.

Suddenly the loud unmistakable thump of rotary blades filled the air. It was coming from behind Oliver and it was so loud that Oliver ducked his head, out of instinct. It was actually a few hundred feet above when it passed over him and it was moving fast. Oliver was sure Kevin had given orders to the pilot to not waste time and he wasn't. He keyed the handheld radio, "Oliver to the Sheriff, can you read, come back."

A static voice replied but Oliver had to adjust the squelch to understand it. "Repeat, come back," Oliver said.

"This is the Sheriff," the familiar voice said. "Did you enjoy your night? Come back."

"Yeah, wise guy," Oliver responded. "I just saw your chopper fly over my head."

He's already spotted them and is about to pick them up. Come back"

"What?" Kevin shouted into the radio. "I'm standing here talking to my pilot. He's not airborne yet, come back."

Oliver felt his knees go weak and his stomach roll. "Shit, somebody is picking them up, come back." Oliver stood helpless and watched four people disappear into the chopper. It rose, turned east and quickly disappeared into the glare of the sun.

The hand held squawked, "Give my pilot your approximate position and stay on the air talking him into your location. It shouldn't be more than five minutes, come back."

"Understood," was Oliver's dejected reply. He started to give the pilot directions to his position while his eyes searched the eastern horizon, but it was empty.

The Sheriff's pilot picked him up in a matter of minutes. Oliver jumped in and quickly buckled the seat harness. "Can we catch them?" he screamed at the pilot.

The pilot slipped his head set off. He looked at Oliver and shook his head. He hollered above the racket of the copter. "If he picked up four passengers he's got a lot more engine and airspeed than my little hedge hopper. Besides the sheriff gave me orders to bring you back pronto." The chopper lifted and immediately dipped into a 180 degree turn and angled for maximum speed. They headed toward Pinedale.

Oliver twisted in his seat and looked over his shoulder eastward in hopes of catching one last glimpse of the helicopter that contained his only reason to exist.

Kevin was at the landing pad as the chopper set down. He handed Oliver a fried egg sandwich and a cup of coffee he'd gotten at Big Mo's. "Sorry, he wouldn't let me take the basket out of the building," he said, trying to lighten the moment.

## THE PAST IS NEVER DEAD

"Thanks," Oliver said, with a look that said I understand and thank you. "I want to know everything you know about this. Start at the beginning. How did you know Betsy was missing?"

Kevin explained how he had called the school looking for Betsy. "I wanted to know when you were coming back."

"They told me Betsy had taken a personal day. I called your house but all I got was the answering machine. I had Jimmy Hawks go up and check it out. He said Betsy's truck was there, but no one was home. While Jimmy and I were investigating, I got a call from Woody. He was in pursuit of a speeder and Betsy was in the back seat."

"What about the helicopter this morning, anything on that? It was a big twin engine. I'm not an expert but from my experience in the Secret Service it looked like a Bell 427. I think they hold six or eight." Oliver said.

"We're checking on it." Kevin said.

When they got back to the Sheriff's office Oliver's Jeep was there. Oliver glanced at Kevin with a surprise look and pointed to the Jeep.

"Two of my deputies followed you last night. They found the Jeep and brought it back here." Kevin smiled. "We have an interest in Betsy's disappearance also."

"I know," Oliver nodded. "Sometimes I forget to say thanks."

"Why don't you go home, shower, and try to rest," Kevin suggested. "Maybe whoever is involved will try to call you." He patted Oliver on the back and guided him toward his Jeep. "I'll keep you informed."

# 24

Oliver went home and showered, but resting was out of the question. Just being in the house alone and knowing Betsy wouldn't be coming home from school was unnerving for him. He had a bowl of cereal while planning his next move. He ate it standing at the kitchen sink. Sitting down wasn't an option.

It would help if Kevin could find out where the helicopter had come from and who it was registered to. Unfortunately, choppers didn't need airports to take off and land. They could fly under the radar, so to speak. Unless you had a visual on them they could disappear rather fast. He was also planning to update his friends in Washington about Yokatory's demise and ask if they could confirm that Sharad Ramadoos was still in India.

He put his bowl in the sink and headed to Pinedale High School. He wanted to talk to the person who told Kevin about Betsy's call that morning.

Oliver sat in the teacher's lounge waiting for Mrs. Best. She worked in administration and was the one who had taken Betsy's call. He was in deep thought about the last time he and Betsy had shared a lunch in this room just days ago.

"Mr. Clearmountain, excuse me, Mr. Clearmountain," Judy Best said.

"Oh, yeah," Oliver jumped. He hadn't heard her come into the room. He rose and greeted her.

"I'm sorry, did I startle you?" she said.

"No, no, you didn't," Oliver declared. "My mind was somewhere else. I won't take much of your time. I just wanted to know exactly what Betsy said when she called in for her personal day."

"Is everything alright?" Judy asked. "The Sheriff just called and asked me the same thing. Is Betsy okay?"

"Well she's missing, but I would appreciate it if you didn't say anything to anyone. She probably told me where she was going and I wasn't paying attention," Oliver confessed.

Judy Best shook her head in disgust. "Men, you're all the same. Why just the other day my husband asked me three times where I had been. I gave him three different answers and each time he nodded, accepting my answers."

Oliver grinned his understanding, "Can you remember exactly what Betsy said when she called? Did she sound upset?"

"Well," she tilted her head and looked up, as if what she wanted to say was written on the ceiling. "She said Judy, I'm taking a personal day and I hope it doesn't cause a problem. And I said no, we have substitutes on standby. You have a nice day. She did sound like she was doing two things at once, you know, preoccupied."

Oliver was about to say is that all, when she continued talking. "She did say something strange," Judy continued. "It didn't make any sense at all. She said make sure Tigree doesn't eat all the Twinkies. And then she hung up before I could ask her what she meant. We don't have anyone here by that name, student or faculty." She looked at Oliver with a puzzled look. "Does it make any sense to you?"

Oliver shook his head slowly, "That was it? That's all she said?"

Judy Best nodded, "That was it, and she hung up immediately after saying that."

"Thank you very much Mrs. Best."

"I hope it helps you find Betsy, she's one of our favorite teachers." She shook Oliver's hand and left.

Oliver slumped into the chair. That doesn't sound like Betsy. She would have been a lot more concerned about missing a day's work. Also, Betsy wasn't one to have brief phone conversations. Betsy was the type of outgoing person who would have told Mrs. Best what she was planning to do on her day off.

Oliver rose from the chair and walked down to the cafeteria. It was before the first lunch period and everyone was busy preparing for the hungry hordes. He walked up to the person putting coins into the cash register.

"Excuse me, do you sell Twinkies?"

The lady made a frown and shook her head, "No nourishment, wasted calories."

Oliver smiled and said, "I know, but they taste good."

The woman realized Oliver was just trying to be nice. "I know," she said. "But the school board won't let us, Sorry."

Oliver thanked her and left. He was heading back to the sheriff's office. He didn't have much to go on. If Kevin didn't turn up any information on the helicopter and the information from Washington was status quo, he'd be clueless. That's what Betsy used to call him when he tried to buy her clothes for her birthday or Christmas, clueless.

He stopped for gas and after filling up went inside to pay. He was glancing all around the store as was his habit, constantly observing his immediate environment. He was taking his change from the counterman when his eyes fell on a Twinkies display. He thought about how he hadn't had one since childhood, but Uncle Tigree never outgrew them. Tigree, Twinkies, suddenly he knew what Betsy was saying. He had given Tigree a Twinkie as a gift when they met in ATLANTIC CITY. Betsy was telling him her abductors were from Atlantic City. But not Wyoming, New Jersey!

He bolted out of the store and ran to his Jeep. His first instinct was from experience, find out all you could about your objective. In this case it was Michael Bondinni aka Mike Bond. He grabbed his cell phone and called his lawyer, Gordon Cundiff.

"Yo Chief," answered Gordon. He recognized Oliver's number. "What up?"

"How soon can you meet me?" Oliver excitedly blurted out.

"Unless you're the sitting judge in the courtroom I'm about to enter, it will have to wait until this evening." Gordon joked.

"Where and when?" Oliver replied.

"You're serious, what's the matter?" Gordon's demeanor sobered.

Oliver didn't want to overload Gordon with worry as he was entering a court room to defend a client. "I just need to talk to you as soon as possible."

"Okay," said Gordon. "I'll meet you half way at the Elk lodge, say 6:00 PM. I believe it's your turn to buy."

Oliver wasn't about to argue with him. "Fine, 6:00 o'clock," then he disconnected. He had a few hours before he had to drive north, so he headed for the Sheriff's office. He had to speak to his guys in DC. And he also needed to buy a plane ticket to Atlantic City.

## THE PAST IS NEVER DEAD

As he recalled Delta stopped in Minneapolis and then Atlanta where he had to switch planes to get to Atlantic City. United on the other hand took him to Denver and then Philadelphia where he could rent a car.

# 25

He drove directly to Kevin's office. As he entered the front door he heard Kevin's booming voice, "Clearmountain, get in here."

Oliver stuck his head in the door, "Any news?"

"I'm glad you're here. "Kevin said, "It saves me sending someone after you. The FBI is on the case. Agent Brann will be here in an hour. She wants to talk to you."

Oliver scrunched up his face like he was in pain, "FBI? Jeez Kevin, I don't need them nosing around. They'll just slow me up with their bureaucratic bullshit."

Kevin nodded knowingly, "I didn't have a choice. We've had a kidnapping in Sublette County and that's a federal offense. It's my duty to inform the feds." His look told Oliver he was sorry.

Oliver put both hands on Kevin's desk and leaned close to him. "I'm pretty sure I know who took Betsy."

Kevin was stunned, his mouth actually went slack. He looked at Oliver in total astonishment, "Who?"

"The wise guys from Atlantic City," he said softly. "But Kevin that information stays between us, understand?"

"I understand. You don't have any facts, so it's just a rumor at this point and the Sheriff's office doesn't deal in rumors," Kevin said with a stupid grin and a wink. "You can trust me."

"Good can I use the phones?" Oliver said as he turned to leave.

"You're still paying your taxes aren't you?"

Deputy Page was sitting at a desk. His arm was in a cast and a sling and he was in civilian clothes. The sleeve of his shirt had been cut away.

"How are you doing Woody?" Oliver said.

"I'll make it," the deputy said.

"What are you doing here? Shouldn't you be home resting?"

Woody jerked his head toward Kevin's office, "Tell that to the slave master. He said just because I can't drive a patrol car, doesn't mean I can't answer the phone. But I have to wear civilian clothes because he didn't want me cutting up the county's uniform." He gestured to his sleeveless shirt.

Oliver contained an understanding chuckle as he shook his head and walked over to a desk and sat down.

He reached his guys in Washington. They appreciated the update on Yokatory, but they weren't as convinced as Oliver about his demise. So the question they had about the camp took thirty minutes. He finally got around to asking his next favor. He wanted to know the exact whereabouts of Ramadoos. Oliver was a professional investigator who knew you followed up every lead even though the case was going in another direction, from the Revolutionist in the Rockies to the Gangetic Plains of India, and now to the Gangsters of America.

He hung up the phone when an FBI suit came through the front door. Oh, it was worn by a rather attractive female, but it said FBI all over it.

She stopped in front of Deputy Page and flipped open her badge, "Agent Dawn Brann to see Sheriff Cahill."

Woody looked at her and then over to Oliver.

She followed Woody's stare. "Are you Sheriff Cahill?" she said, addressing Oliver.

"No and yes," Oliver said, standing up and extending his hand. "I'm not Sheriff Cahill, but I am the person you want to see. I'm Oliver Clearmountain."

She looked Oliver right in the eye. "You're one of the people I want to see. Can you take me to Sheriff Cahill?"

"I'm Cahill," Kevin said. He was leaning against his office door. "Why don't both of you come in to my office."

Agent Brann took the chair in front of Kevin's desk. Oliver sat on the one next to her.

"I don't have a lot of time, Agent Brann. I have an appointment in Jackson at five o'clock," Oliver lied. His appointment with Gordon was for six o'clock, but he needed an excuse to keep this meeting short. All she wanted, he was sure, was to be brought up to date, and hell, Kevin could do that. Besides, going over Betsy's abduction was painful for him.

Agent Brann spoke to Kevin, "We'd like to go over the crime scene. Have you secured it?"

Kevin looked puzzled. "Crime scene?"

Oliver chimed in, "Do you mean my house?"

"If that's where she was abducted," Agent Brann said. If it's locked, I'd like you to give me the keys. My CI unit will be here at 5:00 PM."

Oliver and Kevin exchanged looks of disbelief. "And just how long will your investigation take?" Oliver inquired.

"We should be able to wrap it up in 24 to 36 hours," Agent Brann said.

"And where am I supposed to sleep?" Oliver asked. He was becoming visibly upset.

"The government will reimburse you for any expenses you incur," she said.

Oliver stood up and said, "I have to get going. I'm going to be late."

Agent Brann glanced at her watch. "It's only 3 o'clock. Your appointment isn't until 5."

"Yeah," Oliver countered, "but my appointment is two hours from here." He nodded to Kevin, threw his house keys on the desk and headed out the door. "I'm going to be out of town for a few days, but Kevin knows how to get in touch with me." He glanced back as he exited and caught a glimpse of Agent Brann's head swiveling back and forth between him and Kevin in total bewilderment. She finally focused on Kevin with a look that asked, *aren't you going to stop him?*

# 26

Oliver stopped by the house and used the hidden key he and Betsy kept under a rock, to let himself in. He repacked his suitcase, doing a quick ironing job on his suit. He figured three days worth of clothes would be enough. He searched the house briefly for any hidden clues he might find, something Betsy might have left if she had a chance. Finding nothing, he locked the house and placed the key back under the rock. He thought all burglars must know that everybody hides an extra key under a rock near the door. He didn't move the key, perhaps hoping that Betsy would magically return and need it.

Oliver decided to leave word for Gordon that he would meet him in the Silver Dollar saloon in Jackson. It was silly making Gordon drive half way to Pinedale when Oliver was going to get a flight out of Jackson as soon as possible, hopefully that evening.

Oliver was sitting comfortably in the western saddle that served as bar stool at the Silver Dollar Saloon when Gordon walked up next to him.

"Do you come here often cowboy" Gordon said in his best John Wayne impersonation, as he hopped into the saddle next to Oliver.

Oliver was nursing a beer. He slowly turned and gave Gordon a snide grin. "I'm full-blooded Shoshone, not a cowboy."

"Oh, I didn't know you Indians used saddles," Gordon said continuing their usual banter.

Oliver knew this would go on until one guy made the other laugh. "If you don't know much, you must be a lawyer," Oliver said, turning back to his beer, "cleverly disguised as a responsible adult."

Gordon almost broke to a grin, but quickly added, "I'm sure you know Chief that light travels faster than sound. That's why some Indians appear bright until you hear them speak."

Oliver spit some of his beer on the bar stifling his laugh. He quickly wiped his mouth with the bar napkin. He extended his hand to Gordon. "No fair, you've hired a comedy writer?"

"Okay what is so important? You wouldn't drive to Jackson just to buy me a Wild Turkey," he said, as the bartender walked up. Turning to the bartender he said, "On the rocks."

"Betsy's been kidnapped." Oliver said.

Gordon didn't react. He just looked at Oliver and studied him like he would an opponent in the court room. He had trained himself to show no emotion when an outlandish statement was dropped. It took him only seconds to know Oliver was sincere. "How, when, where and why?" was all he said.

"They took her from the house about 34 hours ago. I haven't the foggiest idea as to why."

Gordon leaned close to his friend, "What do you want me to do?"

"I think she was taken by a gangster by the name of Michael Bondinni also called Mike Bond," Oliver confided. "I need you to get me everything there is to know about the creep. I'm leaving on the first flight out of here. I would like to have all that by the time I get to New Jersey tomorrow morning. Where he lives, what he owns and who are his friends as well as his enemies."

Gordon was writing as he listened. He looked up at Oliver, "Do you want me to go with you?"

"No, but thanks for offering." Oliver clasped his hand on Gordon's arm. "If I need help, I'll call you." Oliver appreciated his friend's offer. The two men stared at each other, words weren't necessary. "The irony is I have traveled all over the world with POTUS security, but the man never went to Atlantic City."

"You've never been there?"

Oliver shook his head as he finished his beer.

"Check with the airport and find out the next flight." Gordon suggested. "I don't think anything is going tonight, it's too late. Come to my house and use my computer to arrange your connections to Philadelphia. Marilyn just made a batch of Roosevelt beans and we'll cook up a couple of extra steaks." He could see fatigue on Oliver's face. "We'll spend some time checking out this Mike Bond character and you can get a good night's sleep. I have a feeling you're going to need it."

Oliver nodded a tired approval. He threw fifteen dollars on the bar, "The next drink is on you at your house." Oliver pushed to get out of the saddle, he slipped and stumbled He suddenly realized how tired he was.

"Now I know why Indians never used saddles," Gordon said. "They were too clumsy."

Oliver lay awake in Gordon's guest room. His stomach was full. The dinner had been outstanding. There was nothing he enjoyed better than a char-broiled steak and a plate of Roosevelt beans. Although he was tired, sleep didn't come easily. He and Gordon had spent a few hours digging into the life of Michael Bondinni. And now, as he was trained, he was reviewing the information in his mind instead of trying to get some overdue sleep. Mike Bond, as he was known, had been listed frequently in the Philadelphia paper with numerous apprehensions and accusations, but nothing ever came of them. To Oliver's knowledge he had never been arrested. He appeared to be very wealthy and lived in a suite at the Borgata. His occupation was listed as president of the High Roller travel agency. His few close friends' names all ended in a vowel. He had a reputation as a ladies man, at least that's the image he projected. Every photo they viewed in the newspaper file showed him with a different woman. He was small in height. Oliver guessed he was about 5'6" and slight of build, maybe 150 pounds. Oliver suspected a Napoleon complex fed by his horde of henchmen and runners better know as gophers. He'd learn more about him when he got to Atlantic City.

Sleep finally slipped into his overworked mind.

# 27

The flight connections went smoothly. He caught an early standby when he arrived in Denver and although flying east consumes and extra two hours, he made excellent time. He arrived in Philly late afternoon and decided to avail himself of the limo service to Atlantic City. He could always rent a car if he needed one, or worst case, borrow one.

He had to keep reminding himself his only objective was finding Betsy, not taking vengeance on Mike Bond. It wouldn't be a good idea since he left his Berretta with Gordon and arrived in Atlantic City unarmed.

The one thing Oliver admired about Gordon and lawyers in general was they knew how to get things done. Gordon had made a reservation for him on-line and established a $5,000 dollar line of credit. His room was costing him $179.00 dollars a night and it was the least expensive Borgata offered. Oliver didn't want to spend anymore since he was using Gordon's money. He checked in as Gordon Cundiff, using one of Gordon's credit cards. They also made a counterfeit copy of Gordon's driver's license with Oliver's picture placed over Gordon's. Using wide scotch tape as laminate they had produced a reasonable phony identification for Oliver. They decided that by using Gordon's name he wouldn't raise any suspicion and if Betsy happened to hear it or see it she would know Oliver was near.

Oliver didn't bother going to his room. He had the bell captain send his bag up, telling him he wanted to look around and get the feel of the place.

The Bell Captain smiled, "Don't lose all your money before you get to the room, Mr. Cundiff."

Oliver handed him a ten dollar bill, smiled and said, "Do I look like a loser?"

It took only an hour for Oliver to thoroughly case the joint. His experience came in handy, enabling him to checkout some areas where the public were not allowed. He had one of the help tell him the name of the Casino General manager; the guy even offered to point him out.

Oliver walked toward the manager, making eye contact from quite a distance and never loosing it as he approached him. By the time Oliver was within ten feet it was obvious the manager was uncomfortable with the rapidly approaching stranger. So much so he quit talking to the pit boss he had been chatting with and was staring at Oliver.

Oliver said to the pit boss "Excuse us," as he took the managers elbow and moved him a few step away.

Working quickly and with authority Oliver said, "Mr. Bryne, Mr. Sal Bryne."

"Yeah, what the hell do you think you're doing?" Sal Bryne said as he swung his elbow free of Oliver's grip

"I'm sorry to manhandle you Mr. Bryne, but I'm with the Secret Service." Oliver flashed an old identity card, careful to hold his thumb over the name, Oliver Clearmountain, along with a phony gold five star badge that he had pinned to his wallet. It looked like the real thing. "I've checked into your hotel under the name of Gordon Cundiff." Oliver paused and stared into the man's eyes, letting what he had just said sink in. "What I'm about to tell you is top secret. Don't even think of repeating it to anyone. You'd be committing an act of treason." Again Oliver paused and watched Sal Bryne process the information he was hearing .Oliver noticed he was starting to perspire. People with something to hide usually do, he continued, "I'm the Advance Agent for the White House and I would like you to assist me. I'm doing a site survey and it needs to be covert."

Sal was now trembling as the magnitude of what Oliver had said hit him. "Sure, what do you need from me?"

"That's very patriotic of you," Oliver winked. "I need you to cover my back so you're security doesn't hassle me." Oliver was now being less formal and friendlier.

Sal Bryne was just nodding now. It was obvious he was very uncomfortable.

Oliver continued, "The advance team will arrive if we're sure POTUS is scheduled to stop."

"POTUS?" Sal looked puzzled.

Oliver smiled, "Code name for the President of the United States."

"Why's the President coming here?"

Oliver shook his head and said with a wry smile, "Mine is not to reason why, mine is just to do or die."

Sal nodded knowingly and Oliver continued, "I won't be any trouble. Mostly I'm observing your traffic flow in the casino and looking for familiar faces. The real work will begin when and if the Advance Team arrives. We'll know in the next forty eight hours." Knowing he had successfully pulled off his charade, he patted Sal on the shoulder and said, "This meeting never happened, okay?"

Sal nodded "Can't I get you anything?"

Oliver shook his head, "I'm fine, but I'm not allowed to gamble so I would appreciate it if you would turn your head if you see me at a table."

Sal laughed, regaining his composure, "Consider it done. Here," he handed Oliver a card. "Let me comp you for dinner, it's on the Borgata."

Oliver took the card, "Thanks, I'll report back to you as often as possible. Thank you and your government appreciates your cooperation."

Oliver walked toward the casino very happy that the first part of his plan worked. He now would have free range to find Betsy.

He found a good chair near the end of the keno area where he had a great view of the casino. There was a lady sitting in the next chair and Oliver acknowledged her as he sat down, "Are you having any luck?"

She was in her late forties and dressed very nicely in a white silk blouse and black slacks. "Luck doesn't have anything to do with it." She had a pleasant smile, "I have a system."

"Is it working?" Oliver asked.

"That's why they call me Keno Lady."

"So you're not a stranger to this place." Oliver stated.

"Honey, I'm in this chair six months out of the year and have been since the place opened," she said.

Oliver observed her. Based on the clothing, jewelry and grooming she wasn't hurting for money. "So I guess your system works."

She nodded, and then continued as if she owed him more of an explanation. "I sit here and people watch, while I play the game. When I tire of it, I take six months off. And go home."

"Where's home?"

"Bozeman Montana."

Oliver nodded knowingly and smiled, "Named the best small town in America in 2006 and home of Montana State University."

Keno Lady's head turned quickly and with a raised eyebrow she said, "You know about Bozeman? I thought it was a well kept secret."

"I've passed through that part of the country." Oliver said. He grinned at the lady. "Why don't you gamble in Las Vegas if you live way out west?"

"Let me repeat myself," she boasted. "I don't gamble, I win, and this is where I win most frequently."

Oliver decided to gather some information, "So you see a lot of what's going on around the Borgata?." Oliver said.

"I saw you manhandle Sal Bryne," she grinned. "He doesn't like to be intimidated."

"I just introduced myself, that's all," Oliver lied.

"Rather firmly," she smiled.

Oliver took out a piece of paper from the chairs pocket. It was a Keno form, "Will you show me how to play this game?"

"Pick out some numbers that you think will come up on the board in the next game and go up to the counter and give the man your money," she said. "Let's see how you do on your own first."

"Do I have to bet a lot of money?" Oliver asked, as he checked a few of the 80 numbers listed on the form.

"It's a risk-reward game," Keno Lady said checking her own Keno slip. "The more you risk the more you win."

"I'm not much of a risk taker." Oliver uttered.

"Then don't quit your day job," she confided.

# 28

Oliver's room was particularly nice. He had unpacked and showered and was now resting on the bed before dressing for dinner. His afternoon had been very productive. He had identified himself to the powers to be while establishing a good cover story. He had also made friends with the most well informed person in the casino. She had told him that Mike Bond lived in a suite. She thought it was on the 25th floor. She also informed Oliver the High Roller travel agency had an office just off the lobby.

She also told him she stayed in the hotel. What puzzled Oliver was how did she afford to cover her expenses while playing Keno? He estimated she had to win $400.00 a day just to break even, unless the hotel picked up her room.

This evening Oliver was going to dine at Bobby Flay's restaurant and gather as much information as he could. He was also going to catch the show. It was a review with a lot of dancing girls. Exactly what Betsy used to do.

Oliver decided to stop for a drink at the bar before dinner. He sat at the end of the bar and noticed a group of four suited characters at a table in the corner. Actually, he heard them before he saw them. They were loud and attention-seekers. The guy with his back to the wall was Mike Bond. At that moment Oliver's dinner plans were put on hold. He decided to shadow the group, at least Mike Bond as long as he could. There was one very quiet woman with them. She was stunningly beautiful in a plum colored, tight fitting, designer dress. Her jewelry was a bit ostentatious. She was wearing a diamond tiara along with a matching, inch thick, diamond choker around her neck. Oliver thought if the diamonds were real her ensemble was worth millions. She smiled when spoken to but for the most part sat quietly like a frightened child. She was sitting to the right of Bond and he occasionally put his hand on her leg. She didn't resist, but Oliver could sense she didn't approve.

## THE PAST IS NEVER DEAD

Oliver was nursing his second beer when the group called for the check which Bond just scratched his name on and left. One of the four handed the waiter some cash which he immediately, without looking at the amount, stuffed in his pocket.

Oliver followed them to Bobby's Flay's Steak House. They were seated immediately. Oliver decided to have his dinner at the buffet knowing he would be finished long before they came out of the Steakhouse.

One half hour later Oliver positioned himself where he could watch the entrance to Bobby's Flay's

Another hour and they appeared, Mike Bond had the arm of the princess in the plum dress. The other three walked behind him. They started toward Oliver. He turned and proceeded ahead of them. Considering the direction they were headed, the only destination could be the casino.

Oliver spotted Keno Lady in her usual seat. He hurried and sat down next to her.

"Still winning?" he whispered as he sat down.

"I'm still here," she smiled.

"Keno Lady," Oliver said to get here attention, "in a moment some people are going to walk past us. I'd appreciate it if you could identify them for me."

She looked up from her form and without a word looked out onto the casino floor. She was scanning the room as Mike Bond came into view. Without being told who Oliver wanted her to identify she said, "Mike Bond and today's arm candy. The fat one is Joey Cucci, they call him Chops. He's Bonds bodyguard. The one in the blue jacket and gray slacks is James Camanetti otherwise known as Jimmy Cricket. The fourth one I'm not sure, but I think he's a cop." She went back to her Keno form.

They were heading for the elevators.

"Excuse me," Oliver said as he stood up. "I'll be back in a moment."

He hurried to the elevator and arrived moments before they did. He pushed the up button. The elevator door opened and Oliver gallantly, with a bow and sweep of his arm offered the lady entrance.

"You go first, clown," Bond's bodyguard said. "The lady is with us."

Oliver noticed when he gestured to the elevator he had what looked like a remote control device in his hand.

Oliver positioned himself in the middle of the elevator and watched to see what floor they pushed.

Bond took a key card and inserted it in a slot, then pressed a button that didn't have a floor number on it, just a P. "What floor, buddy," he said to Oliver without turning around.

"Fifteen," Oliver said.

As the elevator started to move the girl said, "This necklace is hurting, I can't wait to take it off."

"When we get to the room you can take everything off," Bond smirked as his cohorts smirked.

The fifteenth floor indicator lit and the door dinged and opened. Oliver excused himself past the men and exited. He turned toward his room and never looked back until he heard the door close. He hurried back to the elevator and pressed the down button.

He was in luck. Keno Lady was still there. He quickly sat next to her. "Thank you," he said. "You did me a big favor."

Keno Lady nodded but never took her eyes off the Keno board as the random numbers lit one by one. "I just won $3,000," she said. "Now what did you say?"

"That girl that was with Mike Bond, you said she was today's arm candy," Oliver stated. "Do the women change everyday?"

"For the most part," Keno Lady said.

Oliver didn't want to ask the next question so he just stared at Keno Lady. "Well?" she said.

Oliver pulled his wallet from his pocket and removed a picture of Betsy. "Have you seen this woman before?"

"I think so," Keno Lady said as she studied the picture. "She was last night's arm candy I think. The reason I remember is she and Bond started to argue and then suddenly she fainted. It caused a little commotion. Chop's picked her up and carried her to the elevator.

Oliver slumped in the chair. The thought of Betsy being hurt sickened him.

"I assume you know her since you carry her picture." Keno Lady showed concern. "Family?"

Oliver nodded his head in silent reply.

# 29

Oliver lay on his bed staring at the ceiling. The thought of Betsy being in the same building haunted him. How was Betsy being held prisoner? How was he going to find her? She might as well be a thousand miles away. He knew he could find Mike Bond's, but he was reasonably sure the kept women weren't there, near, but not in the same suite. He wondered how many there were.

He finally succumbed to some much needed sleep but was wide awake at 5:45 AM. Oliver looked at the clock on the end table and wondered what time Sal Bryne got to work. He showered slowly, it was four in the morning in Wyoming, too early to call Kevin or Gordon. He went down stairs and wandered around the near empty casino.

He finished a hardy breakfast and was killing time reading the USA Today.

"You don't sleep much," the female voice said.

Oliver glanced over the top of the paper to see a smiling Keno Lady. "I'm alone obviously. Please join me," he said. He picked up the carafe of coffee and shook it. It was more than half full. "Would you care for some coffee?" he said, turning over the extra cup in front of the place setting across from him.

"Thank you, I will join you. I'm tired of eating alone," she said sitting down across from him. She noticed the dirty plate in front of Oliver, "Oh, I see you've already eaten."

"I have, but I'll eat again if it would make you comfortable," Oliver joked.

"That won't be necessary," she said and turned to the approaching waitress. "Just an English muffin and some jam, please."

The waitress nodded and did an about face and walked away.

Keno Lady continued, " What are you doing up so early?"

"Can't sleep, I've a lot on my mind." Oliver replied. He was toying with telling her the truth.

"Oh, what is it you do for a living?"

"I'm a Forest Ranger," Oliver replied.

Keno Lady looked right and left and then smiled and said, "I don't see many trees around here. Are you playing hooky?"

Oliver grinned at her humor, shook his head and looked down at his plate. He decided to tell her the truth. He decided he might just need an ally.

"I'm looking for my wife," he said as he looked up into her eyes. He held her attention and said, "I think she was kidnapped by Mike Bond."

Keno Lady raised an eyebrow and continued to look deep into Oliver's eyes. The moment was broken with a third voice, "Your muffin madam!" Neither one was aware of the waitress's presence.

Keno Lady spread some jam on the muffin then put it down, "I appreciate your confiding in me. I might be able to help. I've suspected all along something wasn't right about Bond's girlfriends."

"Why?" responded an interested Oliver.

"For one thing they never smile. They hardly ever talk. I originally thought they were on drugs," she said as she picked up her muffin. "But after the other evening I think it has something to do with the choker they wear. They all wear the same one. I noticed it because it's so gaudy, it's hard to miss." She took a bite of the muffin, pausing for Oliver's reaction.

"I noticed it last night. Did my wife have it on?"

"Do you mean the woman who fainted? Yes. She was wearing it. Do you suspect they are being held against their will?"

Oliver tightened his jaw and nodded, "I know for a fact one of them is," he said with disgust.

"Do you think they're kept in the hotel?" she said dabbing her lips with her napkin.

Oliver nodded, "It's that thought that's keeping me from sleeping. Now if you'll excuse me, I'm going to find the answer to that question."

"Go right ahead," Keno Lady said. "You know where to find me if you need me."

Oliver walked into the office area of Sal Bryne. The secretary was sitting at her desk reading a magazine.

Oliver said "Is he in?" he gestured to the closed door with Sal Byrne's name on it in gold.

She quickly put the magazine down, 'Umm, he's busy. Whom should I say is calling?"

Oliver continued toward the door. "Is he as busy as you?"

The secretary was searching for a reply as Oliver opened the door of Sal Byrne's office. Bryne was eating breakfast at his desk. "Who the…? Oh it's you," Bryne said as he recognized Oliver and recovered from the surprise of someone barging into his office. "I guess you guys aren't used to knocking."

"I need to know Michael Bondinni's suite." Oliver said with authority.

Wiping egg from his chin, Sal shook his head, "No can do!" he said.

"I can have a warrant faxed to this office in fifteen minutes. Believe me, we don't want that," Oliver said with conviction. He took out his cell phone and paused as if he was going to dial.

"I…can't, I have my orders." Sal said, stuttering.

"You just got new orders," Oliver said, staring him down. He knew he had the element of surprise working for him. It wouldn't pay to give Sal time to think. "Give me the room number and I'm out of here." Oliver said with a friendly smile. "No one will know Sal. I just want to talk to him and see if he would like to leave town for a few days while POTUS is here. He pops up on my list of people we don't want around when POTUS is in the area." Oliver sensed he was making headway, "Otherwise Sal I'll have to have him arrested on some drummed up charge and held until the visit is over." Oliver was now standing right in front of the seated Sal Bryne. He was looming over him. "I could arrange for him to have you as a cell mate."

"Suite 2500 and 2501" Sal said nervously. He uses two. His guests stay in 2501. You can't tell a soul you got this info from me."

"Don't worry, I'll keep my word, no one will ever know, now give me the pass key to get the elevator to that floor." Oliver said, intensifying his glare.

Sal froze for a moment. He was hoping Oliver would forget to ask for the pass key. Their eyes met for a few seconds. For only that brief moment did Sal consider saying no. Then his eyes started involuntarily blinking as he reached into the top drawer of his desk and produced a room key card.

"Thanks," Oliver said as he snatched the card from Sal's hand. "I'll return it when I leave."

Oliver slipped into the chair next to Keno Lady. "I'm going to need you to do something for me."

Keno Lady's eyes sparkled as she smiled, "I hope it's dangerous."

Oliver did a double take and explained what he needed from Keno Lady.

"I've been bored to tears. I could use some excitement. This sounds like fun." She confided.

"I'll make it as exciting as I can," Oliver laughed and patted her arm. "I'll need you to create a distraction when the time is right."

"Just let me know… Well, look at that," she said, looking up at the Keno board. "Oliver, you are bringing me good luck. I just hit the house for 5 grand."

Oliver sat back, shook his head and smiled. "Before you leave here, you are going to have to show me how you do that."

"We'll see," she said, as they both rose from their seats. She headed for the cashier for her payoff and Oliver for the elevators for what he hoped would be his payoff.

# 30

Oliver was reasonably sure there wouldn't be any security or guards on the 25th floor. Knowing the pass key was needed to get the elevator to that floor, was precaution enough for the residences. His heart was beating in anticipation, wondering what awaited him when the elevator doors opened. It had been a long time since he felt the excitement of the unknown. Oliver had to admit he liked the feeling. It kept his mind alert and made him feel alive.

The bell rang announcing the arrival of the elevator as the door slid open. Oliver paused, as he held the door button, keeping the door open. He slowly peeked out, looking up and down the empty hall. A quick glance at the wall told him rooms 2500 and 2501 were at the end of the hall, next to each other. It was obvious the two rooms occupied the entire end of the 25th floor.

Suddenly Oliver realized a painful reality He was letting his heart direct his actions. What the hell was he doing on the 25th floor without a plan? To expose himself now would only hurt his efforts of rescuing Betsy. He couldn't knock on the door of either suite without knowing what was on the other side. He was in a hurry to make sure Betsy was safe, but this wasn't the way to insure her safety.

He stepped back into the elevator and pressed the lobby button.

Oliver was sitting next to Keno Lady, depressed because he realized the time table wasn't controlled by him. He was going to have to wait for Bond to make the first move. He couldn't go after Betsy. He would have to wait for Bond to bring her to him.

"Are you ready to be there for me when the time comes?" Oliver said.

"I'm as ready as rain." Keno Lady smiled as she clutched her purse.

"The casino seems to be crowded this morning," Oliver observed.

Keno Lady nodded and pointed, "Do you see that crowd over by the blackjack tables?

"Yes"

"That's Danielle Fournier's posse" Keno Lady said.

"The academy award winner?"

"Yep," Keno Lady replied. "She's getting married this weekend. She's marrying John Avery, her leading man."

"Just what I need, a bunch of celebrities in town and paparazzi everywhere taking pictures," Oliver moaned.

"Does it make a difference?"

Oliver paused for a moment and then said, "No, it's really just like the deep forest. The more trees there are, the more places to hide. It's the same with people."

"You'll have a lot of trees to hide behind," Keno Lady joked. "She's got a lot of adoring fans."

Because of the crowd, Oliver didn't see Mike Bond get off the elevator. His arm candy this morning was Betsy Clearmountain. They were half way across the casino floor when Oliver saw Betsy. His heart flipped, he jumped to his feet and turned to face Keno Lady. "It's show time, you know what to do."

Keno Lady looked past him and saw Bond. She smiled and said, "You can count on me."

Oliver quickly disappeared into the crowd. He couldn't take a chance that Betsy would see him and react.

He sat in a chair located in the hallway where he could see the exit to the restaurant. It had been forty minutes since Bond escorted Betsy in for brunch. The same crew had accompanied them, Chops and Jimmy Cricket. The cop wasn't with them. Betsy looked stunning in a silk green blouse and beige slacks. The large collar of the blouse was turned up in a stylish fashion, but it didn't completely hide the ever present necklace.

Oliver was pretending to be reading USA Today. Staring at the same page for the last forty minutes he could almost recite it word for word. He finally saw Betsy leaving the restaurant heading for the ladies room in the hallway. Chops escorted her to the door of the rest room and then took his position outside to wait.

Oliver text messaged Keno Lady, "Now."

*THE PAST IS NEVER DEAD*

Suddenly there was a commotion and then screaming at the far end of the hallway. Oliver couldn't hear what the crowd of scrambling people was shouting, but then he clearly heard one word, "RAT!"

Chop's turned toward the commotion, taking a few steps in the direction of the turmoil. His movement enabled Oliver to slip behind him into the ladies room. As he did he saw a very confused rat securing down the center of the hall looking for a place to hide. It looked like Chop's was reaching for his gun. He looked confused, not knowing whether to run or shoot.

Betsy leaned wearily on the vanity. She was exasperated at failing to remove her necklace. She looked very tired. She turned her head as she heard someone enter. Oliver was holding his finger to his lips telling her to be quiet.

Betsy turned and ran to him, breathlessly whispering his name.

They embraced as tears of relief ran down her cheeks.

"It's alright, you're safe now," Oliver comforted her. "We don't have much time. Is that necklace locked on?"

"Yes, and I can't get it off," Betsy said, totally exasperated.

Oliver spun her around and pulled at her collar looking at the locking mechanism. It was a simple lock that only needed a straight pin to open it.

"Relax Legs, we'll get it off." He held up her hair and removed the clasp on her earring. He plucked the stud part of the earring and placed the pin in the back of the necklace. It opened with a click.

"Open the door and call Chops in here. Tell him to hurry." Oliver said. "Tell him there are rats in here."

Betsy went to the door and pulled it open. People were running and screaming. Chops stood his ground in front of the door amidst the flood of people. Betsy beckoned him in. She tried hard to have an urgent look on her face.

"Help me please," Betsy exclaimed. "There's a rat in here."

# 31

Chops came through the door with his pistol in his right hand, "Where?"

Oliver stepped from behind the door and slapped both of Chops ears with open palms as hard as he could.

Chops was stunned. He screamed as his hands went to his ears in a natural reaction.

"Thank you," Oliver said as he took the gun out of Chops loose grip.

The body guard staggered forward, bent in pain. He was holding his ears trying to gain his balance and stop the painful ringing.

Oliver reached into the right front pocket of Chop's jacket and removed the remote control device.

Chops started to regain his balance and turned to face Oliver. With his hands still holding his ears he said, "What the hell is going on?" He was still in pain.

Betsy dropped to her knees behind Chops and tugged at the cuff of his trousers, lifting it up and clamping the necklace on his exposed ankle. She fell back on her butt with a look of satisfaction.

Oliver pressed the control button on the remote device.

They both watched in awe as Chops hopped on one foot and then lost control of his body as the voltage ran through it. Oliver held the button down as Chops convulsed on the tile floor. He released the button only when the uncontrollable mass on the floor started to foam at the mouth.

Oliver took Betsy's hand and said, "Walk out slowly like you own the place. I'll be right behind you. Go to the Keno area."

Betsy exited the ladies room and saw a commotion at the end of the hall to her left. She turned to her right. As she continued to walk, Keno Lady fell into step along side of her. "I'm a friend of the Forest Ranger," she smiled. She slipped a room keycard into Betsy's hand, "Room 312. Don't open the door for anyone except me or your husband."

Betsy nodded and continued to walk. Only now her direction was toward the elevators.

Keno Lady left her side and went to her chair. She sat down and resumed picking numbers for the next keno game.

Oliver didn't follow her. His objective now was Sal Byrne's office.

He passed a nosey group of onlookers, crowded into the hallway watching three security guards fussing over a jacket spread on the floor. They appeared to have something trapped under it.

Oliver barged into the reception area. The same blond was reading the same book as his last visit. "Where's Bryne?"

"He's not here, he had an emergency. He just left," she responded immediately.

"I can see he's not here," Oliver growled. "I asked where he is."

"Mike Bond called him. I think he's in the restaurant."

Oliver turned and walked out. He didn't want to have a confrontation with Bond. He was afraid Bond might know what he looked like. He would make sure Betsy was safe and then wait until Sal Bryne was alone.

A loud shriek greeted Oliver as he emerged from Byrne's office area and diverted the curious onlooker's attention to a new crisis. "There's a dead man in the ladies room," announced a near hysterical lady, who was standing in front of the powder room holding her head in panic. The crowd started moving in the direction of the ladies room.

In moments they'll know Betsy is missing, Oliver concluded,. He knew that their adventure had just begun. He headed for Keno Lady.

He slipped into the chair next to Keno Lady.

"312" she said. "Tell her to take anything she needs. I think my clothes will fit her, might be a little short in the inseam. That girl's derrière is a long way from the sidewalk." She smiled and winked at Oliver.

He was as tight as a drum, trying to stay aware of all that was around him, but Keno Lady made him laugh. "Thanks," he said. He patted her on the knee as he got up and headed for the elevator and room 312.

Betsy flung the door open the moment she saw Oliver through the peep hole.

"Oh, Oliver, I thought I'd never see you again," she said as she hugged his neck.

Oliver didn't bother to say anything. He just returned the hug twofold. He lifted her off her feet and spun her around. They kissed until they were breathless.

Betsy finally pulled her head back, stared him in the eye, "What took you so long?"

"I got here as fast as I could once I figured out your Twinkie clue."

Betsy kissed him again, "Thanks Chief."

"Now take your clothes off!"

Betsy gave him a startled look, then a sexy smile, "Do we have time?"

"No, no, just to change outfits. Keno Lady said to take anything you'd like."

'Oh,' she pouted in disappointment. "Just who is that lady?"

"I'm not too sure, an angel I think. I couldn't have done this without her."

"What should I wear?"

"Something that makes you look short and fat," he joked.

Betsy started to disrobe. "I'm not the only one being held prisoner by that psycho maniac, Bond. There were two other girls, although I haven't seen Tina in three days." Betsy said as she perused through the closet for something to wear. "I think he hurt her."

"I'll deal with him, but my first priority is getting you back to Pinedale."

Betsy searched through the closet and bureau drawers, she settled on a light weight summer sweater and cream colored slacks. "Hum, a little short in the leg."

"It looks great," Oliver said. Not even noticing what she had chosen.

They both froze at the knock on the door. Oliver looked through peep hole and sighed in relief at the distorted face of Keno Lady.

"My clothes never looked so good," Keno Lady said, nodding approval as she checked out Betsy's outfit. "Here, take my car," she tossed keys to Oliver. "It's a rental. Turn it in at any Avis location."

"I can't take…"

"Hush," she interrupted Oliver. "I'm protecting my clothes. If you hang around here they might get blood on them."

## THE PAST IS NEVER DEAD

Oliver and Betsy looked at each other in total surprise. This lady knew how to take charge.

Betsy slowly nodded, "She's right."

"Come on," Keno Lady said, "I've called the valet service. It's probably out front already. It's a red Jaguar, you can't miss it."

Oliver was still questioning her as she pushed the two of them out the door.

"Tip the valet well, I have a reputation to maintain," she laughed as she closed the door.

# 32

The lobby had settled down but was still crowded. With no luggage they didn't draw any attention. Just to be safe they exited on the marina side and walked around to the valet pick-up. Keno Lady had given Oliver the parking ticket. The car was waiting for them just as she said. The runner held the driver's door as Oliver approached. .

With a quizzical look, the youngster hesitated and then said, "This is Ms. Madigan's car!"

"I'm her brother," He handed the kid the ticket and a hundred dollar bill.

As they drove away from Atlantic City, Oliver said, "Let's put some miles on this car before we turn it in. It'll be harder for them to track us."

"They probably know we're heading home. That psycho will just come after us," Betsy said.

'I believe they will come," Oliver agreed, "But it'll be the last place they'll look. His first instinct will be that we're on the run and Wyoming is the last place we'd go." Oliver looked at Betsy and smiled. "That will give us time to get ready for him." He paused, as though he was distracted. "Madigan, Madigan, where have I heard that name before."

"What are you talking about? Who's Madigan?"

"When I gave the valet the ticket, he said this is Ms. Madigan's car."

"Haley Madigan?" Betsy replied with a start. "Oh my god, Keno Lady is Haley Madigan?"

"Who's Haley Madigan?"

She's one of the wealthiest women in the world. She runs Reliable Mutual, America's second largest mutual fund with over a trillion under management. She has a reputation for secrecy and runs the company from a distance. She has few friends and most people don't know anything about her. She prefers it that way. Her worth is estimated at 7 billion. They say she lives out west somewhere.

## THE PAST IS NEVER DEAD

"How do you know so much about her?" Oliver inquired.

"We did a case study on her at Rutgers. She's every girl's hero." Betsy smiled. "And I'm wearing her clothes."

Oliver drove north on the New Jersey Turnpike then west at exit 6 to the Pennsylvania Turnpike. He decided to drive west as far as Harrisburg or maybe even Pittsburgh before they turned in the car and started a roundabout air trip home. He was thinking of changing airlines at least once on the way home.

Haley Madigan sat smugly in her usual chair. She was pleased with herself. She had been a successful diversion for the nice Forrest Ranger. Buying a rat at the local pet shop had been a stroke of genius. Fortunately, she liked rats. She dealt with the two legged ones daily, so keeping one in her purse didn't bother her. She found the entire scenario extremely entertaining. Mike Bond's bodyguard wasn't dead but he was in the hospital with an ill regular heart beat. The casino was buzzing with activity.

Bond was visibly upset. He scurried back and forth past her most of the day, barking orders to underlings. He wasn't the only unhappy one. Sal Bryne was being read the riot act by Danielle Fournier who wasn't happy having rats on her guest list at the reception. It was all Haley could do to keep from laughing out loud. She loved the excitement danger brought. It was a characteristic that contributed to her success in the world of stocks and bonds.

Haley had been planning to go home next week, but that plan was about to change. She was sure Oliver would be back once his wife was safe, and she enjoyed the excitement the Forest Ranger created. Maybe she would just stick around to see if he needed her help.

Suddenly, Jimmy Cricket slid into the chair next to Keno Lady.

"Mike Bond would like to see you," he mumbled without looking at her.

"Well, that should be easy, I'm very visible," she responded without taking her eyes off the board posting results of the current game.

"Don't get wise," Jimmy said as he turned his hatchet face toward her.

"If I was wise I wouldn't even acknowledge you were here." She continued to score the recent game.

"He wants me to bring you to his room."

Keno Lady put her paper and pencil on the tray in front of her. She turned toward Jimmy, "That's not what I want, so listen to me very carefully. I don't let underlings escort me to men's hotel rooms. If your superior wants to talk to me tell him the chair you're occupying is free. I'm here until 5:00PM. After that I'm unavailable."

Jimmy showed his agitation as he rose from the chair. He cast his most threatening look at Haley, "The boss ain't going to be happy."

"With you or me?" Keno Lady said as she returned his glare, only hers contained a mocking grin.

Jimmy Cricket stormed off toward the casino area.

It was 4:50 PM when Haley saw Mike Bond exit the elevator. She smiled to herself. His arrival at the deadline time, set by her, was his show of strength that he was in charge.

"May I sit down?" he gestured to the empty chair next to her.

"If you wish," Haley nodded.

Bond sat down, careful not to wrinkle his jacket. He was dressed is a very expensive Calvin Klein three button charcoal suit. The blue shirt had a white collar which highlighted a dark blue silk tie. He was certainly well groomed.

He adjusted his cuff and unconsciously rubbed his manicured nails with his thumb, "Why are you afraid to come to my room?"

Haley stopped looking at the keno board and unhurriedly turned to face Bond. She checked him out from shoes to shave and then returned the question, "Afraid? Hardly."

"I just wanted to ask you if you were sitting here during the commotion earlier today."

Haley nodded.

"Did you see the rat?" Bond inquired.

"Now you know I did. He asked me to come to your room," she smiled.

"Funny" Bond grinned. "I'm talking about the four legged one that caused all the screaming."

"No, but I certainly heard the commotion. You would think a classy hotel like Borgata would have pest control." She paused for effect and then continued, "But this hotel doesn't control pests, in fact it rents them rooms."

She looked at her wrist watch, "Oops its 5 o'clock. I have to be going." Haley rose quickly from her chair. "Have a nice evening." She strode off, leaving Michael Bondinni conspicuously alone.

"Bitch" he mumbled as he looked around to make sure no one was enjoying his humiliation.

# 33

Oliver adjusted the seatback, trying to get comfortable enough to get some sleep. They had chosen to turn Haley Madigan's car in at Harrisburg. They took the 1:51pm U S Air flight to Charlotte NC, then Northwest flight to Minneapolis/St Paul. Oliver was allowing himself to relax for the first time in three days.

Just as he closed his eyes, Betsy said, "I still don't understand all this changing flights. If Bond is looking for us he'll just go to Pinedale."

Oliver nodded his head, "Eventually, but they will try to find us first. He'll search for us in New Jersey, then he will spread out the search. When all else fails, he'll come to Pinedale. That's why you're going to stay in Jackson with Gordon and Marilyn."

Betsy sat up in her seat, "And just where are you going to be?"

Oliver turned his head and opened his eyes, "I'm going back to the casino and destroy that bastard."

"You can't kill him," she whispered her concern.

"No, I'll just make him wish he was dead." Oliver stated with resolve and closed his eyes.

Betsy was worried. She knew once her husband set an objective, nothing would change his mind. She felt responsible that he was going to put himself in danger. Her mere existence had created the problem and she felt helpless.

"I'm going with you," she said. "I can help."

Oliver opened one eye and peered at Betsy. "How much help would I be in your classroom?"

After a pregnant pause he continued, "This is my classroom."

The plane arrived in Jackson 4:30PM mountain time. Oliver called Gordon at work and arranged to meet at his house. Gordon agreed and said he would head home now.

*THE PAST IS NEVER DEAD*

Marilyn greeted them at the door. She hugged Betsy, "You poor dear, I'm so happy you're alright." She then pushed back and said, "You are alright aren't you?"

Betsy smiled and patted her cheek, "I'm fine Marilyn, just fine."

"Gordon is in the den," Marilyn said. "He's making cocktails."

"Oh, you found something he could do around the house," Oliver said as he headed toward the den.

'Hello Barrister," Oliver said as he entered the room. "You're thirty six hundred dollars in debt to Visa," he said, throwing the credit card on the desk. "Don't know when I can pay you back."

"No sweat, Chief. Here have a Knob Creek," he said handing Oliver a glass. "I'm only charging a thousand dollars a drink today."

"Do you take Visa?" Oliver grinned as he accepted the drink in one hand and put his arm around Gordon with the other. "Thanks Gordon, I couldn't have done this without you. Betsy and I are grateful."

"You didn't waste much time completing your mission."

"It's not over yet. I'm going back east to collect a scalp." Oliver sipped his drink.

"I think it best if you don't give me any details of your plan at this point. If you do, I would be obligated as your consul, to advise against it."

They walked into the kitchen where Marilyn and Betsy were having wine.

"Where are the steaks?" Gordon asked Marilyn. He turned to Betsy, "Black Angus and Roosevelt beans okay with you?"

"Mmmm, sounds great," Betsy said.

They were sitting on the porch drinking coffee. Four pleasantly stuffed adults who were content to enjoy each others silent friendship and the cool evening breeze. It was a pleasant and relaxing finish to a chaotic week.

Gordon's phone extension on the porch rang. He slowly turned to Marilyn with a look that said I'm not answering it.

"Answer the phone," Marilyn said. "It's for you."

"If it was for me they would call my cell phone," he growled. The last thing he wanted was to talk to a needy client.

He begrudgingly picked it up. "State your case," he grumbled.

"Hi," the voice said. "I'm glad you made it home alright."

"Thanks, but it's something I've been doing successfully for years. It's not a difficult trip from the office."

"When did you find time to go to work?" the voice inquired.

"I usually set aside 60 hours a week to do that. Who is this?"

"Room 321," the voice replied. "It's been quiet since you left."

"I think you have a wrong number," Gordon said.

"Is this Gordon Cundiff?"

Gordon took the phone away from his ear and looked at it. He shook his head in disbelief, "Yeah, this is Gordon."

"You don't know who this is, do you?"

"No and how did you get my home number?"

"I have my resources," the voice continued. "You never even told me your name. I had to get it from the desk clerk."

"Is this a shakedown?" Gordon was rapidly losing his temper.

"Oh, maybe I do have the wrong Gordon Cundiff. Are you a Forest Ranger?"

"Forest Ranger? Hell no, I'm a lawyer."

Oliver had been listening to Gordon's half of the conversation. He held his hand out for the phone. "I think that's for me."

Oliver put the phone to his ear, "Keno Lady?"

There was a pause, "Yes is that you Gordon?" Yeah, that was my brother. He thinks he's a comedian. How did you find me?"

"My friend the desk clerk gave me your name. You forgot to check-out."

"We were in a hurry. I returned you car in Pennsylvania, at the Harrisburg Avis" Oliver said.

"Yes I know."

"Listen, can I have your number and a time when I can reach you?" Oliver asked. "I would love to hear what's going on with Bond."

"That's why I called. I was wondering if you were coming back or had I seen the last of you."

"Let me call you tomorrow. It must be eleven o'clock back there. When would be a good time? I have a lot to tell you."

"Call anytime. I'll give you my cell phone number, but please Gordon, don't give it to anyone," Haley pleaded. "Promise?"

"With my life" Oliver assured her. "We'll talk tomorrow, goodnight."

"Who the hell was that?" Gordon demanded.

Oliver winked at Betsy and grinned as he handed Gordon the phone. "That was the wealthiest woman in the world, and she thinks you're an asshole."

# 34

Oliver agreed to let Betsy go home and pack some clothes. She also had to let the school know she was alright and would need a few more days off. She was sure it would be okay. While Betsy was getting her things together Oliver drove over to Kevin's office.

He wanted to tell Kevin about his adventure in person. It just wasn't something you explain on the phone. He also had to call off the FBI and tell Agent Dawn Brann he appreciated all her help. He hoped he wouldn't sound too sarcastic.

As Oliver entered the office he saw Woody sitting at a desk trying to get comfortable. The shoulder cast was making him fidgety.

"This is the same scene I left," Oliver observed.

"Same hell hole," Woody replied.

"Clearmountain! Get in here," Kevin roared from his office.

Oliver peeked in sheepishly. Seeing Agent Brann, he smiled, "I'm glad you're here."

"I'm not," came her curt reply. "I was about to have a warrant put out for your arrest. Where have you been? You have jeopardized a federal investigation."

Oliver felt the tension in the air. "I was out of touch. No satellite signal. The good news is I found my wife. She escaped her captors and got in touch with me. Unfortunately she wandered around in the mountains and it took me a while to find her."

"Why wasn't I notified?" Agent Brann said.

"I just explained, NO signal," Oliver repeated with authority. He knew he was going to have to take charge of this inquisition or get caught in a lie.

Oliver hadn't expected to see the FBI in Kevin's office and wasn't prepared with his excuse. He paused for a moment too long.

"Well," Kevin chimed in, "We're waiting."

*THE PAST IS NEVER DEAD*

"Let me start at the beginning, so I don't have to repeat myself.' Oliver was trying to buy some time.

Oliver was still standing near the door when Woody stuck his head in, "Oliver, your friend in Washington called. He said it was important, and you should call him the first chance you get. He said he would leave a message at your home."

Oliver grasped the moment, "I didn't get the message because I haven't been home" he said. Oliver looked at Kevin and Brann reinforcing his story he'd been rescuing Betsy. "When did he call?"

"Yesterday," Woody said, handing Oliver the phone message.

"This will only take a second." Oliver held the phone message in the air and started out of the office. "We can't keep Washington waiting, can we Agent Brann."

Kevin and Agent Brann sat patiently for ten minutes as Oliver made his call. When he returned, Kevin saw he was upset.

"Jonathan Yokatory isn't dead." Oliver said as he collapsed into the chair next to Agent Brann.

"Then that's who took your wife?" Brann said.

Oliver looked up at her and thought, *agreeing with you isn't lying*. He nodded.

"Did you find Betsy near the Yokatory camp?" Kevin asked.

"Not exactly, but she covered a lot of ground." Oliver was stretching the truth. His mind was racing. *Yokatory was in that camp while I was there. No…he couldn't have been or he wouldn't have let me go.*

"Where's you wife now? I want to talk to her." Agent Brann asked.

"She resting. She has been through a lot. She needs a few days rest."

"Where is she?" Brann persisted.

"I'll tell you after she's had a few days rest. The last few days have been hard on her. She's sleeping, she's not going anywhere."

"I want to talk to her now," Brann demanded.

Oliver eyes deepened as he stared at Agent Brann. "I don't like repeating myself. I said in a few days."

"Now I'm going to go to my wife." Oliver turned to Kevin. "I'll give you a written report the first chance I get." He rose slowly out of the chair staring daggers at Agent Brann, challenging her to say something. She remained quiet.

In the outer office, Oliver walked by Woody and whispered, "Tell Kevin to loose the Fed and meet me at Big Mo's for lunch."

Woody smiled and winked his acknowledgement.

Oliver flipped open his phone as he walked to his Jeep.

Betsy answered, "Hi honey, where are you?"

"I'm in the parking lot of the sheriff's office. Take what you have packed and throw it in your truck and haul your beautiful butt out of there, fast."

"What's up," Betsy wanted to know.

"The FBI is going to show up in a few minutes to question you." Oliver informed her. "And I don't think we're ready to tell them the entire story."

"Okay, I'm outta here."

"Go to Cundiff's and tell Marilyn not to mention to anyone that you're there."

"Oh, there was a phone message from your buddy in the secret service. He said call him first chance you get."

"Thanks, I already took care of it."

"When will I see you?" Betsy said, as she snapped her suitcase shut.

"I'll drive up later tonight when I'm sure no one is tailing me," Oliver said, "Now git, LYL."

"Love you lots also," Betsy said before the phone disconnected.

Oliver was upset that he told Dawn he was going to see Betsy. That was asking for a tail.

Inside Kevin's office, Agent Brann said, "I'm going out to the Clearmountain place. I want to talk to his wife."

"What makes you think she's there?" Kevin asked as Woody entered the office and handed him a phone message slip. "Sorry to interrupt, but I think this is important."

"Where else would she be?" Dawn replied, ignoring Woody. "I want you to come with me."

Kevin glanced at the note Woody handed him. Meet Oliver at Big Mo's—alone! He looked up from the note at Agent Brann, "I can't, I have a district to run." Crumbling the note, he hollered after Woody. "Did she say it was important?"

"Yep" Woody said, "Right away."

Kevin threw his palms up and shrugged his shoulders, "Sorry, but you can find the Clearmountain place without me."

Agent Brann was disappointed, "I suppose I'll have to eat lunch alone."

"Woody," Kevin shouted as he walked to the door. "Get Jimmy Hawk on the radio and tell him to pick up lunch for you and Agent Brann. Tell him to get something for himself also, it's on me."

"You're buying?" Woody looked up to the ceiling, "Well I'll be…Lucifer better put on a jacket, his place is about to freeze over."

# 35

Satisfied that no one was following him, Oliver sat in his Jeep along side of Big Mo's restaurant. He decided to take the free time and call Keno Lady as he had promised. He decided he would continue to call her Keno Lady until she told him otherwise.

"Gordon?" she asked as she answered her phone.

"Yes and no," Oliver replied. "It's time to bring you up to date. My name is Oliver Clearmountain. Gordon Cundiff is the name I used. He's my lawyer."

"Is that who answered the phone last night?" Haley inquired. "I knew something wasn't right."

Oliver spent the next ten minutes explaining to Keno Lady what the truth was.

She listened intently and didn't interrupt once. In fact at one point Oliver had to ask if she was still there. He was just finishing when he saw Kevin's SUV pull in the lot.

"I have to go, my appointment just arrived," Oliver said.

"Just one minute," Haley said. "My real name is Haley Madigan and I want to assist you if you plan to pursue retribution with Mr. Bondinni. What he is doing is not only illegal, it's sick."

"I appreciate that, but this is my responsibility, I don't want anyone getting hurt." Oliver stated.

"Hurt? Listen Gord…Sorry, I mean Oliver. There are two theories about arguing with a woman, neither work. I'll give you a few days to let me know how you're going to take care of Mr. Bondinni. If I don't hear from you I'll open up my own can of whip-ass and let the police sort out his pieces."

Oliver was stunned. He didn't know what to say.

"Got to go," Haley said. "I just hit for four hundred. Talk to me in two days." She hung up.

*I'm glad she's on my side* Oliver thought as he slipped out of his Jeep and waved to Kevin.

They took their usual booth near the back.

Big Mo walked up to their table. "Well if it isn't Pinedale's finest and the phone man."

"Listen Mo," Oliver said. "I'm sorry about being rude to you. Betsy scolded me about phone manners. Please accept my apologies."

Mo made a face and nodded like it was all forgiven, "What can I get you boys?"

"Couple of hamburgers and a large order of fries," Kevin said. "A root beer and," he pointed to Oliver.

"A chocolate shake," Oliver added.

Mo said, "Coming right up" and headed back to the kitchen.

Kevin looked hard at Oliver, "Okay, the truth, the whole truth, and nothing but the truth, starting now."

Oliver looked at his friend and saw genuine concern in his eyes. "Betsy was kidnapped by a New Jersey mob boss," he started. "He was the reason she left the East Coast. He was infatuated by her. She left in the middle of the night, in fear of him. My guess is he has been looking for her ever since. The bikers were the tie to Betsy's past. Betsy worked with Lee Fitzpatrick, the biker that was killed, as a showgirl at a casino back East. I guess she stumbled upon Betsy's whereabouts and informed Bondinni. Apparently she thought there would be a bounty. I believe Bondinni offered them a deal. I think their first plan was to eliminate me and when that didn't work they decided to kidnap Betsy. We are very fortunate they were incompetent.

Kevin shook his head in stunned silence.

Oliver continued, "As you know, at first I thought it was my past that was catching up in the form of Jonathan Yokatory, but it's turned out to be Michael Bondinni, a punk from Atlantic City.

"How did you find out it was him?"

"Betsy had the presence of mind to leave me a clue. Something she said to Mrs. Best at the school. It was a tidbit only I would understand."

"So you went to New Jersey and rescued her." Kevin continued, "It was that simple?"

"Actually, it was easier than I thought, but I had help." Oliver said. "I don't think they were expecting me to react so quickly. I caught them off guard."

"What now?" Kevin said. "Don't you think he'll come after both of you this time?"

Oliver just nodded. Discontinuing the conversation as Big Mo approached the table with their food.

With a devilish grin he slapped two hamburgers down on the table and dumped a load of fries from the tray. The fries slid over the entire table.

"What the heck!" Kevin said, grabbing a napkin.

"I was informed this table takes issue with the baskets we serve our food in." Big Mo declared. "I'm just trying to accommodate my customers. Would you like some soup with your meal?"

Oliver looked up at Big Mo's grinning face and said, "No thank you, this will be fine.

Big Mo turned and walked away. Every waitress in the place was watching the reaction from the booth.

"What the hell's got into him?" Kevin roared.

"Easy Kev," Oliver confided, "We gave him a tough time about serving food in a basket. It's payback time."

Big Mo returned with a Root Beer in one hand and a Milk Shake in the other. He paused at the table with a quizzical look.

"No," screamed Kevin, "We never criticized your glassware." Kevin was pushing back from the table as much as the permanent booth would allow.

Big Mo smiled and gently placed the glasses on the table, "The trouble with using experience as a teacher is the final exam comes first and then the lesson." Pleased with his performance, he walked back to the kitchen.

Kevin sat staring at the array of fries scattered over the table. Oliver was laughing. It appears that he enjoyed Big Mo's performance more than Kevin.

"What the hell was that all about?" Kevin wondered out loud.

"We just got a lesson. Don't tease a prideful man."

Kevin agreed, but then said, "I should put ketchup all over our fries."

"Let's leave well enough alone," Oliver suggested.

Kevin agreed that a truce would be good. Both men placed napkins under their hamburgers and returned to their conversation.

"What about Yokatory? I thought you said he was dead." Kevin said as he took a big bite from his hamburger.

"I don't know." Oliver confided. "I thought he was dead. Evidently it was a sham. If he knows where I am, I'm sure he will come after me."

"He couldn't know where you live." Kevin scooped up some fries. "That State Police escort you received coming home prevented anyone following you."

"If his so called right hand man studied my wallet long enough he'll remember my address." Oliver said wiping his mouth.

"Do you want protection?"

"I may need your help," Oliver said as he noticed Big Mo heading their way.

"Would you fellows like dessert? Maybe a couple scoops of ice cream?" Big Mo was having a hard time containing his laughter.

Both men answered simultaneously, "NO!"

Oliver held up his hands in surrender, "You win, we've learned our lesson. Just the check please."

"Lunch is on me today boys," Big Mo said as he left the table. "Have a nice day."

# 36

Oliver stopped home to pick up a few things including his Berretta and a clean uniform. He then headed to his office. He had to tell his boss, C.M. Rawlings that he needed a few more days off. The C. stood for Colleen.

"Hello O," Colleen said as she greeted him at the door. "I was just leaving. Are you back on the job?"

"I'm going to need an additional week, but I plan to be in the area if you need me." Oliver said.

"We'll manage. Sheriff Cahill explained when I spoke to him the other day. I understand the urgency of the situation. Is Betsy alright?"

"Yes, thanks for asking," Oliver said. "It's just the trouble maker is making himself a nuisance."

"You have obviously reported him to the authorities?" Colleen asked.

"The sheriff and the FBI are aware," Oliver said with a quizzical look.

Colleen laughed. "Agent Brann was around the other day asking questions about you. I think for awhile you were a suspect."

Oliver shook his head in amazement. "I wouldn't want their job. If Christmas presents were missing, they would suspect Santa Claus."

Colleen chuckled, "Stay in touch, I've got to run. We have another fire up near the south entrance to the park."

"Do you need me to help?" Oliver offered.

"Nope, it's a controlled burn. I'm just going to chase a few thrill seeking campers who think they're indestructible. Stay in touch." Colleen headed for her Jeep and waved goodbye.

Oliver spent the next few hours in the office cleaning up his desk and catching up on the backlog of paperwork. Then he headed up to Jackson.

He covered the sixty four mile trip without incident. It was still daylight when he pulled into Gordon's driveway. Betsy met him at the door.

"Hey Chief, I thought you'd be later," she said as she hugged his neck and kissed him. "I've only been here a short time myself."

"Let's take Gordon and Marilyn out to dinner," Oliver said. "They've been a big help through all this."

Marilyn was in the kitchen when Oliver walked in. "Hi Oliver," she said. "I just hung up with Gordon and he's on his way home."

"Great. Betsy and I would like to take you and Gordon out to eat tonight. . We'd just like to acknowledge how much we appreciate everything you've done for us."

Marilyn started to say something and Oliver halted her with, "We won't take no for an answer."

"I was going to say," Marilyn continued, "you had a call earlier, from Ms. Madigan in New Jersey. She left two numbers where you could reach her and said she would appreciate a call the first chance you got."

Oliver looked surprised as he took the note from Marilyn.

"Did it sound urgent?" Oliver inquired.

Marilyn nodded her head, "It did."

Haley picked up on the first ring.

"Hey Keno Lady," Oliver greeted her. "I heard you've been trying to reach me."

"Bond has left town," she announced. "I'll give you two guesses where you think he's headed and the first one doesn't count."

"Pinedale, Wyoming," Oliver stated.

"I can only assume Pinedale, but I'm sure about Wyoming. He chartered a private plane to go to Wyoming."

"Are you sure?" Oliver asked.

"I'm sure, Oliver. After you left he was all over the casino shouting orders and running back and forth. Suddenly things got awful quiet. I couldn't find him anywhere so I started to snoop around. His employees at High Roller Travel like to talk, and I like to listen. When I inquired about a trip to Montana she informed me Mr. Bond had just left for a hunting trip in Wyoming and she was sure he would have been happy to give me a lift. There were four of them. When I asked if they would have room for me she said, "Oh yes, he specifically asked for a plane with a range of 2500 miles and one that could land on a small strip of less than 6000 feet. That's the Hawker 800XP. It'll carry eight."

"When did he leave?" Oliver inquired.

"Long enough ago to be there by now," Haley said. "Wherever there is."

"Thanks Lady, you're a dear."

"What are you going to do?" Haley asked.

"Find them before they find me," Oliver stated.

"Call me when you find them," Haley pleaded. "I'm not very good at waiting."

Oliver hung up the phone and saw Gordon walk through the door.

Gordon looked at his wristwatch "Is it cocktail time?" And with a wink he headed for the den. "Follow me Tonto, and bring the squaws."

Oliver grinned at the attempted humor, shook his head as he took Betsy by the arm and followed Gordon into the den.

"Houston, we have a problem," Oliver announced, getting everyone's attention. "Mike Bond is in Wyoming." He waited for the statement to register with everyone.

"Where?" Betsy said.

"Are you sure?" Marilyn followed.

"I don't know," he said to Betsy and turning to Marilyn, "Yes."

Gordon was behind the small bar putting ice in glasses, "Do we have a plan?"

Oliver picked up a glass of bourbon and looked at the amber glow created when he held it to the light. "Yes, you're going to circle the wagons and protect the women. I'm going to put on my war paint and track him down," he said savoring his first sip. "But first we're taking you to dinner," Oliver put his arm around Betsy. His intent was to defuse the situation. He was worried enough for all of them, but he refused to let Bond have the upper hand. Nothing could be done until dawn and by then Oliver would be in Pinedale.

# 37

The next morning Oliver was up before dawn. He was getting dressed when Betsy rolled over in bed and groggily asked, "What time is it?"

"Time to sleep." Oliver said as he walked over to the bed and kissed her forehead.

"If all goes well I'll be back by tonight, and we can celebrate the future and forget the painful remembrance of our past." He patted her on the butt and said, "Get some sleep."

"I'll worry," Betsy moaned. "Be careful."

"There is nothing to worry about. "When I get to Pinedale I'll tell Kevin and he'll put out an APB. When they grab Bond, I'll press kidnapping charges and we'll get the FBI involved again. It will all be over quickly. When the trial comes up you'll have to testify and he'll go away for a long time. Case closed."

"Sounds good," Betsy cooed as she closed her eyes.

He slipped out of the house trying not to wake Gordon. He was afraid he'd still insist on tagging alone. Oliver preferred to do this alone.

Oliver reached Kevin's office a little before seven. Kevin's SUV was parked in its usual place.

Oliver entered the office. He paused, waiting for Kevin to bellow, "Clearmountain, get in here!" Oliver glanced up at the fisheye mirror to see if he could see into Kevin's office. It appeared Kevin had someone in the office with him but Oliver couldn't see who it was.

Then he heard Kevin's booming voice, "You're late Jimmy, go get me some coffee."

Oliver's heart stopped. He sensed trouble. *I know he saw me come in. He knows I'm not Jimmy Hawk. The deputies park around back and use the rear entrance. Something is wrong.*

"You got it boss." Oliver shouted as he started for the door. But before he could take a step there was a guy standing at the threshold of Kevin's office door. He had a shotgun leveled at Oliver.

"Not so fast, Slick," he said. "Get in here." He was waving the gun barrel.

The man with the shotgun backed up as Oliver entered the office.

Kevin was sitting at his desk with his hands palms down.

There were two additional men in the office. One was standing in front of the desk, holding a pistol on Kevin. The other one was seated in the chair opposite Kevin. It was Jonathan Yokatory. Oliver froze. He knew instantly how desperate the situation was.

Kevin looked sadly at Oliver. "Sorry. They were waiting for me when I got out of my cruiser."

"Well, well," Yokatory said as a sadistic smile crept over his face. "Look who just walked in and saved us a lot of hard work. Secret Service Agent Clearmountain, I've been looking for you."

Oliver didn't reply. He knew anything he said would just provoke the unstable cult leader.

"I'm sorry I wasn't at the camp when you stopped by," Yokatory continued. "I had business elsewhere. My people told me a childhood friend stopped to save me from my wicked path." Yokatory rose from the chair and started pacing. "When they told me my friend's name, I was shocked. I thought we had an unwritten understanding. That we'd leave well enough alone. You know, you don't come looking for me and I won't kill you." He sat on the corner of the desk. "But just like the rest of the government smucks, you can't keep your word."

"You've got it all wrong, Jonathan." Oliver said. "I wasn't coming after you. I don't even work for the Justice Department anymore."

"What were you doing snooping around my camp?" Jonathan said.

"I'm a Forest Ranger. I'm responsible for our national parks and resources." Oliver evaded the direct question.

"A Forest Ranger!" Yokatory laughed. "You expect me to believe that?"

"If you let me put my hand in my pocket I'll show you my ID."

"I don't care what you say you are," Yokatory shouted in anger. "You could be Smokey the Bear. I don't give a shit. I'm still going to kill your righteous ass. I'd do it right here, but I don't want them to find the body. If you turn up missing they'll come after me. You're just going to disappear." He started for the door, "Bring em both," he said to the gunmen.

Oliver and Kevin followed Jonathan Yokatory down the hall past the empty cells. Oliver noticed the feet of a body in the supply room as they went out the back door. Jonathan opened the rear door of a panel truck that was backed up to the building. Oliver felt the barrel of a shotgun painfully push into his lower back and he fell into the panel truck. Kevin was pushed in on top of him and the doors were slammed shut. The van was stripped bare, no seats, no rug, not even side panels. The hard ribbed metal floor was filthy.

As the two gunmen got in the front, one turned and pointed the shotgun. "Don't even think about moving." he demanded. "I told Jonathan we should restrain you but he didn't want any marks on your body."

"Our murder is going to look like an accident?" Oliver inquired.

"You catch on quick, Slick" the gunman said.

Oliver and Kevin both sat up putting their backs against the side of the van facing each other, and the van started moving. Oliver figured Jonathon was in a separate vehicle so that just in case something went wrong he could get away. The driver and gunman were not the two he had the run in with at the camp. He didn't recognize either of them.

"Where are you taking us?" Kevin requested.

The driver laughed. "To your final resting place." When he stopped laughing he started singing "I shot the sheriff, but I didn't shoot no deputy. Oh, no oh."

The gunman said, "Eric Clapton, right?"

"You don't know shit," the driver said. "Bob Marley wrote that song."

# 38

Because it was daylight, Oliver could sense where they were going. They weren't heading back to Colorado. They were heading into the Bridger Wilderness Area due east of Pinedale. They drove for about a half hour, then the road got rough. They had obviously left the paved road. Just by moving his eyes Oliver communicated with Kevin. *'When they open the rear doors we go out the front.'* Kevin nodded. Oliver could only assume Yokatory was following them.

Finally the truck came to a rest. The driver threw the gear shift in park and opens the door. "Cover me," he said to the gunman.

"You got it." he replied as he got out the passenger side.

The driver hollered from the rear of the truck, "If you try any funny stuff when I unlock this door we'll shoot your ass right here and now."

Moving as quietly as they could without rocking the van, Oliver and Kevin were already slipping out the two open front doors. Gathering in front of the van they could hear the driver unlock the rear doors. "Stay with me and don't stop running," Oliver whispered to Kevin." Using the van as cover they ran straight ahead to a group of trees.

Oliver heard the drivers surprise when he saw the rear of the empty truck "What the hell…?"

Oliver and Kevin were heading for the trees when they heard the shotgun roar. Oliver hoped they had covered enough ground to render the range of the shotgun pellets ineffective.

"Ow," Kevin groaned.

"You hit?" Oliver asked as they kept running for protection.

"I don't think so, just stung," Kevin replied as they heard more shots as they slipped into the cover of the trees. This time it included a report of a pistol and a slap of the bullet hitting the tree next to Oliver.

"Stick with me and keep running." Oliver gasped as he ducked around some trees and snaked his way deeper into the woods with Kevin close on his heels struggling for breath.

After five minutes of jogging deeper into the wilderness, Oliver held up his hand and stopped running. Kevin bent over and grabbed the fabric of his pants just above the knee. He was gasping for breath.

"Shhh," Oliver said. "I'm trying to hear them"

"I hope you can't," Kevin blurted between breaths. "I'd like to think we lost them."

Oliver shook his head. "We don't want to lose them. My plan is to wear them out."

"What about me?" Kevin wheezed.

"You'll be fine." Oliver whispered. "The average person can move two miles an hour in this terrain. About half that fast for every 1000 feet they climb. If we can keep them close to us, I can make them travel faster than they should. In which case, I'll have them on their knees in a hour, begging for help." Oliver looked at Kevin's back as he bent over breathlessly. "You're bleeding. Take off your shirt."

"I'm fine," Kevin said straightening up. He put his hand behind his back and winced. There was some blood on his hand. "At least I thought I was."

Oliver lifted the back of Kevin's shirt. "Just as I expected, you got hit with some spent pellets. They just broke the skin." He looked closer, "In fact some are still imbedded just under the surface. You'll be fine."

"Thanks Doc," Kevin smiled at Oliver.

Oliver threw a couple of good size rocks down the hill in the direction of their pursuers, and listened.

"I heard them," yelled a voice from down the hill. "They're up here."

"Let's go, Hoss," Oliver said, as he gently pushed Kevin up the mountain. "I noticed your holster is empty but what else do you have on that belt?"

"Handcuffs, mace, extra shells, and oh yeah, my nightstick," Kevin replied as he started up the mountain.

Every fifteen minutes Oliver would repeat the rock throwing. After awhile he started throwing the rocks off to his left. He and Kevin stopped moving and hid. Over the next few minutes, the direction he threw the rocks led his pursuers around them. He could hear how tired they were by the noise they were making crashing through the brush as they climbed higher. Both were gasping for breath as they shouted to each other. Finally Oliver and Kevin were below their followers. Suddenly a shot rang out.

One of the gunmen had turned around to look down the hill and spotted them. Now the chase was reversed. Crouching as low as they could, Oliver and Kevin started down the hill, struggling not to lose their balance.

"There they go. They're heading back down," the shooter shouted as he started running toward them.

After seventy yards, Oliver noticed the terrain was becoming extremely steep and too difficult to maintain control. He stopped and slipped behind a tree. Kevin saw what Oliver had done. He grabbed at a tree to stop his descent and slipped behind a boulder on the edge of a steep slope.

Their pursuers were gaining ground, they were only moments behind.

The noise got louder as it became apparent the gunmen had lost control and were sliding and stumbling down the hill. "Lookout, awe shit, damn it," came the screams.

Oliver watched the awkward twosome tumble past him totally out of control.

Further down the hill they came to a crashing halt. For a moment neither body moved. Oliver and Kevin carefully climbed down to their dazed chasers.

"Careful," Oliver warned. "I don't see Yokatory."

Kevin placed his size 14 boot in the middle of one of the gunman's back. As he put his weight on his foot he could hear what air was left in the guy's lung escape.

"Oof," the guy moaned, as he fought to catch his breath. Kevin picked up the shotgun and held the barrel to the back of the man's neck.

Oliver rolled the other gunman over onto his back. He was barely conscious. "Hello Slick."

Oliver saw the man's hands were empty. He looked around for the pistol. He must have dropped it rolling down the hill.

The gunman at his feet started to say something. Oliver dropped his knee hard into the man's stomach. The guy rolled into an embryo position clutching his gut. He tried to scream but nothing came out of his mouth.

"Watch him, I'm going to look for the pistol," Oliver said.

Kevin tapped his guy's head with the barrel of the shotgun to get his attention. "Where's Yokatory?"

"I don't know," the guy moaned.

"Wrong answer," Kevin responded, as he hit his head harder. "Where's Yokatory?"

"He stayed with the van," was the quick reply.

"Found it," Oliver said as he tucked the pistol in his belt. "Cuff your guy. This one doesn't have any fight left in him." Oliver dragged his guy to his feet and pushed him down the slope. He fell and rolled about 10 feet further down the hill. "Doing it your way is going to take a lot longer." Oliver stated as he walked toward him. "Get up."

# 39

When they arrived at the tree line Kevin stayed with the two Yokatory men as Oliver scanned the area. He thought he had seen a car behind the van as they made their escape. It wasn't there now. The van sat alone in the field with its doors wide open. It was obvious if anyone had been there, they were now gone. They put their prisoners in the back of the van and drove to Kevin's office.

The parking lot contained three state trooper cars. Deputy Jimmy Hawk was just walking out the rear door when he saw Oliver and Kevin get out of the van.

He hollered back into the office "The sheriffs here." Then he ran to the van. "You guy's okay? What happened?"

"Get the Sheriff over to the hospital, he's been shot." Oliver said.

Kevin gave Oliver a look of disgust. "I'm not going to the hospital," he announced as he looked back into the van. "And neither are either of you, so quit bellyaching."

Oliver walked to the rear of the van to open the door

Jimmy stared at Kevin's back. "Sheriff, your shirt's all bloody."

"Help Oliver, Jimmy, we have some prisoners in the back." He tossed Jimmy the shotgun. "I'll be in my office."

Oliver helped Jimmy lock the two gunmen in their own holding cells and then went to Kevin's office. The outer office was full of Sheriff's Deputies and State Troopers. They were all staring at him.

Oliver smiled and nodded, "Anyone got coffee and maybe a donut or something to eat? I'm starving."

Kevin was sitting at his desk, opening a first aid kit. "Here they are," he said as he held up tweezers. "Somebody get these B-B's out of my back." He stood to take his shirt off and turned to Woody, who was giving him a cup of coffee. "How's Deputy Jenks?"

"Hospital say's he has a concussion, but he'll be okay." Woody said. "They hit him with a pipe or something."

"More than likely the barrel of a shotgun," Kevin said.

"Was it just those two you brought in?" Woody asked.

"No, one got away. Put out an APB on Jonathan Yokatory."

"Do we have a description?" Woody said.

"I'll get a picture from Washington. You'll have it in 5 minutes." Oliver said as he picked up the phone.

Oliver hung up the phone. "The picture's on the way," he said as he reached for the tweezers and pushed Kevin's head down on the desk. "This will be painless. I won't feel a thing." He laughed.

"Take it easy, medicine man." Kevin groaned. "My back feels like it's on fire. How many buckshot can you see?"

Oliver paused for a second, counting. "It looks like five maybe six. You have about 15 wounds, but only six shot penetrated the skin." If you had run a little faster, like I told you, none of them would have stuck."

Oliver cleaned up Kevin's back and put bandages on the puncture wounds.

Kevin's deputies and the state troopers gathered in the conference room with Kevin and Oliver. Kevin clicked on the recorder in the center of the conference table. "I unlocked the front door at six thirty this morning. Seeing no one in the outer office, I called out for Deputy Jinks. I heard someone say, 'Down here Sheriff.' I walked down the back hall to the supply room and there was a guy standing with a shotgun pointed at my belly. I saw a pair of legs behind him on the floor. I knew they belonged to Jinks. Two more mugs appeared behind me and then the one named Jonathan Yokatory said 'Let's go to your office.' At first they just asked questions about when the other deputies would come in, and then the leader, Yokatory, wanted to know where Oliver Clearmountain lived. I told him they didn't have to hold a gun on a County Sheriff to get that information. It was in the phone book."

"Why did they come here first if they wanted me?" Oliver interjected.

"Their plan was to use me to get to you," Kevin said. "Yokatory said you were the suspicious type and a hard polecat to corner, but you would relax when you saw them with me." Kevin turned to Oliver. "The simple fact of you showing up here threw a wrench into their plans. What made you come here this morning anyway?"

Oliver chuckled, "The funny thing is, I was on my way to tell you some thugs were in town looking for me and Betsy. Only it wasn't Yokatory's group I was worried about, it was the crowd from New Jersey."

Kevin turned off the recorder. "Okay people that's it," he said standing up. "Get out there and find me that Yokatory jerk, before he hurts himself." Kevin had a you know what I mean grin on his face.

Oliver and Kevin were finally alone in Kevin's office. Oliver had explained to Kevin the entire scenario of the New Jersey trip at Big Mo's. Now the two men sat quietly and stared at each other, each one silently putting the pieces together.

Kevin spoke first. "So where is Betsy now?"

"She's staying with Marilyn and Gordon up in Jackson." Oliver said.

A concerned look came over Kevin's face. "What makes you think this Bond guy is in Pinedale?"

"I'm sure he's coming after me," Oliver said. "Keno Lady said he chartered a plane for Wyoming and if he wants me, he's got to come to Pinedale.

"He doesn't want you." Kevin stated grimly. "He wants Betsy and her rescuer, Gordon Cundiff!"

Oliver's jaw dropped as the reality of Kevin's statement hit him. His eyes closed in repentance. "How could I be so stupid?" Oliver jumped to his feet. "Betsy and Marilyn are in Jackson unprotected." He reached for the phone on Kevin's desk and dialed Gordon's cell phone.

# 40

Betsy smiled as she entered the room. She had showered and looked fresh, ready to face a new day and get her life back to normal.

"Well Betsy, what should we do today? Would Oliver get mad if we went shopping?" Marilyn was sitting at the kitchen counter having her second cup of coffee.

"What Oliver doesn't know won't hurt him." Betsy smiled. She placed her cup under the spout and pressed the button. "I sure do love this coffee machine, a freshly ground and brewed cup of coffee in less than a minute."

"Its one of Gordon's toys, although I must admit I like it." Marilyn said. "What time did Oliver leave?"

"Before dawn," Betsy replied, taking her coffee and joining Marilyn at the counter. "I worry about him. At times he thinks he's invincible."

"He'll do fine. When he starts tracking something he usually finds what he's looking for." Marilyn said as she drank her coffee.

"It's what he does, after he finds his prey that worries me. Sometimes he's recklessly fearless, and with this particular hunt, he's very upset. He might revert to his ancestral way of thinking and tie Bond to an ant hill." Betsy stared into her black coffee. "This won't have a happy ending." She looked into the black abyss as if she could see the future.

"When it's over, we'll all be happy," Marilyn was trying to lighten the moment. "Let me take a shower and we'll find something fun to do." She headed out of the kitchen. "There's juice and eggs in the fridge, cereal in the pantry and muffins in the bread drawer. Make yourself at home. I won't take long."

Betsy searched for jam as her muffin toasted.

The Cundiff home was a beautiful two story brick structure, much larger than Betsy and Oliver's home. It sat back off the main road and was situated perfectly on a choice lot, just minutes from the Jackson Hole ski area.

Having finished her muffin, Betsy refreshed her coffee and wandered out to the rear patio. It was warming up quickly. The morning sun was shinning brightly as she admired the Grand Teton range. With no foothills obstructing the view she marveled at the rugged snow veined peaks rising majestically from the flat valley. A red tailed hawk was pumping its wings hard as it headed back up the mountain with breakfast clutched in its talons. It was probably a poor pika or field mouse who zigged when he should have zagged. Imagine having this view in your back yard, Betsy thought. It was quite a contrast from South Jersey.

She actually heard it before she saw the large Class A, RV pull to the rear of the house. It turned slightly away from her into the vast area in front of the three car garage. Its back was toward the patio and the front was facing Gordon's gentleman's barn. Betsy couldn't see who was driving but she half expected Gordon to step out.

A very large metallic gray and black mobile home the size of a greyhound bus sat in the driveway rumbling as a slight hint of diesel exhaust drifted out the rear. It looked as if it was a city bus, waiting at a bus stop for a passenger. Nothing happened, no one stepped out, it just sat there as if it was driven by a ghost.

Finally curiosity took over and Betsy stood up and decided to see just who it was.

"Where did that thing come from?" Marilyn inquired, as she came out of the house. And then as if answering her own question she said, "Oh no, he better not have!"

"What?" Betsy exclaimed.

"Gordon." Marilyn replied. "He's been after me for months to look at one of these mobile homes. No, he wouldn't have," she cried out, shaking her head. They both started walking toward the large, imposing bus. As they neared the side door, it opened, and a well dressed man stepped out.

"RUN," Betsy screamed. Her coffee cup shattered on the ground as she turned away, tugging at Marilyn's arm with both hands.

"If you run, I'll shoot your friend," Jimmy Cricket replied as he pulled a pistol from his jacket and pointed it at Marilyn's head. Betsy felt ill. She couldn't have run if she tried. Her legs felt like rubber and her feet like lead.

## THE PAST IS NEVER DEAD

The nearside window slid open. Betsy couldn't see in but she didn't have to, she knew who was peering out. "Good morning, gorgeous. Why don't you and your friend come on in and join us for brunch?"

"No," screamed Betsy, "It can't be you."

"Show our guests inside Jimmy." It was Mike Bondinni.

Marilyn clutched Betsy trying not to show fear, but her hands were shaking. "It will be alright."

"I'll come in if you let my friend stay here," Betsy offered.

"Right," was the sarcastic reply. Then in a harsh, commanding voice Bond shouted, "Get in."

Betsy and Marilyn made eye contact as they both heard the phone ringing in the house. It was a distant glimmer of hope, but moments too late.

"Now," screamed Bond.

Jimmy grabbed Betsy and pushed her in the open door.

She stumbled going up the steps.

He shoved the gun in Marilyn's face and screamed "Help her."

Marilyn realized this must be the nut from New Jersey. She was also aware the Jimmy guy was nervous and looked to be very unstable and dangerous. Betsy had regained her feet and hurried into the coach while Marilyn followed.

# 41

"Slow down Oliver," Gordon said into the phone. "I'll call home, hang on." Gordon put Oliver on hold and punched an open line on his desk console. The phone rang until he heard Marilyn's voice informing the caller that the Cundiffs were unable to answer the phone right now, please leave a message.

He punched Oliver's line, "They must be out, or maybe Marilyn ran down to the store for milk and Betsy's in the shower." He lied, he knew there was plenty of milk in the fridge.

"Get to your house and wait for me. I'm on my way," Oliver said as he hung up the phone.

"Kevin."

"Got it, I've already notified the police in Jackson. They're sending a car over to check out Gordon's house." Kevin rose from his desk and followed Oliver out of his office. "Let's use my vehicle. It has more lights and a loud siren.

Kevin pulled into the Cundiff's driveway in record time. The trip had taken 47 minutes. He parked behind a white SUV that had a rack of red and blue lights above the windshield. "Cop's are still here," he said.

Oliver hardly heard him. He was unbuckled and out of the vehicle before it came to a complete stop. Oliver ran to Gordon who was standing in the driveway talking to a police officer.

"What have we got?" he asked both men.

"They're not here," Gordon said. "We've been through the entire house and everything is normal, no sign of a struggle or anything suspicious."

"Do you have an APB out on them?" he asked the Jackson policeman.

"Not yet, Mr. Clearmountain, as far as the law is concerned they're not missing." The policeman said.

Oliver turned to Gordon, "Have you tried Marilyn's cell phone?"

'It's on the kitchen counter," Gordon replied. "What about Betsy's?"

"I've been calling her all the way up here, no answer. It's either off or no signal.".

"Maybe they just went shopping?" The policeman suggested.

"How many web cams do you have in the area?" Oliver inquired.

The officer looked pensive as he tried to recall. "Ten or twelve between the village and Old Faithful, but not many focused on the highway. I'll check," he said, as he slid into the patrol SUV and clicked his radio microphone.

Oliver looked at Gordon, "Do you have any idea what happened?"

"The house is in order. Everything looks normal," he said, shrugging his shoulders.

"Is her car still here?" Oliver said, hurrying toward the garage.

Gordon's answer was a boy am I dumb look. "I'll get the remote from my car." Gordon said.

Oliver suddenly stopped. "Don't bother, her car is still here."

"How do you know until you open the door?" Gordon said.

"Look," Oliver pointed to the smashed cup on the driveway in front of the garage door. "Unless Marilyn drinks her coffee and smashes the cups like she's at a Greek wedding, they've been abducted."

Marilyn and Betsy were seated on the end of the queen size bed in the rear of the mobile home. Jimmy Cricket was sitting up front with a clear view of both of them. He was staring at them, nervously twirling his pistol on his finger. Mike Bond was sitting in the passenger seat, giving the driver directions.

Betsy motioned to Jimmy, making a drinking motion. "Can we have some coffee? I dropped mine."

Jimmy nodded and walked to the sink.

"What are you crazy, I don't want coffee." Marilyn said softly.

"Shhh," Betsy whispered. "Just follow my lead."

Jimmy walked to the rear with two mugs of steaming hot coffee in his hands and his pistol stuck in his belt. "Here," he handed each a mug. "Black will have to do. I ain't no waiter and this ain't no restaurant."

"Black is fine, thank you." Betsy said taking a mug with both hands. She was tempted to grab for the gun in his belt, but she knew it wasn't the prudent thing to do. The hot coffee would surely burn Jimmy's hand, but more likely she'd catch a lot of it in her face.

When Jimmy returned to the front, Betsy turned to Marilyn. "Stand in front of me like we're talking."

As Marilyn stepped in front of her, Betsy moved over to the side window and slid the glass and screen back. She threw her cup, coffee and all, out the window.

"What are you doing?" Marilyn exclaimed. "Have you lost your mind?"

"I'm dropping bread crumbs, just like Hansel and Gretel." Betsy said.

"Give me your cup and go to the bathroom. Stay there and if anyone knocks on the door, tell them you're sick." She took the mug from Marilyn.

Marilyn went into the bathroom and Betsy sat on the bed drinking coffee. She didn't like black coffee, but it would have to do. The maniacal stare from Jimmy Cricket was disturbing. Betsy realized they were in serious trouble and she was aware she needed an escape plan. The appearance of Mike Bond worried her. He had the look of a crazed psychopath. He was drawn, pale and unkempt. It appeared he hadn't slept in days. This was not the same cool dude that ran the roost in Atlantic City. Betsy suspected drugs were involved and if she was right, it intensified their terrifying predicament. Although she hadn't noticed, she was sure the driver was Joey (Chops) Cucci. He was the least stable of the three of them, plus he had a score to settle with Betsy for the shock treatment she had administered to him in the ladies room.

# 42

Oliver had given Kevin the nod to distract the Jackson policeman. He then pulled Gordon aside. "Look, the cops aren't going to help us for the first 48 hours or until we can prove they have been kidnapped." He looked at Kevin talking to the policeman. "So dismiss this cop and tell him we'll be in touch when our wives return."

Gordon went over to Kevin and the policeman. "Kevin, Oliver wants to talk to you."

Oliver walked around the patio looking for anything that would tell him what happened. Suddenly his cell phone vibrated. He flipped it open and stared at the screen.

Kevin edged up next to him, "Who ya calling, Chief?"

Oliver didn't answer. He continued to gape at his phone.

"I can get some deputies to set up road blocks south of here." Kevin offered. "We're going to have to stop every vehicle. Can you get the Rangers to be on the lookout in the park?"

Oliver didn't answer him. He finally looked up to Kevin and held his phone so Kevin could see the screen. "What's that?"

"It's a text message from Betsy."

Kevin looked harder at the screen. He saw two letters, r v. He looked to Oliver for an explanation.

"They're in a RV," Oliver shouted as Gordon, having dismissed the policeman, walked up to him.

"What? How do you know?" exclaimed a surprised Gordon.

Oliver held up his phone, "Text message from Betsy," he said. "I don't know how she did it, there's no quit in that girl."

"Is that all it said?" Gordon looked at him. He didn't quite comprehend what was going on, since he hadn't seen the message.

"Yes," Oliver responded. He was already weighing the idea of calling her back, but he dismissed the thought knowing his call would bring attention to

her phone. Even if he responded with a text it would give her secret away.
"Kevin, can you track cell phones?"

"No, but the state has the equipment. Let me get on it." Kevin said.

"Do you have Betsy's cell number?"

Kevin walked away holding his phone to his ear, nodding as people do when they are making cell phone calls.

"Kevin," Oliver shouted, "get your guys set up in the south. Gordon and I are driving north." He grabbed Gordon. "Let's move."

Kevin waved, acknowledging he heard Oliver.

Betsy was pleased with herself. Text messaging Oliver had been a chore. Moving her fingers over the keyboard of her phone while it was in her tight fitting jeans was next to impossible. She wished she could have said more but just two letters nearly broke her fingers. It took her ten minutes. Marilyn was still in the bathroom. It was time to deposit the second coffee mug out the window. She slid the window and dropped the mug.

"What the hell are you doing?" Jimmy screamed. The road noise had prevented her from hearing him come up behind her.

Her heart sunk. She had been caught. She snapped around mustering up as much courage as she could. "I don't like doing dishes."

Jimmy backhanded her across the cheek. She fell on the bed. Instantly she could taste the blood flowing from the inside of her cheek.

"I guess it's time for the necklace," Jimmy smirked.

Betsy's body trembled at the sound of the word. She wanted to kick out at him and fight back but she knew it would be useless. She heard Oliver's voice in her head, 'Pick your fights. Don't let them pick you.'

He stepped back to the bathroom door and banged on it. "Get out here, NOW."

"I'm sick" Marilyn responded in a weak voice.

"NOW," Jimmy screamed, "or I'll start beating on your friend."

"Leave her alone," shouted Marilyn as she rushed out of the bathroom.

Jimmy pushed her on the bed next to Betsy. He turned and walked up front.

Betsy wiped a little blood from the corner of her mouth.

Seeing this, Marilyn said. "Are you hurt?"

## THE PAST IS NEVER DEAD

Betsy shook her head.

Jimmy Cricket returned with two jeweled, choker/necklaces in his hand. He yanked Marilyn off the bed by the hair and spun her around. Before she could protest he snapped the jeweled choker around her neck.

"What's this?" Marilyn grabbed at the necklace.

Jimmy said, "Let me show you."

"NO!" Betsy pleaded.

Marilyn's hands stiffened at her throat as her eyes rolled back in her head. Her mouth opened as she tried to scream, but nothing came out but drool. She collapsed on the bed, twisting as her entire body convulsed.

"Please stop," Betsy begged Jimmy.

Marilyn's body went limp and a soft moan escaped her lips. She appeared semi-conscious.

Jimmy tossed the second necklace on the bed next to Betsy. "You know the drill." Betsy snapped the all too familiar necklace around her neck.

# 43

"Just keep driving north until you get to the airport," Oliver told Gordon.

"Then what?" Gordon asked.

"We'll check the airport lot for RV's. If we don't see any we'll continue north."

"Do you have any idea where they're headed?"

Oliver shook his head. "I don't think they went to the airport, but we'll check it out. The last thing we want to do is pass them." Oliver's eyes were glued on the road as he talked. "It seems like Bond went to a lot of trouble to look like a vacationer, using the RV as cover. I'm thinking he plans to hole up somewhere in the mountains."

"Why?"

"Because he knows the minute I discovered Betsy missing I'd head to Atlantic City, just like I did the first time he took her."

Gordon nodded.

"Pull over," Oliver yelled, unbuckling his seat belt before the car stopped.

By the time Gordon got out and walked to the curb behind the car, Oliver was kneeling in the gutter holding pieces of broken glass. He searched along the curb and picked up the remains of a cup handle. He glanced up to Gordon holding the piece in his hands. "This isn't a coincidence." Oliver said as he stood up. "Lets go, but slower this time."

Gordon got behind the wheel and turned to Oliver. "Do you mean to tell me you think Betsy dropped that cup?"

"She knows a broken mug in the driveway was the only clue she left behind. She's doing all she can. Keep driving" Oliver said. "I'll bet we'll find another one."

Gordon shook his head in disbelief.

Oliver's heart jumped as his cell phone beeped. The thought that it was Betsy was short lived.

## THE PAST IS NEVER DEAD

"Good news, I've got a few blocks set up," Kevin announced before Oliver said hello. "Bad news is the State boys have to inform the FBI if they are going to search the airways for phone activity."

"I understand." Oliver replied. "Listen Kev, we don't need the southern road blocks. I'm convinced they're heading into Yellowstone."

"How do you know? Never mind, I'm on my way." Kevin said.

"My gut feeling tells me they're going northeast toward the lake and the lodge. There's an RV campground at Fishing Bridge," Oliver said. "We can meet up there or I'll leave word if you miss us. Stay in touch." Oliver shut off his phone.

Gordon looked out of the corner of his eye at Oliver. "So now I'm to drive slow looking for broken coffee cups?"

"Just drive barrister, I'll look."

"What happened" Marilyn sobbed, "I hurt all over." She was curled up on the bed and Betsy was rubbing her back.

"It's the necklace; it gives you an electric shock. It's remote controlled so while you have it on, do as you're told. They love to use it."

"Oh Betsy, what are we going to do?" Marilyn was still shaking.

"Stay strong, you know Oliver and Gordon will find us. It's only a matter of time."

"If they do," it was Mike Bonds voice. Betsy looked up to see him standing in the hall, "you two will be widows."

Betsy stared at him with disgust. "Let Marilyn go. She's not part of this."

Bond studied Marilyn trembling on the bed. "I'm not too sure. My harem can always use an attractive addition."

"You're a crazy..." Betsy stopped, knowing it was the wrong thing to say.

The pain that shot through her neck and up the back of her skull also crushed her chest. The room went black for a second and Betsy couldn't control her burning muscles. She heard a moan escape from her throat as she rolled off the bed and crashed on the floor. She was conscious and hurt all over, but couldn't move.

"Stop, please stop," Marilyn cried.

Betsy regained some control of her cramped muscles and pulled herself to the bed. "Oliver is already in Atlantic City, just waiting for you. He'll kill you the minute you set foot back in the casino."

"We're not going back to Atlantic City," Bond said as he turned and started to the front of the RV. "That's part of my past. My future is in the slave trade. Have you ever been to the Far East?" His cynical laugh lingered as he left.

Bond slipped into the passenger seat. "Keep heading north, Chops. We'll take turns driving so we can drive all night. I have one more pick-up to make in Bozeman Montana."

Chops nodded without taking his eyes off the narrow road that wound through Yellowstone National Park. "What then?"

"I have our chopper waiting to take us to Canada where we'll meet up with my Chinese partner."

"Hmm," Chops acknowledged, "We're not going to operate out of the casino anymore?"

Bond smiled, "We're going to establish a new base of operations in British Columbia. It's closer to the action." Bond slipped off his loafers and put his feet up on the dash. "These three will bring top dollar."

"Why are the Chinese willing to pay so much for American broads?" Chop's said.

"The forbidden fruit, the Chinese love the Western world," Bond said. "And I'm going to deliver it to them," Bond grinned, "for a price."

# 44

"Don't bother to stop, but there's another busted mug on the road." Oliver pointed through the windshield.

Gordon started to slow but then kept going. "I'll be damned," he muttered.

They were about to enter the park. "Pull over at the entrance gate. I want to talk to the ranger."

Standing in the toll booth, Oliver said, "Tell me Roy, how many RV's have entered the park today?"

The ranger shook his head. "I don't know Oliver; I'd guess forty or fifty since I came on at nine this morning. Half of them were rentals from Cruise America. The rest privately owned. I guess a few of those babies are special."

"Anything stand out as unusual about any of them?"

Roy shook his head again, "Not that I recall."

Oliver described Mike Bond and Roy continued shaking his head. "Nope, I don't recall seeing anybody like that."

Oliver paused. It suddenly dawned on him that Bond wouldn't be driving. "How about a fat guy, thirty five or forty, Mediterranean complexion, slicked back hair, with large meaty hands."

Roy's eyes brightened, "Yeah, big fat hands. He paid with a fifty. He could hardly hold the change I gave him. He was driving a black and grey Class A. Fleetwood Revolution LE, top of the line. You don't forget when you see one of those. It had a huge front windshield, I could see right in. It was a beauty. Come to think of it, the guy in the passenger seat fit your first description. He had his feet on the dash board when they pulled up. I had to tell him to put on his seat belt."

"Did you get the plates?"

"Our cameras did, I'm sure."

Oliver could hardly contain his excitement, "Did they ask for directions?"

"Nope."

"How long will it take you to retrieve the plate number?"

"Half hour, forty-five minutes at the most." Roy said. "Why?"

"The guy owes me money."

Roy accepted the offhand answer with a nod. He knew there was more to the story.

"When you get the number, advise all the stations to be on the look out for it, but tell them to just report, its not official business. " Oliver said. He started for the door. "I can't rely on my cell phone in the park. Call the Lake Yellowstone Lodge and leave me a message. Thanks Roy, you've been a big help." Oliver ran to the car.

As he slid into the passenger seat Gordon said, "You scored didn't you? What have you got?"

"Black and grey Class A. We'll know the license plate number when we get to the Lodge. Go"

Betsy sat on the side of the bed looking out the window for familiar sights. She knew how to take the necklace off but that would have to wait until they had a chance to escape. Removing the necklace would accomplish nothing as long as they were prisoners. She no longer had the luxury of just worrying about herself. Marilyn was also her concern.

The 'OLD FAITHFUL NEXT RIGHT' sign flashed by. We're going west, Betsy thought. I guess Bond was telling the truth when he said we weren't going back to Atlantic City. Where are we going?

She couldn't just sit and do nothing. She patted Marilyn's leg. "Stay here. I'm going to see if I can find out where we're going."

"Be careful," Marilyn said as Betsy headed up front.

Jimmy Cricket was sitting on the sofa. "What do you think you're doing?"

Betsy slipped into the bench seat at the kitchen table. "I'd like to talk to Michael."

Bond twisted around in the passenger seat and looked at her. "Talk."

He looks like hell, Betsy thought. "What are you planning to do with us?"

Bond smirked. "You wouldn't believe me if I told you."

"Try me."

"You and your friend are worth fifty thousand to me and that's just the beginning."

"What are you talking about? Oliver doesn't have that kind of money."

"My business associates in the Pacific rim and China do. In fact, its petty cash for them." Bond explained. "A sexually active Caucasian woman is worth her weight in gold."

"A what?" Betsy was speechless. "You don't mean me and Marilyn? We'll never-"

"Yes you will," came his stern reply, "willingly, when you see your choices."

Betsy sat very still trying not to show her new found fear. Bond was truly mad, she thought. Her stomach's impulsive flip almost betrayed her. She swallowed hard and turned away so Bond couldn't read the horror she was feeling. She tried to gather the courage to continue the conversation, but was unsuccessful. She got up and slowly walked back to the bedroom, hoping her knees wouldn't give out.

Bond turned around in the seat and smugly enjoyed the results his remarks had on Betsy Clearmountain.

"When we leave the park at the West exit we'll be in West Yellowstone, Montana. We'll stop and get supplies and then head to Bozeman."

Bond turned to Jimmy. "Take our guests some of your special juice. Make sure they drink it, its time for them to take a nap."

# 45

The Lake Lodge wasn't crowded when Oliver walked in. He walked to the registration desk. He wasn't in uniform, so he identified himself.

"My name is Oliver Clearmountain, I'm a Forest Ranger. I'm expecting a message from my office. Do you have anything for me?"

The desk clerk smiled. "You're not staying here, are you Ranger?"

Oliver checked the name tag pinned on his shirt, "No Ryan, I'm just using you as a secretary."

Ryan grinned at Oliver's humor, "I've been used for worse Ranger, let me check." He disappeared into the adjoining office.

He reappeared with a yellow slip of paper in his hand. "Yes I do,"

Oliver took the note. Written on the paper was his name and below it read, Wyoming license 2 – 7230. Oliver knew the number two meant the license was issued in Natrona County. He was sure the license was being traced in Casper.

"May I use your phone?"

"Sure, come on back," Ryan gestured to the adjoining door. "Can't get a signal, huh?"

Oliver felt now that he had the license plate, things would get easier. "You wouldn't happen to have the number of the RV camp ground at Fishing Bridge, would you Ryan?"

"Sure, I'll get it."

Oliver hung up the phone in disgust. There wasn't any record of Bond's RV at the camp ground. There weren't any reservations for future nights and it certainly wasn't there now. Oliver sat at the desk with his hand on the phone. Although he had hung it up, letting go would make the bad information final.

"Not what you wanted to hear, huh?" Ryan offered.

Oliver nodded. Just when he thought he was getting close, now he had no idea where Betsy and Marilyn were. Had he made a mistake by thinking they were heading this way? Maybe they kept going toward the North or East gate. Maybe they were holed up in some out of the way canyon. Great! If they were still in the park he only had 2.2 million acres to search and eighty percent of it was forest. The possibility of them getting out of the park was unthinkable. He still had his hand on the phone when it rang, startling him back to the present.

"I'll get it." Ryan said. He picked up the phone. "Lake Lodge, Ryan, how may I help you?" After a pause he continued. "I don't have to take a message. He's sitting right next to me." Ryan extended the phone to Oliver, "It's for you."

It was the Ranger from the South gate. "We got a look see," Roy said. "They were spotted leaving the West gate."

"They're no longer in the park?" was Oliver's rhetoric reply. "Do you still have them under surveillance?"

"No, they're in Montana."

"Great, and I'm on the other side of the park." Oliver groaned.

'Anything I can do to help?" Roy offered.

"No, but thanks Roy, you've already been a big help. I'll be in touch." Oliver hung up the phone. He was in a positive frame of mind again.

"That call was more to your liking," Ryan laughed.

"You bet," Oliver jumped up. "How far is it to the West gate?"

"Sixty miles," Ryan said. "And drive careful. "The Rangers are S.O.B.'s."

Oliver smiled, "Can I use you as a secretary again?" He picked up a pen and scratched a note to Kevin. "Give this to Sheriff Kevin Cahill."

Ryan smiled as he took the note. "Will do and I wish you luck."

Gordon was still parked at the front entrance.

"I hope we're close, I'm starting to worry," he said as Oliver slipped into the car.

"They were seen at the West gate. Let's go."

After driving for a few unspoken minutes Gordon broke the silence, "I'm sure it's nothing but I think someone is following us."

Resisting the natural instinct to turn around, Oliver said. "When did you first notice them?"

"Back when I pulled over, suddenly, for the broken coffee mug," Gordon said. "A pick-up truck pulled over quickly behind us. And then it pulled away from the curb right after we did. It didn't stop at the South gate like we did, but now I've noticed it again. It's just an old blue truck." Gordon glanced into the rear view mirror. "It's not there now."

"Let me know when you see it again." Oliver said. "It's probably just a tourist. There aren't a lot of roads in the park."

Jimmy Cricket was putting away the groceries as Chops came out of the bedroom. "Our sleeping beauties are out for the night."

"They should be. I hit them hard with chloral hydrate." Jimmy said. "That stuff will knock out a gorilla." Looking at Chops he smirked. "It might even make you drowsy."

"Funny," Chops mumbled. "What did you get to eat? I want some pasta. Did ya get some good Romano cheese and fresh Italian bread?"

Bond was sitting at the table looking at a map. "Chops get over here. I want to show you where we're going in the morning."

# 46

Haley Madigan had been home only twenty-four hours and she was already busy working her two jobs, which occupied most of her time in Bozeman. The first order of the day was to get an update of results for the first quarter and projections for the second quarter for Reliable Mutual. While on the East coast, Haley spent a lot of time observing her company as an outsider. Playing the customer she would scrutinize her company's service level as well as the competition. She would then make the personnel changes she saw fit. Then she was going to wade into her pet projects around the house. She loved to putter around with decorating changes and fixer-up projects. Although she had hired help to do the heavy stuff, she loved to roll up her sleeves and get involved. She called it therapy.

She had a great couple to house sit her Bozeman mansion. Manny and Marge Olivari had both worked for Reliable Mutual before retiring and moving to the Madigan estate. They have been married as long as Haley had been alive. She looked at them as family. The Olivari's had an in-law type apartment located on the lower level of the 20,000 square foot, three story home. The house sat on the highest point of the 90 acre domain. Haley had recently installed a 7000 foot long runway that was capable of handling a large commercial jet if necessary. The end of the runway finished just below the immense garage, separated by a twenty foot grassy knoll. It was her intention to make her trips to Atlantic City easier.

Manny and Marge managed the manor for Haley, even when she was there they supervise the staff that ran her home. During the course of an average day there could be a staff of five or six in the house, and as many as two or three strange vehicles in the driveway. Although Manny and Marge ran a well-organized operation it was a very busy single resident home and at times a bit confusing.

That's why Bond's RV sat in the driveway unnoticed for 45 minute that morning without being disturbed. The first one to notice the black and grey Fleetwood loitering in the driveway was Marge.

She walked up and rapped heavily on the door.

The door opened and Jimmy said, "Good morning. Are you Ms Madigan?"

"No," Marge said. "What do you want?"

"Ms Madigan ordered this RV and all I'm doing is delivering it?"

Marge scrutinized Jimmy from tip to toe with a stern look. "Wait here I'll let her know."

As Marge walked away, Jimmy turned back into the interior of the RV. "This is working just like you said it would, boss."

Bond smiled, "Just wait until you see who we're picking up."

"Does the broad work here?" Chops wanted to know.

"She lives here," Bond said.

"Jesus boss, she must be rich," Chops responded, as he looked out the window at the imposing mansion.

"She's one of the richest in the world," Bond scoffed. "In fact, I think she's the richest broad in the States."

"Why don't we just take her money?" Jimmy chimed in.

"It's not that easy my friend" Bond said. "She doesn't have it lying around the house." He was delighted the way his plan was rolling out.

"LOOK, LOOK," shouted Chops, looking out the window. "I'll be damned, it's Keno Lady"

"Okay Mrs. Cundiff, get up here and greet our visitor." Bond gestured to Marilyn. "And remember, do as I told you. If you screw up, I'll juice your friend." He flipped the remote in his hand. Marilyn nodded and stepped down the steps to greet Haley.

Marilyn stepped from the RV. "Hello Ms. Madigan."

"Why are you in my driveway?" Haley said as she sized up Marilyn.

"I was told by my company to come out and show you the new Revolution LE from Fleetwood. It's the top of our line. Please step in."

Haley backed slowly up as Marilyn was talking. Her eyes were fixed on the jeweled necklace Marilyn wore. She was taken aback and very perplexed, but she knew she was in trouble. She continued to retreat, "Get it out of my driveway," she said. After a few more steps backward, she turned and ran as fast as she could to the nearby open garage door.

"GET HER" Bond shouted.

Jimmy jumped from the RV in hot pursuit.

Haley was nowhere in sight as Jimmy entered the four car garage. Two spaces were occupied by cars. Closest to him was a green Jeep and on the other side of it was a black Suburban. He heard a door close. There were two doors. One on the back wall that led to the rear of the house and one at the far wall that looked as if it led into the house.

Haley ran through the kitchen. The Cook was chopping at the counter. She pushed her as she ran past, "Run, hide, we're in danger. Follow me."

Haley's mind was racing as fast as she was. That had to be Bond in the RV. Where did he come from? Who was that woman? What the hell does he want?

She continued to the den with her Cook right behind her.

"Why are we running, Miss Haley," the Cook asked.

Haley opened a desk drawer and pulled out a snub nosed .38 cal. revolver.

"Run, go this way." Haley pointed to the far door. "Find Manny or Marge and tell them to call the police. There are killers in the house."

The Cook took off running, still carrying the 9 inch chef's knife she had been using in the kitchen.

Haley heard the door from the garage close. Someone was in the kitchen. She looked at the gun in her hand. Could she actually shoot someone?

She walked over to the phone. Would she dare make a call?

She was standing at the desk with her hand on the phone when she saw a shadow on the wall in the hall. Suddenly, standing in the doorway was Jimmy Cricket with a big smile on his face and a gun in his hand.

"Well, if it isn't Keno Lady," He scoffed.

Haley fired.

Jimmy dropped the gun in shock as he grabbed his side. His face went blank in shock as he sagged to his knees. He fell back into the hallway.

Haley walked out to the hall and stood over him. She was trembling as the adrenalin sped through her body.

She felt the pain on the back of her head as the walls spun and the floor came up to greet her, then darkness.

# 47

Oliver and Gordon slept in the car in the town of West Yellowstone. During the night while Oliver had time to think, between Gordon's snoring, he realized the RV could be heading to Bozeman. That meant only one thing to him, Bond was heading to Keno Lady, but why?

He called the police in Bozeman. They said they would keep a lookout for the RV and in the morning they would send a patrol car out to the Madigan estate.

He and Gordon had a drive-thru breakfast and were eating in the car.

He then took a chance and called Kevin. The signal was bad but Kevin answered.

"I got your message from Ryan," Kevin said through the broken transmission. "I've notified the Montana state police. They'll let me know if they see the RV."

"Great," Oliver noted. "We're on our way to Bozeman…hello, hello, can you hear me Kev?"

Gordon glanced at Oliver "Did you lose him?"

Oliver nodded his head and closed his phone. "We're on our own."

"Why do you think they've gone to Bozeman?"

"Because that's where Keno Lady lives."

"That's your friend from Atlantic City?"

"Yeah," Oliver said deep in thought. "Do you have any guns in the car?"

"I keep my hunting rifle in the trunk. I think I have about half a box of shells. Do you think we'll need it?"

"I hope so. Because if we do, it'll mean we caught them." Oliver said.

A sinful expression crept across Gordon's face. "I also have my hunting knife back there. Maybe I'll get a chance to use that."

Oliver pushed back in the seat to stretch his legs. "Have you seen the pick-up truck this morning?"

Gordon looked at Oliver with a blank stare.

"You know, the one you think is following us."

"Oh, no not this morning." Gordon said. "I thought I saw it last night. But now I'm beginning to think you're right. Besides all trucks are starting to look alike."

Haley opened her eyes. The light hurt her head. She quickly closed them tight. Was that Betsy's face I saw? She braved the pain and peeked with one eye.

"How do you feel?" Betsy said. She was holding a cold washcloth on Haley's head.

"The back of my head is numb, but the inside hurts like hell." She then moaned "What happened? Where are we?"

"Shhh, take it easy," Betsy whispered. "You're in the RV and we're still in your driveway. I'm not sure, but I think Chops hit you. He carried you out here on his shoulder."

"Mmm," Haley nodded. "I shot that Jimmy creep."

"We thought so. I saw Chops helping him into the coach," Betsy said. "Unfortunately, he's still alive. He's up front whimpering like a baby. He sure is mad."

"Who was that other woman? She was wearing the necklace." Haley flinched as she touched the back of her head.

"That's Marilyn Cundiff, my friend. She's up front taking care of Jimmy the Creep. She's an RN."

Haley rose up on one elbow. "What's going on Betsy?" It was then she saw the necklace on Betsy's neck. The thought leaped into her pain racked brain, as her hands grabbed at her own neck. She felt the jeweled choker. "NO!"

"You're going to be alright Mr. Cricket," Marilyn said trying to be as professional as possible. This was no time to be disrespectful. "The bullet passed cleanly through your side. It missed your kidney. It's merely tore some muscle and left two puncture wounds. You just need to rest until the wounds heals." She looked over to Bond. "The dressing should be changed every twenty-four hours and he could use some pain killers or at least aspirin."

## THE PAST IS NEVER DEAD

"Yea, yea, let me worry about that. Get to the back with your friends." Marilyn walked to the bathroom to wash her hands.

"Chops, get over here," Bond said. "How many people are in the house?"

"Chops moved into the seat next to Bond. "I don't know. It looked like someone was working in the kitchen. You know stuff lying around and the burner was on, but I didn't see anybody."

"Okay," Bond said. "We're going to have to make a slight change in our plans."

He walked to the door. "Jimmy, keep an eye on the broads. Chops and I are going to check out the house."

The Cook had found Manny. He directed Marge and the Cook out the back door and told them to take cover in the woods. He heard the gun shot and crept up the backstairs just in time to see Chops carry Haley out on his shoulder while helping Jimmy Cricket. Challenging Chops, unarmed, was out of the question. Although Manny was a young sixty seven, the truth was he was still sixty seven. After they left, he found the maid upstairs and directed her to run to safety. He then called 911 but before he could explain the nature of the call he hung up because he heard the door from the garage open and Bond and Chops come into the kitchen. He returned to the lower level and left the house, hurrying to find his wife. Staying out of sight he headed for the safety of the woods. He felt helpless because he didn't do anything to help Haley.

# 48

Bond and Chops started to search the house. They stared at each other in panic as they heard the police siren. It sounded very close.

Chops looked out the kitchen window. "Cops, they just pulled up the driveway."

Bond answered the front door. Two policemen were standing on the front steps.

"Yes, how may I help you?"

"We received a 911 call from this address," the cop said. "If you would place your hands on your head," the policeman requested. His hand was on his gun.

"What's this all about? Are you arresting me?" Bond feigned in annoyance. "I work for Ms Madigan."

"You're not under arrest. We're just being safe. Is Ms Madigan home?"

"No"

"Did you call 911?"

"No, why would I do that? I'm here alone."

The policeman nodded suspiciously. "Sir, would you please step outside for a moment."

Chops stepped into the threshold pushing Bond aside. He had his pistol pointed at the policeman. "Why don't you come in?" He noticed both cops had bulletproof vests under their shirts.

The second officer pulled his gun.

Chops automatic, spit out three rapid shots at the cop's legs. The officer crashed hard on the cement steps. His pistol fell clattering to the ground. He had been hit twice in the legs. "The next one is in the head." Chops snarled.

Bond had pulled his pistol from the back of his waistband and was pointing it at the other cop's head. "Like my friend said, why don't you come in?"

Chops dragged the wounded officer into the house.

Oliver pointed to the road on the left. "That's Haley's driveway. I can't see the house from here, but this is the address. Block the entrance with the car. We'll go on foot from here." Oliver was out of the car when he said, "Open the trunk."

Gordon parked broadside on the driveway and popped the trunk.

Oliver unsheathed Gordon's Winchester hunting rifle. He tossed it to Gordon. "Are you up for this?"

Gordon cast a quizzical look at Oliver. "Rescuing Marilyn and Betsy?"

"No," Oliver said. He picked up the hunting knife and ran his thumb across the blade testing for sharpness. "Killing people!"

When they came out of the tree lined turn in the driveway. They could now see the house up on the hill.

"The RV is still there." Gordon noted.

"So is a police car." Oliver said.

"Do you think the cops got them?"

"I don't know," Oliver said as he scanned the entire surrounding area.

"All that patrol car tells me is there are more guns involved. Be careful and assume nothing." Oliver started up toward the house. "Cover me and shoot anyone who points a weapon at me."

Gordon cocked his rifle, chambering a round, and fell in ten yards behind Oliver.

"I'm going to the house," Oliver said, "but keep your eyes on the RV. I can't see in those windows. Remember you don't know what Bond looks like, so if I shout his name, you shoot, even if he looks like a cop to you."

With that statement Gordon realized the intensity of the moment.

Oliver entered through the garage. He carefully moved past the Jeep and looked through the rear door into the back yard. It was quiet. He cautiously entered the house through the kitchen door, as quiet as a church mouse. Gordon was right behind him. Oliver was crouched low like a cat ready to spring. He turned to Gordon and put his finger to his lips. Listening, he thought he heard a noise. He turned and looked down the back hall. He saw a snub nose .38cal pistol lying on the rug. He moved down the hall sticking close to the wall. He was trying to give Gordon a clear view, past him, of the entire length.

He peeked carefully into the den. Seeing it was empty, he crossed in front of the doorway, and retrieved the pistol. He flipped the cylinder out. It had been fired.

Gordon smiled in relief knowing now that Oliver was armed.

Oliver pointed toward the end of the hall, signaling his new destination. Gordon nodded that he understood.

Creeping as close as he could to the doorway into the living room Oliver sensed someone in the room. He thought he heard labored breathing.

Bond and Chops sat silently next to each other, neither wanted to speak. They both realized just how close their escape had been.

Betsy, Marilyn, and Haley sat crowded in the rear seat of the speeding Suburban. Jimmy was lying in the back. He had a blanket and pillow and was resting comfortably.

Chops finally spoke. "How much further is it to the pick-up area?"

"Only a few miles," Bond said. "If he's on time we should be in Canada in an hour or so."

"I hated leaving the RV behind. I was getting used to it," Chops said. "Maybe we can buy another one, huh boss?"

"Yea sure, I never paid for that one," Bond chuckled. "High Roller Travel bought it, and they're out of business." He continued his uneasy snicker while he unfolded a ten dollar bill and sniffed the powder that was in the crease.

Chops noticed how the long adventure was taking its toll on Bond. "You need to get some sleep, boss."

"You drive, I'll think. That's how it works," Bond said, sniffing, he put the crushed up bill in his pocket.

# 49

Resting on the floor, Oliver chanced a look into the room. He saw two policemen spread out on the rug. They appeared to be restrained because their hands were behind their backs. He resisted the urge of rushing into the room to their aid. He slowly got to his feet and evaluated the situation. He called Gordon up to cover him as he guardedly entered the room.

One cop turned his head, "Help us, my partners been shot."

Oliver moved quickly to his side, "Where did they go?"

"Don't know," he said. "They used our handcuffs on us. I have an extra key in my right-hand shirt pocket." The uninjured policeman sat up and offered his pocket to Oliver.

"They shot Chad in the leg," he said as Oliver unlocked his cuffs.

Oliver became aware of movement in the archway at the other end of the room.

He saw an elderly man slowly enter the room. His hands were above his head. "Don't shoot," he said. "My name is Manny Olivari. I work for Haley Madigan."

Gordon treated Chad's leg. Oliver and the healthy policeman went out to search the RV. It was empty. The cop slipped into his patrol car, reported the shooting and requested backup. Oliver went back into the kitchen and sat down with Manny.

Gordon stayed with the wounded officer.

"Manny, tell me what happened here?" Oliver said.

Manny was explaining what happened when more police cars came screaming up the driveway.

A police sergeant stepped into the kitchen and introduced herself. "I'm Sergeant Caryn Hanna. This scene is my responsibility. Are you Oliver Clearmountain?"

"Yes ma'am, I am." Oliver said, somewhat surprised she knew his name.

"We got a call from your friend Sheriff Cahill. Apparently you're one of the good guys," she smiled. Turning to Manny she said, "Hi Manny. Are you okay?"

"I'm fine, Caryn, now that you and your people are here." Manny took a drink of water.

Addressing Oliver, Sergeant Hanna said. "Oh, by the way, we moved your car. It was blocking the driveway. Their vehicle is still here. We think they're on foot. I have a search party being set up. We'll go in after them in the next twenty minutes. How much of a head start do you think they have?"

"Your officers said they were handcuffed for forty minutes. I un-cuffed them...," Oliver looked at the kitchen clock, "fifteen minutes ago. That would mean they have a fifty-five minute head start. If they are on foot, they can't have gotten far."

"What do you think happened?" Sergeant Hanna said.

"Well, I found a ladies gun in the hall." Pulling it from his waistband he showed it to Manny. "Does this belong to Haley?"

Manny nodded yes.

"It's been fired and with what Manny saw, I think Haley wounded one of them."

"Good," Sergeant Hanna said, "That will slow them down. I'm about to coordinate the search. I would appreciate it if you would stay here."

Oliver gave a fatigued nod.

She turned and left.

Gordon had been standing against the threshold of the hall door. "Stay here, like hell I will. What are you crazy?"

Oliver grinned at Gordon. "Shhh, don't tell the world." he turned to Manny, "That's a big garage out there. How many cars does Haley own?"

Manny said, "Three. The BMW that's in for a check up, the Jeep and her black Suburban."

"Where's the Suburban?" Oliver asked.

"It's in the garage." Manny said.

Oliver jumped out of his chair. "Come on," he said to Gordon, "They're on the road again."

They both jogged down the quarter mile driveway. When they got to Gordon's car it had been pushed aside. Gordon started the car as Oliver placed the hunting rifle in the trunk.

"Head back up the driveway," Oliver said as he got in the car.

"Why? What did you forget?"

"They didn't leave this way."

An empty gaze crossed Gordon's face. It was obvious he wanted an explanation.

Oliver continued, "Sergeant Hanna said the police moved your car when they came in. It was blocking the driveway, remember? The Suburban couldn't have exited this way."

"Where the hell did they go?" Gordon was confused.

"Go back to the house. I think I know." Oliver said.

Gordon passed two squad cars that were leaving the estate.

"The manhunt has started. The police are setting up a perimeter." A smiling Sergeant Hanna waved as her patrol car passed. "She's happy we're doing what we were told." Oliver waved back. They continued back to the house.

Gordon pulled in behind the RV on the large paved area in front of the four car garage.

"Now what?" Gordon said.

"Drive down that grass terrace on your left."

Gordon cut the wheel and pointed the nose of his Chrysler 300C over the edge of the driveway, "This isn't my off road vehicle. Where are you taking me?" Gordon anxiously asked.

"To a super highway below," Oliver said. "I noticed a runway behind the house,"

The heavy car slipped slightly on the manicured lawn as it headed down the grassy slope along side the terrace steps. The car came to rest on the end of a very wide and long tarmac.

"Step on it" Oliver said. "I think they left the estate at the other end of this airstrip."

The Hemi engine roared as the Chrysler screamed down the blacktop.

# 50

A mile and a quarter later the Chrysler came to a halt, "Now what." Gordon said.

"The highway is to our left," Oliver pointed. "See where that tall brush is matted down."

"This isn't an all terrain vehicle," Gordon stated.

"If I'm right it's a short distance to the road." Oliver stated.

Gordon drove slowly off the tarmac and onto the flats. He followed the path where the brush had been flattened. After a few minutes of a rough ride through the silver-green sagebrush that caused the car to bottom out a few times, Gordon said, "Yep there's the highway. It looks like they turned right."

Betsy sat in the rear seat on the passenger side of the Suburban. Her mind raced, full of ideas to escape. Having successfully unlocked the door without anyone seeing, she was considering jumping when the car slowed. Depending on how much separation she could achieve from Bond and the remote, maybe the electric collar wouldn't function. She could then run into the lodgepole pines and escape. What she didn't know was how Bond would react. Would he chase her, or would he punish Marilyn and Haley?

She decided any attempt to escape would have to include all three of them, but three people were much slower to react, thus slowing the element of surprise. Even with Jimmy wounded, overpowering their armed captors was out of the question. She wondered what Oliver was doing. Was he close, or had Bond successfully eluded him? She was sure of one thing. The longer they traveled the less chance they had of being found. She must do something to help her rescuers find them. All she had done so far was the feeble attempt with the coffee mugs and she was sure that went unnoticed.

"I have to use the restroom" Betsy announced.

"We'll be stopping soon." Bond said.

"Where are we going?" Betsy responded.

Bond turned, looked over his shoulder, "I'm going to the high life, and you're going to your own personal hell," he replied sardonically.

Marilyn said, "Why don't you let us go?"

Bond squared himself in the seat and said to Chops,. "Remind me to shoot her first."

Marilyn gasped as Betsy patted her on the arm. "Easy Marilyn, he won't shoot anybody who is worth more alive."

Haley said, "How much money do you want? I have more than you can dream of, more than you can spend in a lifetime."

"Yeah, the only catch is I would have to let you go to get it, right?" Bond said. "And then I'd have to find a way to spend it in prison." He laughed. "How can you have so much money and be so stupid? Right Chops?" He playfully punched Chops in the arm.

"Yeah, right boss." Chops said. He then turned the Suburban into an unpaved vacant parking lot. At the far side of the lot was a small white cinderblock building that sat on the edge of an open field. The faded, limp windsock that hung on a lonesome pole gave it the appearance of an abandoned private air field.

Chops got out of the Suburban and disappeared behind the building.

"Can we get out?" Betsy asked.

"Stay right where you are." Bond responded as he let himself out. He mumbled to himself. "Where is the dumb bastard? He was supposed to be here an hour ago."

Chops reappeared. "It's open."

"Come on," Bond said, as he gestured for the women to get out. The feared remote was in his hand. Betsy knew that Chops and Jimmy carried their own remotes.

"What about Jimmy?" Chops said. "He's sleeping."

"You snooze, you lose." Bond said.

They entered the windowless dark and dank structure, which was poorly lit by a florescent overhead with only one tube working. The bathroom was a small, square, closed room in the corner.

Betsy started toward the bathroom.

"Where you going?" Chops asked.

"Restroom."

She entered the filthy lavatory and pulled the chain on the single overhead bulb. A quick glance around the area left her wishing she could leave the light off. The toilet bowl was empty and stained beyond cleaning. Thankfully, her reason for being there wasn't to relieve herself. She needed to be alone.

She removed her earring. And using the stud just like Oliver did the last time he removed the necklace, she probed for the hole in the back of the choker. How did Oliver do this, she wondered? Stabbing with the pin she searched for the hole to release the lock. Finding the hole among the costume jewelry was nearly impossible. She was getting nervous when she heard a click and felt the choker release the grip on her neck. She removed the necklace and bent the cheap alloy that held the encrusted cut glass. She worked the material back and forth, a few fake rubies and diamonds popped out and fell on the filthy concrete floor. Finally, her efforts exposed the wires. She pulled on the black and red wires until she felt them break loose from their connection.

A loud bang on the door startled her and she dropped the chocker. "What the hell you doing in there?" It was Bond.

She hurriedly picked up the necklace and reshaped it, making sure the broken wires didn't show. She snapped it back on her neck and grabbed the door handle just as Bond knocked again. "Hurry up—"

He was taken aback when she pulled the door open.

"The toilet doesn't work," Betsy said, as she stormed past Bond and walked to Marilyn and Haley. She still had her pierced earring in her hand.

"Don't give me any trouble. Just sit in the corner and shut-up or you all will be doing the electric flop." Bond was noticeably upset but he smiled at his own humor.

# 51

Gordon drove in silence for several minutes on a secondary road which was absent of traffic. Oliver was focused on everything around them. He had instructed Gordon to stay under 40 mph. Finally Gordon brought the car to a halt in the middle of the road.

"Do you have any idea what we're doing?" Gordon said.

Oliver didn't take his eyes off the surrounding area. "We're trying to find Betsy, Marilyn and Haley."

"I mean do you have a clue as to where they are?"

"I believe they are somewhere in front of us" Oliver said "Although I must admit at this moment I don't have a trail sign to follow." Oliver turned to Gordon. "Do you have any ideas?"

Before Gordon could answer Oliver held up his hand signifying silence. "Do you see that?" Oliver pointed to the sky in front of them.

"A helicopter?" Gordon observed.

"Not just a helicopter Gordon, it's a Bell 427." Oliver responded with excitement, "It's the same one that picked Betsy up, in the Popo Agie Wilderness Area. Do you think you can keep it in sight?" The Chrysler lunged forward before Oliver finished.

"I can try," Gordon said.

The helicopter was flying at about 1000ft and was a half mile in front of them. Fortunately it was flying parallel to the road they were on.

Unfortunately it was traveling twice as fast as the car.

"Can we go any faster?" Oliver urged.

"Not and keep it on this road." Gordon responded. He glanced at the speedometer. It showed ninety-three mph. "I hope he sets it down soon or we'll lose him."

"We might get lucky. It looks like he's using the road for dead reckoning." Oliver observed.

The next few minutes were anxious as Gordon fought to keep the copter in sight and the car intact. He was using the entire surface of the road trying to maintain his speed and stay connected with the helicopter and the highway.

"I can't go any faster," Gordon announced. "Can you still see it?"

"Yeah, but he's losing us." Oliver said. "Just keep going. You're doing great."

"Here he comes," Chops announced. He had been standing outside searching the sky.

"Let's go ladies," Bond said, motioning menacingly with the ever present remote. He was unaware it didn't represent the chilling threat to Betsy it once did.

The three women moved slowly to the door. Each one knowing, once they set foot in the helicopter, their fate would most likely be sealed. But they also were aware there wasn't anything they could do to prevent it.

"Come on," Bond urged. "I'm taking you to a private lodge where you can soak in a bubble bath and pamper yourselves."

"And then what? Sold to the highest bidder?" Marilyn said.

"Yep, for a lot of cash, because you'll be looking sharp and smelling nice." Bond said as he pushed her out of the building. "Maybe I'll give you a farewell bonk myself."

Betsy saw the gun sticking out of Bonds belt. If I could only grab it, we'd be free, she thought.

"I'll get Jimmy," Chops said. He went to the Suburban.

Betsy's optimism increased as Bond turned his head. She grabbed the butt of the gun and pushed Bond away simultaneously.

"What the..."Bond blurted out as he stumbled. He regained his balance after a few steps, then turned back to Betsy. She was holding the gun on him. "You dumb broad."

He pushed the button on the remote that charged Betsy's necklace.

The relief that the necklace didn't work caused her to smirk, "You're the dumb one, Michael Bondinni." Betsy then scowled as she pointed the pistol at his gut. "Don't think I won't shoot. In fact, I don't know what's stopping me from shooting you right now."

Chops came around the corner of the building. "Jimmy's really sick, boss."

"Put your hands up, Fat man." Betsy said pointing, the gun at him.

Chops grinned at Betsy and put his hands up.

He's one cool customer, Betsy thought. He has ice water running through his veins. He's not scared at all.

Haley and Marilyn were standing behind her when she heard them shriek in pain. She felt Haley fall into her. Betsy turned to see Jimmy standing ten feet behind her. He had come around the backside of the building. Both Marilyn and Haley were twitching on the ground in pain. She swung the gun around, but before she could fire, she was lifted off her feet by Chops and thrown to the ground with a vicious force. The gun went sliding from her grip as all the air escaped her lungs when she slammed into the walkway. Betsy thought she was going to die. She couldn't breathe. She tried to fill her lungs, but to no avail. She flopped like a fish out of water, gasping for air. Nothing worked. Her mouth was open but nothing came in. She felt she was suffocating, but her air passages were open. It was like she was drowning in water except she was surrounded by air. Slowly, her breath returned and she realized she would live. Her shoulder and side ached as she looked at the prone bodies of Marilyn and Haley.

Haley sat up. She had her hands at her neck and her eyes were wide open. It was evident she was astonished about what had just happened. Marilyn was still on the ground, moaning, "No, no. Don't do this." Pleading with her captors.

Out of the blue, the thumping roar of the chopper dominated the scene, kicking up a strong wind. The women turned their backs as it touched down.

Picking up his discarded pistol, Bond shouted above the roar, "Let's go." He grabbed Haley by the hair and lifted her to her feet. Simultaneously, he kicked Marilyn in the rear. "Keep your gun on them, I'll check out the chopper.

Chops was getting something out of the Suburban. The three women were facing the highway as Jimmy held a gun on them. Bond ran the thirty yards to the helicopter.

Marilyn was the first one to notice the speeding Chrysler as it came screaming around the bend in the road. "It's Gordon," she said.

# 52

They both saw the black Suburban at the same time.

"There they are," Oliver shouted with alarm, as Gordon slammed on the brakes.

The car's front end dipped as the anti-lock braking system brought the speeding automobile to a hasty stop about fifty yards from the entrance to the unpaved lot.

"Back up," Oliver screamed. "Back up, quick."

Gordon gave Oliver a puzzled look and then threw the car in reverse. He backed up twice as far from the lot.

"Stop. Stop right here," Oliver said as he leaped from the car. "Pop the trunk," he screamed as he ran to the rear of the car.

Chops was unloading the Suburban when he heard the Chrysler's abrupt stop. He turned to see the car back up the road and stop a hundred yards away. He stood staring at the car, wondering why it backed up. Jimmy took notice from his spot, guarding the girls.

Chops drew his gun when he recognized Oliver getting out of the car. Jimmy yelled to warn Bond, but the helicopters spinning blades drowned him out.

Oliver unsheathed the hunting rifle, and walked to the left side of the automobile and rested the Winchester on top of the car. He drew a bead on Chops, who stood a hundred yards away, helplessly out of pistol range.

His first shot shattered Chops sternum knocking him into the back of the Suburban. He slipped to the ground, dead.

Jimmy didn't hear the shot over the chopper noise. He was extremely nervous and didn't know what to do. Bond couldn't hear him and he couldn't see Chops. His instinct was to help Chops. He started forward, moving in front of the three women.

That was a mistake.

Oliver made the mental adjustment. This shot would be thirty yards further. Hardly a problem. He waited until the women were out of the line of fire and placed the 30.06 caliber round squarely into Jimmy's chest. The hit caused Jimmy to spin around before he fell. He laid spread eagle on his back. His open eyes were staring at the Montana Big Sky, but he didn't see any of it.

"Run," Betsy commanded, as she started for the Chrysler with Marilyn and Haley right on her heels. Oliver waved for them to change direction as they ran toward him. He swore under his breath. They were preventing a clear shot at the chopper.

Bond emerged from the door of the helicopter to signal Jimmy to bring the women aboard. At first, he didn't see anyone at the shack. Then he saw the women running for the road. His first thought was to reach for his pistol, but then he decided the remote was a better idea. The women were out of range for either weapon. It was then he saw Jimmy flat on his back in the lot. He was frantic, searching for Chops when he saw the Red Chrysler sitting in the middle of the road two hundred yards away.

He was sure it was Clearmountain standing next to the driver's door. He jumped back into the helicopter as he heard a slug sink into the fuselage. He hollered for the pilot to take off and he heard some glass break.

"I'm hit," the pilot shrieked.

"Get us up, get us up," Bond screamed.

The helicopter lifted, wobbly from the ground, leaned hard to the right and started for the mountain range away from the road.

Oliver fired one more shot at the top mounted motor as the chopper flew away. He wasn't sure if he hit it or not.

"Oliver," Betsy shouted breathlessly, as she threw her arms around him. He grabbed her with his left arm. Holding the rifle in his right and not taking his eyes off the fading helicopter, he gave her an air kiss.

Betsy was about to protest when she realized he hadn't given up the hunt.

"In a minute, honey," Oliver said. He squinted his eyes, keeping them locked on his fading target. Oliver walked away from the commotion around the car and remained focused on the distance.

Was it his imagination or was that helicopter flying erratically. It needed altitude or it wasn't going to clear the hills. After a moment, Oliver thought he saw it go into the trees. He couldn't tell if it was a crash or an unexpected landing. Either way he had to get up there to see for himself. He made a mental note of the area and then turned to his wife, "Are you okay, babe?" He kissed her and hugged her so hard Betsy thought she was going to run out of oxygen again.

Placing Chops body in the back of the Suburban was a chore. Jimmy's was much easier. Oliver, Betsy and Haley took it back to the Madigan estate. Marilyn and Gordon followed in the Chrysler.

As Oliver started to pull out of the lot Gordon said with a grin, "We might be a little late."

Oliver spent the next hour explaining the rest of what happened to Sergeant Hanna. It was evident that without Haley's clout he could have been in trouble and tied up with police procedure for a long time. Sergeant Hanna asked Oliver, "Do you know where the helicopter was going?"

Oliver shook his head, "When he took off, he was heading East."

Haley told Sergeant Hanna everything was okay and she would tell the Governor what a find job Hanna and her team had done. "Tell Police Commissioner Brooks we'll be in touch." Haley said, pleasantly escorting Sergeant Hanna to the front door.

Over her shoulder Hanna said, "I'll be in touch."

Haley's hand was placed firmly in Hanna's back, now she was actually pushing her to the door.

Haley waved goodbye and closed the door. Leaning with her back on the door she asked, "Who wants a drink?"

Betsy said, "Wine would be fine and I don't need a glass, just a corkscrew."

Both girls linked arms as they walked down the hall. Oliver followed.

"Haley, do you own a rifle?"

She turned and said, "Let's have our drink. Betsy has earned it, and then I will make available to you anything you need. I know what you're planning."

Gordon and Marilyn showed up looking like the Cheshire cat.

"Car trouble?" Oliver asked. He then winked, letting Gordon know he knew the real reason for their delay.

"Yeah," Gordon acknowledged with a smug grin. "Had to check the shocks."

Marilyn slapped Gordon on the arm, playfully. "You men like to blow your own horn."

Gordon and Oliver looked at Marilyn in mock astonishment.

Realizing her double entendre, Marilyn blushed as she turned and walked away.

Haley had the cook make dinner and they invited Manny and Marge. It was an enjoyable evening with many stories to recount. Marge's story was the shortest when Oliver asked her what she did. She said, "Manny said run and I ran like hell."

After a delightful dessert of Cinnamon Bread Pudding, the Olivari's retired to their apartment and Oliver, Betsy, Gordon, Marilyn and Haley went into the den to hear Oliver's plan.

"Would you like some coffee?" Haley offered.

"I'll pass," Oliver said. "I don't want the taste of that cinnamon bread pudding to ever leave my mouth. I'd like the recipe." He turned to Betsy, saying. "I'll give it to Big Mo. It'll double his business at the restaurant."

# 53

Bond didn't have his headset on so he could hardly hear the pilot, but he could see he was hurting. He slid into the co-pilot seat. There was blood on the pilot's sleeve and he was having difficulty holding the copter level.

"I'm going to have to put her down. I can't hold it," the pilot said. "I feel like I'm going to pass out and if I do, we'll crash."

They were only thirty feet off the ground, searching for a clearing, when one of the blades clipped some branches. At first it acted like a hedge clipper, cutting the branches, and then it caught heavier branches and turned toward the tree. It was impossible for a weakened pilot to control the helicopter as it dipped to the ground. Some of the branches actually slowed its descent. In a last ditch attempt to prevent a fire the pilot switched off the engine and fuel pumps and engaged the engine's fire extinguishers.

When Bond stopped bouncing around, he realized he had survived the crash. The helicopter laid on its side. The pilot was hanging above him, supported by his seatbelt and shoulder harness. "Help me," the pilot moaned.

Bond climbed out of his seat. He had to crawl backward in order to stand, to avoid bumping the pilot. He checked to make sure his legs weren't hurt and quickly examined his arms. He then flexed and was amazed that he wasn't even sore. He found his pistol still tucked in his belt. He removed it and placed it behind the pilot's ear and pulled the trigger. A large part of the pilot's skull splattered into the broken windshield.

"That's what happens to incompetent jerks."

He made his way out of the wreckage, searching his pockets for a folded ten dollar bill. He was alone, no one to see to his needs. He needed a blow badly.

He sat on the ground leaning against a tree after he had sniffed the powder, from every fold and wrinkle of the ten dollar bill, up his nose. He even licked it clean. In a few minutes he found he was energized and thinking about how to get off the mountain. He decided to spend the night in the passenger section of the helicopter. He searched the chopper for anything he would need for survival.

He found four thin blankets and four tiny airliner type pillows. In the bulkhead compartment there was a plastic bag full of peanuts and pretzels. He also found twelve bottles of fresh water and twelve small cans of soda. There was even the liter of Knob Creek he had asked for. In the built in ice chest he found a bag of ice.

Well, things weren't so bad. Other than the dead pilot hanging off his seat in the flight deck, he was quite comfortable in the passenger section. He decided, later, he would move the pilot outside before he attempted to get some sleep, but for now he would gather what he needed for his journey. He took two blankets and loaded them with the water, soda, whiskey and the snacks he found. He tied the blankets into bundles and then attached them together with rope he found in the luggage area.

Bond looked at his handy work, two sacks linked together. He was proud of his makeshift backpack. He intended to carry it over his shoulder because it was fairly heavy. This outdoor living is easy, he thought. Why does everybody make such a big deal out of it? Tomorrow morning he would walk over the mountain until he found a highway. He was prepared for it to take a few days. He would then commandeer a vehicle and head for the Canadian border. He still had plenty of money stashed. He could still live the good life.

Oliver couldn't believe the way Haley handled the helicopter pilot who had arrived an hour late that morning. Oliver, Betsy and the Cundiffs stood in amazement as she verbally dressed him down. This was not the mild mannered Keno Lady he'd met in Atlantic City. He was watching a professional business person explaining very precisely what she expected from people in her employment. Oliver guessed it was why she had the pilot shut the engine down. She didn't want him to miss anything she had to say. Finally, she turned and beckoned for Oliver to join her.

"Charlie is ready to take you wherever you'd like to go, aren't you Charlie?

"Yes ma'am," Charlie replied. He looked at Oliver. "Hop aboard."

Oliver slipped the rifle behind the seat of the two passenger Robinson R22 Viper Red helicopter. He kissed Haley on the cheek and whispered, "Thank you, I'll never be able to repay you."

"You already have." Haley said. "You've made my life exhilarating again."

Oliver looked back at Betsy and blew her a kiss.

Gordon gave him a thumbs up and shouted, "Kick him once for me."

Oliver pointed to a clearing, "Put me down there."

"I don't see any wreckage," Charlie replied, as he scanned the surrounding area. "I thought you said there was a crash."

"There was," Oliver acknowledged. "It's about a half mile further up. I want to go in on foot, in case there were any survivors. I'd rather not announce my arrival. The passenger was a pretty dangerous guy."

Charlie turned to Oliver and grinned, "Just like you, Huh?"

Oliver covered the distance up to where he thought the crash occurred. He slowed his pace and proceeded cautiously. He heard thrashing in the trees but was too far away to see anything. He took the rifle off his shoulder and checked the wind. He wanted to approach the commotion downwind. He crept slowly forward, then confirmed what he had suspected. A grizzly bear was playing with what was left of a human carcass as if it was a rag doll. Oliver waited. Confronting the bear during its feeding frenzy would only result in him killing the bear or the less attractive results, the bear killing him. He moved back down the hill so he wouldn't have to watch the bear tear into the remains.

Thirty minutes later the commotion stopped. Oliver returned to his vantage point. The bear was gone, so he approached the crash site cautiously. He saw an arm near the helicopter and a workman's boot with the foot still in it. He walked the perimeter around the wreckage and then slowly wound closer to the crumbled copter.

Once inside he was able to establish what had happened. The blood in and around the pilot's chair, along with the brain matter speckled on the windshield told him Bond had shot the pilot from behind while the pilot was still strapped in his seat. He knew Bond was gone because he'd seen tracks leading away from the area.

A quick check in the passenger section informed Oliver that Bond had spent the night. Oliver even established where Bond had relieved himself during the night. Oliver smiled when he realized Bond had taken all the provisions that were in the copter. Oliver was sure the load was at least thirty pounds.

Oliver smiled as he looked up the hill. "You're making this awful easy, Mr. Bond."

# 54

Bond had walked for only an hour and he was exhausted. His makeshift knapsack was much too heavy. He was warm in his sport coat, but afraid to discard it. He'd need it when the temperature dropped during the evening, like it had last night. The pretzels, peanuts and soda just didn't make a very satisfying breakfast. But the worst of his problems were his leather soled loafers. He slipped every step he took. A few long pulls from the bottle of bourbon had helped, but only temporarily. He was now resting every ten minutes for every ten minutes he walked. His breathing had become labored in the thin mountain air. He decided to leave one of the blanket bundles behind. His load was simply too heavy. What he hadn't paid any attention to was his heading. He was unaware he was drifting to his right as he walked, partly because he was going uphill and to a certain extent because it's a natural phenomenon for people unconsciously to turn to their strong side as they walk. He didn't know it but was walking in a large circle.

Oliver slipped the 30.06 rifle over his shoulder, took a drink from his water bottle and started up the hill keeping Bond's visible tracks in sight to his right. Oliver knew the trip for Bond was going to get more difficult every step he took. The terrain would get steeper and the day would get warmer. Bond's natural instinct would be to hurry. That would be a big mistake. Depending on Bonds physical condition and his experience in the outdoors, Oliver felt sure he would overtake him in a matter of hours.

Bond was still in the forest area just above the sagebrush flats. The forest area was habitat for many life forms as opposed to the higher alpine desert like area that had a brief growing season and persistent cold winds. Oliver knew Bond would never make it that high. Other than confusion and exhaustion Bond was going to have to concern himself with black bear and grizzly bear. If he gets hurt and becomes immobile, his list of predators would increase to wolves and coyotes. Bond's luck had run out. He had stumbled toward the Gallatin Range and was heading toward Granite Peak, the highest elevation in Montana.

Oliver realized as he followed the tracks that if he didn't get to Bond quickly, the mountain would eat him alive and deprive Oliver of his revenge.

It took only fifteen minutes of tracking for Oliver to become aware of Bond drifting to the right as he walked. He also observed that his prey was slipping almost every step he took.

He saw a light blue bundle 40 yards in front of him. Oliver was aware it could be a trap but he was confident it was just Bond lightening his load. Just to be cautious he circled up the mountain and approached the package from above.

He opened the bundled up blanket and exposed its content. He was surprised to see it was loaded with water and soda. Why would he drop his supplies? Maybe this was only part of what he was carrying. If so, what would be more precious to keep than water? Oliver drank his water and replaced it with a fresh bottle and took off in the direction of the tracks.

Bond collapsed to the ground. He couldn't go any further, but he knew if he turned downhill, back toward the highway, the authorities would be waiting for him. He guessed the road was five miles away. He wasn't sure he could make it that far, but he didn't have a choice, he could no longer go up.

He started down and began laughing nervously in relief. This was much easier but his legs reminded him he was dog tired. After fifty yards he dropped his remaining bundle. He was now stumbling on weak legs but he felt he was making progress. He fell a few times and tore the knee of his trousers. He was out of everything, even cocaine. All he had left was his pistol. His shoes were now a big detriment. He couldn't get any traction at all. He continued stumbling toward the sagebrush flats.

Oliver paused and looked downhill where the tracks were now leading.

Fatigue had made him quit trying, Oliver thought. Was it Vince Lombardi that once said, 'Fatigue makes cowards of us all?' He's now in a hurry to be arrested.

Oliver had been walking in the new direction when he thought he saw something. He hesitated, moving to his left for a better view, he saw Bond struggling to keep his feet. He was four hundred yards down the slope. He took the Winchester off his shoulder. He wasn't going to try to hit him he was just going to make him run faster.

The shot kicked up the dirt five feet to Bond's left. He spun around and looked back up the mountain. Oliver just shook his head. "That's not very smart Mr. Bond."

Oliver knew Bond couldn't see him amongst the pines. He could tell Bond was exhausted. His shoulders slouched. His movement was slow and clumsy. However, because of the shot Oliver had fired he was trying to run. He stumbled and went sprawling further down the hill.

Oliver walked slowly down toward his beaten prey.

Fifteen minutes later Oliver came upon a sniveling, broken man. Bond wasn't even aware of Oliver's presence.

Bond was sprawled facedown gasping for breath between sobs.

"Get up," Oliver demanded.

Bond was stunned at the sound of his voice, but couldn't respond. He tried to reach for his pistol but Oliver kicked him in the elbow.

He yelped at the pain and rolled over holding his arm.

Oliver bent over and took the gun from Bonds belt.

"Are you enjoying your outing?" Oliver said.

"Water," Bond moaned, "I need a drink." He extended his hand, as if reaching for water.

Oliver pointed over his shoulder with his thumb, "You left yours up there."

# 55

Haley decided to take Marilyn and Betsy shopping for some much needed clothes. They asked Gordon if he wanted to come.

"Sitting here waiting for Oliver to do the yeoman's work is demeaning enough," Gordon said "Going shopping with the girls is out of the question."

"We'll be back about five," Haley said, "Make yourself at home."

Gordon waved as the green Jeep went down the driveway.

He wasn't going to sit around all day like a helpless eunuch. Being unable to help Oliver go after Bond was testosterone draining enough. There must be something he could do. He decided to drive back to the abandoned airstrip. He was sure Oliver would come out that way once he found Bond and he might just be a help.

Gordon parked his Chrysler in the unpaved lot and was sitting on the roof scanning the sagebrush with binoculars he'd borrowed from Haley's den.

He thought he saw someone tumble in the tall grass. Then, for the next ten minutes he saw nothing. No movement at all. He was just about to give up when he saw a lone figure with a rifle balanced on his shoulder walking leisurely along. He was sure it was Oliver.

The figure paused, bent down, and now there were two figures.

Now he saw what he was sure was Oliver, pushing a staggering figure in front of him. They were heading right toward him. The figure staggered and fell numerous times. It had to be Bond.

He was enjoying the show when a truck pulled up next to him. He looked down and saw that the driver was watching the same scene he was. Gordon couldn't see the license on the vehicle, but his camouflaged shirt and hunting cap made Gordon think he was a local.

Gordon looked down from his perch above the windshield. "Can I help you?"

The driver kept looking straight ahead.

"Excuse me, I said, CAN I HELP YOU?" he said forcefully.

The driver ignored Gordon and kept looking at the two figures that were getting closer.

Gordon was not in the mood to be toyed with. His manhood had been tested enough today. He started to climb down when the driver said, "Stay right where you are."

He had his left arm resting out the open window and in the crook of his elbow, Gordon saw the barrel of a gun, a very large caliber gun. "Smile and wave to your friend," the driver instructed.

Gordon leaped off the car to his left, putting the Chrysler between him and the truck. He landed on the ground facing the rear of his car. Standing at the rear fender was a gunman with a shotgun pointed at Gordon's waist. He said nothing, but gazed at Gordon with a toothless grin.

Just by rotating the barrel of the shotgun Gordon realized the man wanted him to turn around.

Oliver walked out of the sagebrush and hollered to Gordon. "Thanks for coming, Bond needs a ride."

As they reached the lot, Bond fell to his knees, "I need water."

Oliver stopped in front of the two vehicles and quickly surmised the situation. The rifle was resting on his shoulder and he was holding it by the grip part of the stock. His finger was in the trigger guard.

Looking at the driver of the truck Oliver said, "Hello Jonathan."

"Hello Clearmountain." Yokatory replied. "Have you decided what you're going to do?"

Oliver quickly looked at the man behind Gordon. He was sure he had a gun on Gordon although he couldn't see it. He looked back to Yokatory and saw the barrel of the pistol resting on his forearm. Oliver slowly nodded and put the rifle on the ground.

Bond was on all fours and not aware of what was going on.

Gordon shrugged his shoulders as if saying, 'Sorry.'

Getting out of the truck, Yokatory said, "Who's the city creep?"

"He hurt my wife," Oliver said.

"Not to smart," Jonathan said, as he put his boot on Bond and pushed him over. "What were you planning to do with him?"

"Not too sure," Oliver said. "My Indian heart says kill him, but I would have probably turned him in."

"How did he hurt your wife."

"Electric shock." He tortured her by shocking her with a neck device."

Bond was on the ground, listening to the conversation. "Who are you?" he said to Yokatory. Bond was still gasping for breath. "I'll give you ten thousand to shoot this piece of shit right now."

Yokatory looked down at Bond with lazy, unemotional eyes. "I think I'd shoot you for a nickel."

"I've got a nickel." Gordon said. He felt the shotgun poke into his back "Shut up" the gunman behind him said.

Oliver looked intently at Yokatory. "How did you happen to be here in Montana?"

"I've been following your sorry butt all over this mountain range. Do you think you're going to get away with invading my camp? And now your Sheriff friend is holding two of my men against their will."

"You and your thugs were trying to kill me?" Oliver said.

Gordon spoke up from the other side of the car, "I think this is the truck I saw following us."

Yokatory turned to Gordon. "That red Chrysler is easier to follow than a pig in snow." Turning back to Oliver he said. "Only lost you once. That was in Bozeman. We were just about to give it up when we saw the car parked sideways, blocking the driveway of that mansion. We watched you drive it back up to the house. That evening we were just about to go up to the house and get you, when a black Suburban pulled in the driveway and shortly after, the cops. After the cops left, the Chrysler pulled into the driveway. At first we thought it was another one. Then I recognized him." Yokatory pointed to Gordon. "He had a woman with him."

Oliver was starting to realize just how lucky Yokatory had been, trailing him.

"What puzzles me is how did you get out of the driveway without us seeing you?"

Oliver realized what happened. "The great spirit helped us," he said.

Yokatory didn't appreciate the humor. "He'd better be watching over you now, because you're going to stand trial"

"Trial?" Gordon cried out. "Under whose jurisdiction?"

"Mine, as the President and Chief Justice of the LTL." Yokatory proudly announced.

"LTL?" Gordon questioned.

"Loyalist to Liberty," Yokatory stated with authority.

Gordon was driving and Oliver was in the passenger seat. Jonathan Yokatory was in the back seat. He had a shotgun on his lap and his pistol on the seat next to him. His friend Josh was following them in the pick-up truck. He'd put Bond kicking and screaming in the trunk.

"So where is the trial going to take place?" Gordon said.

"Colorado" was the lethargic reply.

Gordon looked at Yokatory in the rear view mirror. "You're not going to try and take us all the way to Colorado, are you?"

"That's where my courthouse is." Yokatory replied in a lazy twang.

"How are you going to stay awake that long?" Oliver wondered out loud.

"I'm not," Yokatory said. "I'm going to sleep in the car. And you boys are going to sleep in the back of the truck. You'll find those cages we keep the hunting dogs in quite comfortable."

# 56

They traveled the rest of the day and into the night, primarily on secondary roads. Finally Yokatory told Gordon to pull off the road, behind some cottonwoods, out of sight from the road. True to his threat, Yokatory made them crawl into two, three x three foot cages that were approximately six foot long, in the bed of the truck. He took two grimy wool blankets from the bed box and stuffed them in each cage before he locked them.

"Is he leaving Bond in the trunk?" Gordon said.

"I certainly hope so." Oliver said. "There's no room for him in here."

"This truck bed smells like dog shit."

"It won't kill ya," Oliver said, "but you're going to freeze your butt off before the nights over. Try and stay warm."

Five hours later, Oliver felt the truck move. Gordon opened his eyes and looked at Oliver through the wire cage. It was dark.

"He's going to leave us here for the rest of the trip." Gordon said. "He must be driving."

Oliver pondered the situation. A tarp had been tied down over the top of them.

"Unless he's got Bond driving."

"Why?"

"So he can talk to him. Find out about him," Oliver said thoughtfully. "But what worries me is it gives that little bastard a chance to talk his way out of this."

"Do you think he can convince Yokatory to let him go?" Gordon pondered.

Oliver nodded, "He's got money and Yokatory needs money. I think our situation has just gotten worse."

"We need a plan." Gordon said. "Maybe we can bust out of here and jump off the truck."

Oliver made a face. "You first," he said." We're going sixty miles an hour."

"I'm sure the girls have reported us missing to the police."

Oliver nodded, "We're not officially missing for forty-eight hours. You remember how that goes?"

"Yeah, but our wives are smart. They'll report my car stolen. The cops will jump on that." Gordon asserted.

"I wonder if Yokatory has changed the plates on your car."

"Knock it off Oliver, you're depressing me."

"Think, Marilyn," Haley urged. "You can remember."

"I know my license plate number, I just can't remember his," she said, shaking her head.

Marilyn and Haley were sitting at the kitchen counter having coffee. Betsy was pacing.

'I'm calling the Governor," Haley said. "Oliver could still be on the hunt. Maybe it's taking him longer than he thought it would, but Gordon's disappearance worries me. Where would he have gone?"

"Well, at first I thought he went for a ride. I know he was feeling useless not being able to go with Oliver, but when he didn't come back last night I was concerned. It's so unlike Gordon."

Betsy stopped pacing, "And besides, Oliver should have caught that creep by now." She started pacing and then stopped again. It was like she couldn't walk and talk at the same time. "Maybe they're taking him back to Wyoming and can't get a signal to call."

"We registered both cars' at the same time…that's it," Marilyn exclaimed. "My plate is 7-8820 his is 7- 8821."

Haley was dialing before she finished.

Betsy took out her cell phone and dialed Oliver's number for the fifth time. She received the same message every time. Gordon's phone was not in service.

She called Kevin's cell phone.

"Yeah, Cahill go," he said answering on the first ring.

"Kev, it's Betsy," she said.

"Hi beautiful, I'm glad to hear you're okay. I must say, when Gordon called me yesterday, to tell me you and Marilyn were safe, I was relieved. He told me he was on his way to pick up the Bondinni guy. He said he was pretty sure it wouldn't take long."

"That's why I'm calling. He's not back yet and I'm worried," Betsy confided.

"About what? The Chief getting lost in the woods?" Kevin kidded.

"Gordon's missing also," she said.

There was a long moment of silence. Now in a much more serious tone, Kevin said, "Did Gordon go with him to track down Bondinni?"

"No, Gordon stayed here at Madigan's while we went to buy some clothes. He wasn't there when we came back. His car is gone," she continued. "And Oliver hasn't returned. It's been twenty four hours."

Kevin took down Gordon's license number and said he'd put an APB on it. He was glad to hear Haley had notified the authorities in Montana.

He told Betsy he'd get back to her as soon as he had something and hung up.

Betsy and Haley hung up at the same time. The three women looked at each other with empty stares. Finally Marilyn broke the ice. "What do we do now?"

Haley and Betsy answered simultaneously. "Wait!"

# 57

The ride in the back of the truck was becoming intolerable. The truck must have been set up to carry heavy loads. The springs and shocks were very tight, making the ride extremely firm. Not being able to sit up forced Oliver and Gordon to absorb every painful bump from head to toe. "It hurts when we run over bubble gum." Gordon said. "Do you have any ideas where we are?"

Gordon's head bounced hard off the bottom of the cage. "Ow," he cried out as he folded his hands under the side of his head. "My best guess is Jackson, or maybe a little further south. I don't think we're on 191. If I'm right, we have at least another ten hours to go."

Gordon moaned.

The heat building under the tarp, made hours seem like days.

"Are you okay?" Oliver asked.

"Don't worry about me, although I am feeling a little melancholy.

"Are you crazy? Melancholy about what?" Oliver asked.

"Football two-a-days in South Bend in the August heat, being treated like a dog." Gordon smiled.

Oliver smiled and shook his head at Gordon's attempt at humor. His expression quickly changed. He felt the truck turn and the engine slow, "I think we're stopping."

A few minutes later the tarp was peeled back. They squinted in the bright sunlight.

Bond came up to the cage. "Hello savage," Yokatory pushed him aside and unlocked the cages. "Get out, we're changing trucks."

As he slipped out of the cage, Oliver had to support himself on the tailgate as his knees buckled. He was in no position to attempt an escape. Bond appeared to have made a deal. He was walking freely and Josh's shotgun was firmly focused on Oliver and Gordon.

## THE PAST IS NEVER DEAD

Parked in front of Gordon's Chrysler was a panel truck with Colorado plates. Yokatory had apparently contacted his camp and told them to meet him. Oliver and Gordon were directed to the windowless van.

Scanning the surrounding mountains Oliver figured he was in lower Central Wyoming, probably not too far from the Colorado border and Yokatory's camp. He and Gordon were directed to the windowless van. Oliver wondered if it was the same one he and Kevin had been imprisoned in.

Oliver was aware of Gordon's irritation. He hoped he didn't lose control and strike out at one of their captors.

"Where are you going to put the midget?" Gordon asked Yokatory as he nodded his head at Bond. "This van doesn't have a trunk."

Bond kicked out at Gordon. "Shut up pig."

Gordon caught Bond's leg at the ankle and threw it up. Bond went sprawling in the air in an almost complete flip. He landed on his head and shoulder with a thud.

Bond lay flat on the ground moaning and then shouted, "Shoot the bastard."

Yokatory held up his hand, halting any idea Josh had of shooting. "Hold it." He turned to the prone Bond. "Shut up and keep your distance from these two. You might get hurt." One could detect a slight grin on his face.

The grin disappeared when he addressed Gordon. "Try something like that again and I'll let Josh shoot your ass."

As they entered the van Oliver whispered, "Ease off Gordon. That shotgun makes them the odds on favorite in a fight."

"I can't help it if I want to kill that bastard." Gordon said.

"I understand, but you'll get your opportunity. Oliver said softly. "He'll never closes."

This van had three rows of seats and a new driver.

"Sit in the center row," Yokatory directed.

Josh slipped into the rear seat with the shotgun.

Bond dusted himself off and, rubbing his neck, got into the front passenger seat.

Oliver surveyed their new surroundings. Apparently, the antagonist's force had increased by two, a new driver for them and someone to drive the pick-up. It appeared they were leaving Gordon's well hidden Chrysler behind.

"Is there any chance of us getting something to eat?" Oliver said.

Yokatory threw two plastic baggies with cheese sandwiches and a couple of bottles of water into their laps. "Shut up and eat."

"Ya got any chips back there?" Gordon said and immediately felt the butt of the shotgun crash into the back of his head. It was hard enough to hurt like hell but not knock him unconscious.

Oliver looked over at Gordon and shook his head in compassion.

Gordon shot a painful grin at Oliver as he rubbed his head.

Oliver understood the message. "I can take a lot more than he's got, Chief. Don't worry about me."

Oliver started to plan. Unless an opportunity presented itself, it looked like the camp would be their opportunity for escape.

He was familiar with the surroundings at the camp and he knew getting free was only the first part of getting away. They were going to have to escape and survive with out getting innocent people hurt. He believed there were no blamelessness people at the camp.

After a while Oliver fell into a much needed sleep. He continued planning in his dreams and there, everything worked out well.

# 58

A jarring bump woke both Gordon and Oliver from a deep sleep.
Oliver glanced around at familiar scenery.
"Have a good sleep, Clearmountain?" Yokatory said. "You and your friend slept like babies."
Oliver looked over his shoulder to see Yokatory slouched in his seat. "Nothing else to do, I was through eating and was told not to talk."
Gordon rubbed his head and grunted his agreement.
"We're almost there," Yokatory announced. "It's too late to start the trial today and besides I have some camp business to attend to. We'll have the trial tomorrow. It will give you time to prepare your defense."
"You're serious aren't you? You're really going to go through with this kangaroo court?" Gordon said.
"You'll have a trial by a jury of your peers, sentence and execution, when you're found guilty." Yokatory said. "And maybe I'll bury Clearmountain under my headstone, seems fitting. Why waste a perfectly good grave?"
"Do we get to represent ourselves?" Gordon wanted to know.
Yokatory chuckled. "The court will appoint a public defender for you."
Gordon shot a painful look to Oliver. Oliver understood the message. "We gotta get out of here."

The van came to a halt in the familiar area of the moving hedges. Oliver looked up the slope where he had encountered the bear.
"Look," Gordon grabbed his arm. "The bushes are moving."
Oliver acknowledged with a wink, "We've arrived in the land of liberty."
The van pulled between the two large boulders and passed the swinging hedge gate. The camp looked the same as Oliver remembered.

They were yanked out of the van by several loyalists. Oliver guessed there were thirty people in the crowed surrounding them. He was surprised no one bothered to restrain them. They were simply held captive by the encircling mass of people. Josh pushed Oliver in the back and pointed to a small hut. It had wooden sidewalls and a canvas roof. The ever present crowed moved with them. Any chance for escape was out of the question. Oliver looked at the few people closest to him. His eyes were scanning for weapons although he realized this mob didn't need any. They could easily overpower Gordon and him and stone them to death.

The ten by twelve foot musty tent contained two cots and a crude hardwood floor. Gordon was sitting on one cot, rubbing his legs, trying to induce circulation.

"That was a long trip. I could use some water. I'm starting to cramp up."

Oliver nodded as he peeked out a hole in the canvas. "We're fifty yards from the nearest cover. And there's a gunman at each side of us. The nearest tent is forty yards away."

"It'll be getting dark soon,." Gordon said. "Do you think they'll feed us?"

Oliver nodded, "Yeah, they'll want to keep us healthy for the trial."

At dusk a guard brought in two bowls, each covered with a slice of bread.

They ate in the shadowy silence. Dinner consisted of some kind of stew, probably deer, or antelope. Bear stew would have been tougher and grainier, Oliver thought, although it could have been anything. Oh well, the potatoes and carrots were good. They had also been given a plastic quart bottle of water.

By the time they'd finished eating, the last hint of light had slipped away.

They were sitting facing each other on the cots, but it was too dark to see.

"Here, take this," Oliver said.

Gordon held out his hand feeling for whatever it was Oliver wanted him to take.

Oliver handed the remaining water to Gordon. "Finish it and give me the bottle."

Gordon knocked back the water and handed Oliver the empty bottle. "What are you thinking? I can't see your face, but I can smell the smoke. You're up to something."

"Just getting ready for the morning. Go to sleep, hope soothes the tired heart."

They were both awake before dawn but chose to lie in their cots until morning light. As daylight crept slowly into the tent, Gordon saw Oliver tossing the plastic bottle up in the air and catching it. The bottle had something in it.

"What ya got there, a football?" Gordon inquired.

"Yep, you want to play?" Oliver asked.

"What's in the bottle?"

"Dirt," Oliver said. "I found it under the lose floor board. I needed to give it some weight."

"You're not going to hurt anybody with that." Gordon informed him.

"I don't plan to hurt anyone with it. You and I are going to play catch." Oliver smiled.

It was 6:00 am and Betsy and Marilyn were sitting in the kitchen drinking coffee.

"I can tell by looking at you that you didn't get any sleep," Betsy said.

Marilyn nodded drowsily. "The bed was comfortable but I couldn't sleep. I couldn't turn my mind off, if you know what I mean."

"I think I do," Haley said, as she plodded into the kitchen. "I couldn't sleep either and it's my house."

All three women turned in surprise and stared at the phone as it rang. "Haley snatched it off the kitchen wall before it completed the second ring. "Madigans." After a pause, she handed it to Betsy. "It's Sheriff Cahill."

She put the phone to her ear. "This is Betsy, what have you got Kev?"

"Sorry to wake you,"

"You didn't."

"Well, that makes one of us," Kevin groaned. "The State Police just woke me up. They found Gordon's car but no sign of the guys."

"Where?"

"It's south of here. Just east of Rock Springs."

"We're coming home," Betsy announced with urgency. "We'll meet you at your office."

Haley picked up her cell phone. "Tell the Sheriff we'll be there in two hours." She was calling someone as she spoke.

Betsy responded with a puzzled look and then shrugged her shoulders and said. "We'll be there by eight thirty."

"I better get in the shower and get dressed or you'll beat me there," Kevin joked.

She hung up and looked at Haley queerly. "Two hours?"

Haley nodded as she spoke into her phone. "Make it ten minutes." She disconnected and announced. "You have nine minutes to get dressed and one minute to get to the runway. "We're flying."

"To Jackson?" Marilyn said.

Haley was running down the hall as she shouted back. "To Sheriff Cahill's parking lot in Pinedale."

# 59

Oliver stuck his head out of the tent. The guard was only ten yards away. He looked around the camp. It looked desolate. He assumed everyone was still sleeping.

"Can we stretch our legs," he asked the guard.

The guard shouted down to the other guard, "I'm going to let the condemned men get some exercise."

The other guard waved, "I hope they make a break for it. I could use some target practice."

The first guard beckoned Oliver out.

Oliver was tossing the plastic bottle in his hands.

"What's that?" The guard stepped back and leveled his rifle at Oliver.

"Football," Oliver replied.

Gordon exited the tent and Oliver tossed him the bottle. He jogged into the open field. "See if you can throw a spiral."

"Not bad," Oliver said catching the bottle and throwing a wobbling spiral back to Gordon.

The guards watched intently as Oliver and Gordon played catch with their makeshift football. Each time they threw the ball there was more distance between them as they kept drifting further apart, but closer to the guards.

After a few minutes, Oliver shouted, "Here comes a Hail Mary." He threw the bottle as hard and as high as he could. Both guards followed their natural instinct and looked up at the sailing bottle.

The moment Oliver released the pass he broke toward the guard. That few seconds of distraction was all he needed. The guard suddenly realized what was happening a second too late. Oliver's shoulder crashed into his chest. The force lifted the guard off his feet. The groan he emitted was all the air escaping his lungs. Oliver crashed on top of him and smashed a right fist into the man's temple. His left hand grabbed the rifle. He was quickly on his feet and turned to see if Gordon needed assistance.

Gordon stood over his fallen guard and held his rifle by the barrel. The guard was struggling to get to his feet when Gordon swung the rifle like a bat and hit a home run. The man collapsed in a heap.

Gordon turned and dashed toward Oliver who was only twenty yards from a rock formation that would provide cover. Further beyond that were larger boulders and plenty of scrub pines.

Oliver could hear Gordon's footfalls behind him. He listened for a shot that would signify they had been seen. He scanned the area in front of him. There was enough dense cover to protect them and aide their escape. A quick glance over his shoulder confirmed that Gordon was still gaining on him. He swung his arm in a follow me motion and headed into the thick forest.

"How long have we been running?" Gordon gasped as they rested on a waist high boulder.

"Fifteen minutes," Oliver said.

"It feels like a lot longer than that," Gordon wheezed.

They were both struggling for breath. "Check your weapon. How many bullets do you have?"

Gordon looked at the rifle in his hand. It was a lever action, Winchester model 94. Oliver glanced at it and said. "It has a full length magazine. It'll hold six."

Gordon repeatedly worked the lever action and four shells popped out "I only got four 30 calibers. He examined the rifle for the first time. "And a broken stock."

"You must have hit him awfully hard."

"It would have been a ground rule double in most parks," Gordon said.

The rifle Oliver was carrying was a Savage model 170 pump-action. "This one is also a 30 caliber but it only held three rounds."

"So between us we have seven bullets," Gordon said. "Hell, I bet there are more than seven people chasing us."

"It doesn't matter," Oliver said. "Having a firefight with those guys isn't the answer."

"Oh, so you have an answer?" Gordon asked.

"We need to ditch the guys chasing us and get back to the camp."

## THE PAST IS NEVER DEAD

"Sort of an out of the frying pan into the fire approach." Gordon gasped, still catching his breath

"We have to prevent Yokatory and Bond from escaping," Oliver said as he looked behind them.

"You're losing me, Chief. I thought they were trying to prevent us from escaping." Gordon looked puzzled.

Oliver explained, "Those two are not in the posse that's chasing us. I'm sure they're back in camp waiting to hear if we've been caught. If they don't hear anything positive from the guys chasing us, they'll split, assuming we've made it to safety and called in the Calvary."

Gordon nodded. "Gotcha."

"Come on, let's keep moving. I'll explain my idea." Oliver started walking. "Kick up a lot of dirt. I want it to be easy for them to follow us."

Gordon walked behind Oliver kicking up the dirt and mumbling, "This is not making any sense."

# 60

The helicopter descended rapidly into the Sheriffs parking lot, nose first. Everyone but the pilot held their breath. At the very last minute he pulled up and the chopper settled gently on the parking lot asphalt.

"Whew," said Betsy, "I thought we were going to crash."

Haley cast a stern look at the pilot. "Did you have to scare us to death?"

He glanced at his watch. "Eight thirty on the nose," he said. "I know what a stickler you are for being punctual, Ms. Madigan. Sorry for the scare."

Kevin was in his office as the three of them walked in. "Ladies," Kevin said. "Let me introduce you to Agent Dawn Brann. Dawn is with the Federal Bureau of Investigation. You must be Haley Madigan." He rose from his chair and extended his hand.

"Just call me Haley" she said, shaking his hand.

"FBI?" Betsy blurted out.

"We're treating your husband's disappearance as a kidnapping, a federal offense," Dawn said. She looked intently at Betsy. "The last time I was searching for a Clearmountain, it was you."

Betsy grunted and turned to Kevin, "Any idea where Oliver and Gordon are?"

"We have a good idea," Kevin said as he sat back down. "We think they're in Yokatory's camp in Colorado."

"What? Oliver was in Montana chasing Bond," Betsy said. "Now you say he's in Colorado?"

"I think so," Kevin said. "We found footprint's in the area of the car. The print matches the Merrell Gemini's that Oliver wears. And since we found Gordon's car we assume they're together. Where we found it indicates they were headed for Colorado. That's where Jonathan Yokatory's camp is and we know he has already made one attempt on Oliver's life."

"How do you know that?" Betsy responded.

"Because I was with him," Kevin said. "I was almost collateral damage."

"I'm waiting for Washington to get back to us," Agent Brann interjected. "They are taking a look at Yokatory's Camp using SI."

Betsy turned to Kevin with a 'what did she say look?'

"Satellite Imagery," Kevin said. "They are taking digital photos of the camp. I'm told they can identify people on the ground. In a few hours we might have an idea if the guys are there."

"What if they have them locked up inside?" Haley said.

"The sky eye will give the camp a good look." Agent Brann said.

"Then what?"

"They'll determine if it's a go or no-go. I'm on my way to Fort Collins now."

"Do you need a lift?" Haley said.

Gordon was finding it difficult to keep up with Oliver

"Slow down," Gordon said. "These shoes aren't made for this kind of hiking."

Oliver looked at Gordon's brown Italian, leather soled loafers. "What size are they?"

Gordon paused and gave Oliver a troubled look. "Why?"

Oliver was already taking off his Merrill's. "Here, try these, they're 10 ½"

"That's my size," Gordon said as he caught the sneaker. He slipped off his loafers. "What are you going to wear?"

"I'll do fine." He took Gordon's loafers. "These are flimsy and the soles are slick. It's a wonder you didn't break your neck in these or at least your ankle."

"Are you going to wear them?"

"Only for a while. I don't want to change the appearance of our tracks just yet." Oliver slipped them on his feet.

Thirty minutes later they were standing in front of a large boulder that was at least twelve foot in height.

Oliver said, "This is what I've been looking for." He pointed off to his right. "Go that way for at least a hundred yards and leave plenty of tracks. When you think you've gone far enough, throw this shoe in front of you."

Oliver handed him one of the loafers. Then start back here, walking backwards. Take care that any foot prints you leave are pointing away from this spot."

"What are you going to do? You're not going to try to jump them when they come past here?"

"No, I'll meet you back here. Now hurry."

Oliver started in the opposite direction. With only one shoe on he was careful to leave only a shoe print track.

When he was far enough away he tossed the shoe further down the trail. Unlike Gordon, he was careful not to leave any tracks as he came back to the boulder.

Oliver heard the noisy mob coming toward them as he saw Gordon returning. He was walking backwards very carefully.

"Hurry," he whispered.

Pointing to the top of the boulder he said, "Give me a leg up." He leaned the rifle against the boulder and placed his foot into Gordon's cupped hands. Using Gordon's strength as a spring board, he leaped to the top of the boulder. After catching both rifles, he reached down grasped Gordon's hand and pulled him up just in time.

The brush was crashing with the noise of the oncoming army of pursuers. "This way," someone shouted. "The tracks are heading for that big rock."

There was just enough room on top of the boulder for two men to lay prone and remain out of sight from anyone at ground level.

# 61

Betsy, Marilyn and Haley followed Agent Brann into the Fort Collins City Hall.

The guard at the desk looked up at Agent Brann. She flashed her badge. "FBI," She nodded toward the ladies. "They're with me."

The guard directed them to the security threshold screener. Agent Brann walked around it.

Betsy threw her cell phone on the conveyer belt and walked through, thankful she didn't have her purse with her. That normally took awhile longer.

When they cleared security the guard said, "Your guys are set up in the third door on the right." He pointed down the hall.

As Betsy entered the room she saw three young men in shirtsleeves working on laptops at one end of a conference table. At the other end of the room were two men, still wearing their suit jackets, deep in conversation. The two agents looked up when the four women entered. The three working on the laptops paid no attention.

"Agent Brann," one of them said. "I didn't expect you so soon."

"Ms Madigan flew us down in her helicopter," she said pointing to Haley. "These two ladies are the wives. Clearmountain and Cundiff."

The entire scene reminded Betsy of a cop flick. The abbreviated language and the solemn faces. Even the air was stuffy.

Both of the suits nodded, "Ladies." They made no effort to introduce themselves.

"Who's in charge?" Haley demanded.

"I'm the Special Agent in charge," one of the men said. "My name is Ash, Ed Ash."

"How many are reporting to you," Haley asked.

"Excuse me?" Ash said.

"Your staff, how big is your staff, you know, direct reports," Haley demanded.

"The four in this room and Agent Brann, why?"

"Not enough," Haley snapped. "Have you found them in the camp?"

"Not yet, we're taking a look at the camp now," he said curiously. "What do you mean not enough?"

"If you haven't found them it means you don't have enough people looking," she replied. "It's simple." She looked around the room. "Does the Governor know about this? Has the National Guard been notified?"

"This is our case. Mrs...." He had forgotten which one Haley was.

"It's his state," she said. She flipped open her cell phone, selected a number in her directory and placed the call.

The Agents exchanged perplexed looks. Finally, the other agent said, "We're going to have to ask you to leave the room."

Haley's stare was cold and unemotional as she waited for an answer. "Governor Leeder please Haley Madigan calling. I'll hold."

The agent was at a loss for words. "I'm going to have to ask you to hang up the phone and leave the building."

Haley's expression changed to a grin. "Oh, hello Warren, it's Haley Madigan. I'm in your wonderful state. Where? Well, actually I'm in Fort Collins' city hall. I could use your help."

Haley turned and walked out of the room, seeking privacy.

The second Agent gestured to the door. "Why don't you join your friend?" He said to Betsy and Marilyn.

"Because we want to know about our husbands." Marilyn said.

"Give us your cell phone number and we'll keep you advised." He responded.

Betsy was about to explode in frustration when Haley returned to the room. She handed Agent Ash her cell phone. "The Governor would like to speak to you."

It was all Betsy and Marilyn could do to keep from laughing out loud.

# 62

Agent Ash asked them what they wanted for lunch. He had become more receptive to the ladies since he spoke to Governor Leeder. They were waiting for salads and pizza when one of the computer operators spoke, "We're getting nothing Ed."

"You can't get a good picture?" Ed asked. "Can you improve the signal?"

The operator, whose eyes were glued to his monitor, said," Signal's fine, picture is High Def. I can't find any movement in the camp. It appears the camp is empty."

Everyone urgently moved toward the operator. Two of the monitors had pictures of the camp. Each one had a different perspective. One was scanning very close, while the other was more distant, showing the entire camp. The third was a screen full of numbers and graphs.

"No movement at all?" Agent Ash asked.

"I've been spying for twelve minutes now and zilch, nadda, bupkis, nothing." The operator said. "There are a few vehicles, but I can't tell if they are operational or just junks. They haven't moved."

The terminal operator on the other monitor said, "This place is a ghost town."

"How long can you stay locked on the camp?" Ash inquired.

"We can hold the signal for another ten minutes," he said. "What we need, to confirm our findings, is the AM-1 satellite platform with thermal infrared. I could sense the heat dissipation from any creature in the area. I could tell if there is any life in that camp."

"You can see all that on this screen?" Betsy said.

"Lady, I could tell you what kind of crops they were growing, wheat, corn or oats by reading the spectral signature each plant reflects." He leaned back and rubbed his eyes.

"Can you get linked to that satellite?" Ash asked.

"I don't think so. The military probably has it tied up. I'll check."

"We need to get into that camp." Betsy said.

"I have to wait for orders from the Attorney General before I enter a camp like this. Remember Waco, Texas?"

Haley picked up her phone.

"You don't have the Attorney General's number on that phone, do you?" Agent Ash joked.

"No," Haley laughed. "I was going to rent us a car and find us a hotel. We might be here for awhile."

"What does the military use that satellite for?" Betsy asked.

The operator looked up at Betsy with a grin and said. "So they can tell who farts first, Kim Jong or Putin."

Lying deathly still Oliver and Gordon could not only hear the annoyed hunters standing just below them, they could smell them. They were within four yards of them.

"They went this way," one shouted. "Careful, don't step on the tracks."

Another piped up. "There are tracks going this way."

Silence.

"Do you think they split up to confuse us?"

"The only way to find out is for you take half the boys and I'll take the rest with me."

"Okay and if I find one of them I'm going to shoot his ass for cracking Ray's head open."

"Just remember they're armed."

Oliver could hear them separate as the noise became surround sound. He estimated each group now contained five or six men as they trucked off in separate directions. That meant there were at least twenty people back in camp, the majority being female. However, he was now sure Bond and Yokatory were not part of the group stalking them. He amused himself with the thought of each group finding one shoe. They would argue for hours about how that happened. He was comfortable he and Gordon could get back to the camp undetected.

He could hear them in the distance as he nudged Gordon. "Let's go, and try to stay in the tracks they made coming up. Let's not give them any more signs to follow."

"They never suspected us up here," Gordon said in amazement.

"That's what I was counting on," Oliver said as he prepared to jump down. "It seems that after a while trackers are so intent in following signs, they never look up."

They started backtracking to the camp at a quick but controlled pace.

As if wondering out loud, Gordon said. "What do we do when we get to the camp?"

"I don't know." Oliver said, "I was hoping you'd come up with something."

"We're in your courtroom Chief, not mine. I'll sustain your judgment."

Bond was sitting at a table in the main tent. It had plywood floors and was about 600 sq feet. It was used for a cafeteria and a meeting hall. The tent was quite comfortable. The flap windows on both sides allowed a nice flow of air.

"How long do we have to stay inside," Bond said. "I don't see why I can't go out and see what's going on."

"One of the reasons is because we're vulnerable," Yokatory uttered in a slow drawl. "The camp is short handed. Most of my men are chasing Clearmountain and his lawyer friend, so we're on lock down." He looked intently at Bond and then bellowed, "But the main reason is because I said so! Got it?"

Bond nodded because he knew he was playing with fire. Yokatory was unstable and Bond no longer had Chops to fight for him. Yokatory was mean and lean, six foot two inches of sinew muscle. Bond knew the type. They were much stronger than they looked.

Yokatory went on. "The government has been watching us for years. There are spies everywhere." He was starting to get impatient. His men had been gone for two hours and if they didn't make radio contact with him soon he was going to make a run for it.

"If I don't hear from my guys in the next half hour, you and I are leaving." Yokatory said. "We're going to need some money. How much cash do you have on you?"

"About a thousand," he said. Bond knew money was his negotiating point. It was the only reason he was still alive. "But I can get my hands on plenty more once we get out of here. I'll take you to a place in Canada where you'll be safe." He was trying to establish a rapport with Yokatory. Although there weren't any guns pointed at him, he was still a prisoner.

"How are the two guards that got hurt," Bond said, trying to sound concerned.

"They're being tended too. It's none of your business."

Just then, Yokatory's radio squawked. "Jonathan, come in Jonathan."

Yokatory keyed the microphone. "Did you get 'em?"

There was no reply at first. Yokatory stared at the hand held radio, willing it to respond. Then, finally, a voice said, "We lost them."

Yokatory threw the radio on the table. "We're out of here."

Oliver stayed in the rocky area and started circling the camp. He was trying to make his way closer to the main tent, hoping he could hear someone talking. The camp was deathly still. The sky was getting darker as a thunderstorm was brewing to the west.

# 63

"I got something," the operator on the second monitor said. Turning to his co-worker he said, "Focus on quad 4, just east of the group of large tents. Tell me what you see with your tight shot. I don't think its animals."

Everyone focused their attention on the close up monitor.

"Got'em. It looks like two guys, moving cautiously thru the rocks. One has a white shirt and dark trousers the other tan shirt and pants."

"It's them, I know it," Marilyn shouted as she stretched to see the screen.

"If it's the two we're looking for boss, they don't need our help." The operator looked up from the screen to Agent Ash. "They're both armed and seem to be infiltrating the camp."

Betsy collapsed in a chair. "Whew, they're alive and safe."

Haley patted her on the shoulder.

"I'm not sure how safe they are," Agent Ash interjected. He was looking at the screen. "They're still in that camp."

"If Oliver is armed and in the wilderness, he's safe." She smiled.

Oliver and Gordon had successfully made their way to the rear of the main tent.

"This is where I think Yokatory will be." Oliver whispered as both men crouched behind the tent. He directed Gordon to crawl to the front on the left side. "Stay low and be prepared to shoot anyone that's armed. They will." Oliver instructed.

Oliver reached the front of the right side of the tent and scanned the camp. There was no movement, though his instinct told him he and Gordon weren't alone. Gordon was lying in wait on the opposite side of the entrance to the tent.

With a nod of his head Oliver indicated for Gordon to crawl to the front entrance.

It was a wooden framed door, but the wood siding only extended up four feet. The top of the frame was attached to the canvas enclosure.

Oliver met him at the door in a crouch. "You ready?"

Gordon nodded as he got to his feet.

"When we enter, the left side of the tent is your responsibility." Oliver said in a low voice. "You only have four shots. Make them count."

He tested the door knob, it wasn't locked. He yanked it open as Gordon entered quickly crossing to the left. Oliver rushed behind him searching the right.

The center of the room was a cluster of tables and chairs, apparently used for lunch. Oliver dropped to a prone position so he could see under them. Gordon moved to the left corner of the tent. He couldn't find a target.

The silence surprised both men. They remained motionless searching for movement. Finally Oliver got to his knee and shot a quizzical look to Gordon.

"It's empty!"

Both men started to move slowly to the rear of the tent. Oliver kept glancing back to the front door, suspecting it might be a trap. After a moment Gordon realized he had been holding his breath and let out a long sigh.

"Let's check the next tent. We'll do a thorough search in here later. I know there are people in this camp," Oliver said.

Bond followed Yokatory down the dark tunnel keeping one hand on Yokatory's back for stability, while he wiped away spider webs with the other. Yokatory had a flashlight that provided little if any light.

"Damn batteries are dying," Yokatory mumbled.

Bond didn't reply because Yokatory had made it very clear if he said a word or even made a noise he would run his knife up his belly to his throat. That was just after he was looking out through one of the tent flaps and just before he lifted the plywood square off the floor, in the corner, and motioned Bond down the ladder.

Bond guessed they had traveled a hundred yards when he saw a beam of light shinning through a crack up ahead.

Bond could no longer contain himself. "Where are we?"

## THE PAST IS NEVER DEAD

Yokatory slowly turned and shined the flashlight on his own face, exposing a wicked smirk. He then shined the light down. It reflected off the blade of his hunting knife, poised one inch in front of Bonds belt. "Shhh."

He was listening to see if they had been followed.

Finally he turned and very softly said, "Help me clear this brush"

Pushing back some brush and old boards, Bond could see they were coming out the side of the hill on a steep slope that leveled out ten feet below them.

Bond followed Yokatory's example and sat down and slid the remaining ten feet to level ground.

Exasperated, Bond blurted out. "What the hell are we doing?"

Yokatory dusted himself off and grinned "Escaping."

"From who?" Bond asked.

"Clearmountain." Yokatory explained.

"I thought we were chasing him."

"When I told you to climb down that ladder into the tunnel, Clearmountain and his friend were right outside the tent."

"You should have shot them right then. I would have if you had given me back my gun," Bond bragged.

"They have weapons and I didn't like the odds of defending a canvas fort."

# 64

Oliver and Gordon approached another large tent across the camps common area from the cafeteria/meeting tent. There were voices coming from this tent.

"There are people in this one," Gordon said, "sounds like a bunch."

"That noise tells me they aren't expecting visitors," Oliver said.

"Are we going in?" Gordon said.

Oliver nodded, "Stay alert." He opened the door normally and stepped in. Gordon was right behind him.

Only the four men nearest the door noticed him. They were playing cards at a table near the door. The rest of the fourteen people were mostly women. Two were sitting on the side of bed, tending an injured person. Before any of the card players could holler, Oliver calmly pointed his rifle at them and shook his head. They understood they were to remain quiet and still.

Gordon was now standing in the corner of the tent behind the card players so he could cover the entire area.

"Who are you?" one woman shouted.

"It's the prisoners," another barked.

The room went quiet as what was happening sunk in.

A woman sitting on one of the beds shouted, "You're the bastard that cracked my husband's skull." She got up and started toward Oliver in a rage. She was dressed in Levi's and a sweat shirt and had the look of a hard woman.

He shook his head and pointed the rifle at her, "Don't come any closer."

She continued walking toward him, "You wouldn't shoot an unarmed women would you?"

Oliver realized her rage had given her false bravado. With a stern glare Oliver nodded he would.

She continued walking, challenging him.

The explosion the gun made was deafening, followed by a scream as the woman spun completely around and crashed to the floor.

"He shot me," she screeched. She was holding her left leg, moaning and swearing.

The four at the table started to react and Gordon warned them, "He's a better shot when it comes to armed men." They slowly settled back in their seats.

"Someone help her," Oliver said, looking at the room.

Three women jumped to their feet.

"I said ONE!" Oliver bellowed.

He cocked his rifle for effect and pointed it at one of the standing women. "Where's Jonathan Yokatory?"

"In the meeting tent with that city boy," she responded fearfully.

"Guess again," Oliver said.

"He's in the tent, I swear," she repeated. "Unless he…"

"Unless he what?" Oliver shouted and fired a shot just over her head.

"Unless he used the tunnel," she blurted out, as she collapsed to the floor.

Oliver pointed his rifle to another woman. "Get a blanket and spread it out on the floor." He looked around the room. "Everyone take your shoes off and throw them in the blanket along with your cell phones and any weapons you might think could be hazardous to your health." He turned to one of the men at the table, "Not you, I'll take your shoes."

Oliver noticed one of the card players was the shotgun toting Josh.

"Stand up," Oliver demanded.

Josh rose with his hands in the air.

"Just as I thought." Oliver said, as he pulled his trusty Berretta from Josh's belt.

Gordon poked him in the small of the back with the barrel of his rifle. "Where's my hunting rifle?"

"In my truck," Josh said.

They gathered the blanket and went outside. The sun was gone and dark thunder clouds were rolling in. Oliver rummaged through the shoes in the gathered blanket and removed three cell phones. He flipped one open got a signal and dialed Betsy's cell phone.

It was answered immediately.

"Hi Legs" Oliver said.

"Hello yourself, Chief," Betsy replied.

"Tell Marilyn that Gordon and I are safe," he said. "We just don't want you to worry."

"We know," Betsy said matter of factly.

"You know?"

"I'm looking at you," Betsy laughed.

Oliver's head snapped around scanning the camp, "Where are you?"

"I'm in Fort Collins, not far from you, looking at you on satellite. Wave to me."

"Have the authorities send help, ASAP. Gordon and I have prisoners and a couple need medical help."

"Consider it done," Betsy said. "We're losing the picture. It looks like we're in for a thunderstorm."

"Okay, I have to go. Gordon is going to call you right back, so you have both cell phones numbers. We still have a few things to do. See you soon."

"Did you hear that? It sounded like gun shots." Bond said. "Maybe your guys got them?"

"And maybe they didn't." Yokatory said. "Why don't you go back and find out." Yokatory complacently turned and continued down the slope, away from the tunnel exit.

"No, I've had enough of your camp and Clearmountain," Bond said, hustling after him mumbling, "If I get out of these damn boondocks I'm never going to look at another tree. Hell, I won't even go to Central Park. How much further do we have to go?"

"Another ten miles," Yokatory said, without looking back at Bond.

Fifteen minutes later Bond was struggling through the brush when he announced "I've got to rest." He plopped down on a large rock.

"I don't have time to waste sitting around," Yokatory said as he continued.

"Yeah, well as you're walking, start thinking about entering the civilized world broke. How long do you think you'll last before the FBI picks you up?" Bond shouted after him.

Yokatory slowed and glanced back at Bond, "I'll give you ten minutes to catch your breath." He settled down on a fallen tree trunk. "And while you're resting I want you to ask yourself a question. "Why doesn't he kill me right now and take my money?"

# 65

Oliver had his Berretta, a cell phone and a loaded rifle. He also had his most valuable asset, his K-1 fire starter looped on his belt. The leather case was no larger than his belt was wide and went unnoticed most of the time. It was just a magnesium fire stick no bigger than a pair of nail clippers.

"Find yourself some cover, to get out of the rain, and watch that tent. If someone tries to come out, shoot them." He looked hardheartedly at Gordon, "I mean it. No warning shots. Shoot them, do you understand?"
Gordon nodded as he stared at the front of the tent. He was wondering if he could do what Oliver was saying.
Oliver said, "They'll try you, so don't shoot to wound, shoot to kill."
Oliver knew he was being dramatic, but it was important that Gordon realized he was going to be alone in a precarious situation.
"Tell the cops I'll be back as soon as I can." Oliver patted Gordon on the shoulder and ran back to the cafeteria/meeting tent.

The tunnel opening had to be in a less traveled part of the floor. He found it in the second corner he looked. He found a battery operated lantern and lit it before he went down the ladder. The tunnel had strong beams supporting it. This wasn't an old mine shaft. This was built as an escape tunnel which meant it was a planned way out. Oliver's concern was that the other end of the tunnel had an escape vehicle as part of the plan. He knew time was his enemy as he hurried down the tunnel.

Betsy closed up her phone as the picture on the monitor went black.
"We lost the signal," the operator said.
Betsy relayed Oliver's message to Agent Ash.
"Our men are on the way," he said. "Once we knew friendlies were in control of the camp, I sent in our assault team."

Haley reacted sarcastically to Ash's remark. "Once the camp was secure, Oh, how daring of you."

Betsy admonished her friend with a look "How long will it take them to get there?" Betsy asked.

"They are twenty minutes away," Ash replied.

Haley was now pacing back and forth. "What are we supposed to do? Wait?"

"And stay out of trouble," the second agent added.

Haley smiled at him, "That may be why you went to work for the government, but it's not my style." She turned to Marilyn and Betsy. "Come on girls. I had a car delivered to City Hall. It should be out front waiting for us." She strode to the door. "Good day gents."

Parked directly in front of City Hall was a Porsche Cayenne S. The gun metal gray SUV looked brand new. Anxiously standing along side was a nervous young man.

As Haley walked directly toward him, he said, "Ms. Madigan?"

"I am," she replied, "Thank you." She took the keys from his hand. "Is the tank full?"

He held the passenger door open for Betsy as Haley ran to the driver's side. He then helped Marilyn in the rear seat as he said, "She's fully prepped and ready to go."

"I'll be in touch," Haley acknowledged as she pulled away from the curb.

"If you rented this I can't wait to see what our hotel room looks like," Marilyn said.

"I didn't rent this," Haley grinned. "I bought it and we don't have any rooms." She drove around to the rear of City Hall and parked near the parking lot exit.

"What are we doing?" Betsy asked.

"Following the FBI, unless you know where the camp is located."

"Call Gordon and get an update," Marilyn said.

Betsy tossed the phone to the rear seat. "You speak to your husband."

Gordon answered on the first few notes of Dixie.

"Yea"

"Hi honey, are you safe?"

"I'm not high and dry but I'm fine. Where are the cops?"

"Ten minutes away," Marilyn said. "How can we help?"

"Oliver took off after Yokatory and Bond. Give him a call and find out where he is and how he's doing." Gordon said.

"Will do honey, take care. Help is on the way."

Marilyn closed the phone and gave it back to Betsy. "Gordon said Oliver went after Bond and Yokatory and we should call him."

Betsy shook her head in disagreement. "I don't want to interfere with his chase. An untimely call could expose him. He'll call if he needs us."

Haley started the Porsche and pointed to a car pulling out of the parking lot. "There goes Ash, Brann and the yes man."

# 66

It was raining much harder as Oliver exited the tunnel. He half fell and half slid down the rain drenched slope. He rose to his feet and wiped the clumps of mud he had accumulated on his hands, using them for brakes, in his ten foot slide.

Tracking someone or something involves the senses of sight, smell, hearing and touch. The increasing downpour was diminishing all four. He knew Yokatory was an experienced backwoods man, so the best Oliver could do was force himself to think like his prey and do what he thought Yokatory would do. If the rain maintained this intensity he would have to seek cover. A soaking wet person who was forced to spend the night in this mountain range would risk hypothermia. Oliver was keenly aware of his error in judgment. In his haste to follow Yokatory he had failed to bring with him the necessary supplies for an extended stay in the woods. He didn't even bring water, let alone a food supply. His focus had been on an immediate capture of Yokatory and Bond. He knew he had underestimated Yokatory's survival skills.

The rain had thoroughly drenched him in a matter of minutes and as the water dripped off his nose, he cursed himself for not bringing a poncho or space blanket.

Oliver started down the trail. The loud clap of thunder and the brilliant flash of light were simultaneously intense. He had a nanosecond of warning when the hair on the back of his neck stood up. A tree fifty feet in front of him exploded halfway up the trunk. It momentarily caught fire but the driving rains extinguished it.

Oliver continued his pursuit aware that lightning was just one more thing to worry about. He saw another flash of light followed by a rolling thunder less than a mile away.

He was jogging through the forest at what he liked to call a warrior's pace. Moving quicker than a walk but not expending a lot of energy. His Shoshone ancestors could maintain this pace all day. Oliver felt he could sustain it for a couple of hours.

He paused when he came to a clearing. Barely visible through the rain he saw a man plodding through the waist high sagebrush. He looked like a drowned rat. It was Bond. Oliver was sure Yokatory was somewhere in front of him obliterated by the rain. Oliver quickened his pace. A brilliant flash of light allowed him to see Yokatory fifty yards in front of Bond entering the lodgepole pine trees. Oliver broke into a run, hoping to catch Bond before he reached the pines. Another brilliant flash of light and a tremendous crack of thunder made him halt in his tracks. The lightning stabbed at the ground like a luminous dagger. This storm was turning Bond into Oliver's second priority. The weather had become dangerous. Oliver didn't like the idea of carrying a lightning rod in his right hand in the form of a rifle. He crouched and laid the rifle on the ground. Another bolt darted from the sky and lingered on the ground for a moment. That one hit very close to where he thought Bond was. 'The little thug must be scared shitless,' Oliver thought.

Leaving his rifle in the brush, he continued forward in a crouch, offering less of a target for Tlaloc, the rain god, and his lightning arrows.

He finally rose and scanned the area. He could no longer see Bond. Oliver was sure he couldn't have made the pines, so he must be waiting in the sagebrush. Cautiously, he continued through the sagebrush. He could smell the rain and the burnt grass and sage where the lightning struck. The rain eased a little, so Oliver stood up again. There, ten feet in front of him lay Bond. His hair was still smoldering and smoke was coming out of his open mouth. His gaudy gold chain had been welded to his neck by the intense heat. The lightning bolt had struck him directly.

"Justice," Oliver said to no one.

He hurried to the edge of the pine forest, picked up a broken portion of a burned tree branch and carried it back to the body. It stuck easily in the saturated ground. It was the best he could do to mark the area of Bond's body. He didn't have the tools, the time, or the inclination to bury him. The marker might help the authorities to find it but it didn't make any difference to Oliver. A quick search of the body uncovered a money belt that contained ten one hundred dollar bills plus numerous wadded up tens in his pocket.

## THE PAST IS NEVER DEAD

The cash was no use to Bond now. Oliver threw the belt over his shoulder and quickly headed to the Lodgepole pines. One down, one to go, he thought.

Yokatory was crouched between the pines waiting for Bond to catch up when he saw Oliver enter the tree line. He was only forty yards away. He watched the Indian select a long straight pole and return to the open meadow. He followed him carefully. When he saw Oliver stick the pole into the ground he knew Bond was dead. He was marking the whereabouts of the body.

Yokatory turned and ran. He was mumbling under his breath, 'Damn, there go my finances.' His brain went into high gear. He thought, without money I can't go to the highway. I need a new plan. The first part of the plan was to elude Oliver. He was only a hundred yards behind. Yokatory came to a new rain induced stream. It was nothing more than a runoff from the downpour, but it would serve the purpose of hiding his tracks. It was less than a foot deep. He jumped in it and started walking upstream. If Bond had still been alive they would have headed down stream for the highway. He hoped Clearmountain would still think the highway was his destination. He struggled for a hundred yards upstream and then slipped out of the stream into a rocky area. Careful to not leave any tracks he continued back up the mountain. The rain had slowed.

Gordon had worked his way around the tent a few times making sure no one cut their way out the back of the tent. He had even managed to cover the sixty yards to the front gate and swung it open. To his amazement, no one had tried an escape. He was very relieved to see a Humvee come speeding through the gate and four armed men depart from it before it had come to rest. They were encased in full body armor. Their helmets had faceplates giving them the look of something out of Star Wars except they were all black instead of white. Gordon felt all four guns pointed at him as one of them ran to him.

The second vehicle through the gate was an SUV. It swerved off to the side and more agents poured out.

"Gordon Cundiff? FBI" he said. "You may stand down."

Gordon pointed to the tent. "There are 18 people in the tent, two are injured. There may be a few still armed." He felt his entire body relax. He walked over to a stump and sat down. He was drenched to the skin. As he placed the rifle on the ground, his hands started shaking. He was relieved he hadn't had to shoot anyone. He didn't know if it was the cold rain or reality setting in, but he was suddenly very cold and trembling.

It had stopped raining and Gordon needed a place to dry off. He noticed a tent next to a water tower. He thought that might be a washroom and with a little luck there would be some clean towels.

Haley was grinning to herself as they bounced and slipped through the sloppy unpaved mountain trail.

"What's so funny?" Betsy said.

"That FBI car I'm following isn't going to make it much further in this muck. I believe it's about to bog down."

Haley stopped on the next rise. There in front of them was the Ford sedan, stuck in mud up to its hub caps. Ash stepped out into six inches of mud, soaking his pant cuffs.

He looked back at the Porsche

"He's spotted us," Betsy said.

"I certainly hope so," Haley replied as she threw the Cayenne into low range.

The front tires of the Porsche settled into a puddle as Haley pulled up next to Ash, splashing his trousers with mud. He bellowed in rage. "What the hell are you doing here?"

"I'm just trying to serve my government. Would you like a lift?" Haley beamed.

"I'll send help," Ash said to Brann and the other agent as he climbed into the back seat of the Porsche.

# 67

Although his clothes were still damp Gordon felt better having toweled off and dried his hair. The rain had stopped and the afternoon sun broke through and was warming things up nicely, but Gordon was still cold and clammy. He was very pleased to see the FBI had started a fire in the huge fire pit in the center of the camp.

They'd efficiently rounded up the remaining camp followers and were marching them out the gate.

"You making them walk back?" Gordon asked.

"No" the agent said. "We have a Department of Corrections prisoner bus parked down at the clearing. Didn't want to take the chance of getting it stuck trying to get in here."

Gordon was standing at the fire trying to dry out. "Thanks for the fire."

"No problem, saw you were wet. Agent Ash told us to take good care of you. He said you have powerful, well connected, friends," the agent winked.

"Is Ash the guy in charge?" Gordon asked.

"That's who we're waiting for," the agent said. "He wants to see the camp. I wish he'd hurry because we're all done here."

"What about the group wandering around the mountain looking for us?" Gordon asked.

"We've got most of them rounded up, there might be a straggler or two, but I think we got them," the agent said. "We herded them with helicopters and they didn't give us much of a fight. Armed choppers are very intimidating," he chuckled. "Do you want us to give you a ride or are you staying here?"

"No, I'm staying here. Where is Ash?" Gordon was becoming impatient.

The Agent looked at his watch. "He should have been here by now."

The camp was empty except for the Suburban and the two remaining agents. They had on bullet proof vests and blue jackets with FBI lettering across the back. The heavily protected storm troopers were gone.

Out of nowhere a Porsche Cayenne came roaring through the entrance gate and slid to a stop. It's wheels were caked with fresh mud and it's chassis was dripping with wet sludge.

Not a bad government car, Gordon thought.

Oliver was frustrated. He never lost tracks and even though the rain had stopped, all tracks that had been made during the rain had been obliterated. He literally was walking in circles as he tried to find any signs telling him which direction Yokatory had gone. Think like the enemy, he said to himself. He's got to head for the highway, that's the only choice he has. He was convinced Yokatory hadn't had time to outfit himself, so he wasn't going to spend a prolonged time in the mountains. If Oliver found tracks going up the range that would mean it was going to be a long hunt. If the tracks went down the hill, Oliver could call for help and the troopers could pick him up once he reached the highway. He finally made up his mind. If I don't find tracks soon I'll know I made the wrong decision. He started down the slope.

Yokatory was laboring in the thin air but he couldn't stop and rest. He was comfortable in thinking that Oliver would continue down the slope, but he couldn't risk stopping. He was confident his new plan would insure his escape. He slowed his pace because he knew from this moment on timing was the most important element of his getaway. The change in the weather had left Jonathan a sweaty, muddy mess. He was going to need fresh clothes. The thought of stopping and waiting for Clearmountain, just in case he stumbled onto Jonathan's tracks, was tempting. He could pick a spot with good cover and shoot him as he walked into view.

Gordon was still hugging Marilyn when he asked,"How did you guys get here so fast?"

"We have to thank Haley for that." Marilyn said. "Gordon, you should see that girl operate. She can get things done in a mountain minute."

"We have a lot to thank you for," Gordon said to Haley.

"So this is where you were held prisoner?" Betsy said. "It looks like a girl scout camp." She was watching Agent Ash check out the camp. She turned to Gordon. "Did Oliver tell you he'd meet you here?"

"The plan was he would call you when he hit the highway or he'd return here with Yokatory and Bond. Have you called him?"

Betsy shook her head. "I didn't want to disturbed him."

Agent Ash walked up to the group. "We're all wrapped here," he said to Gordon. "I'll want to take your statement back in Fort Collins."

"As soon as I can get there," Gordon said.

"Well, we're all leaving now." Ash announced.

Haley turned to one of the blue jacketed agents. "Can you guys see that Agent Ash gets a ride back? I'll have to charge the government 35 cents a mile if he insists on riding with us."

This caused a smile from everyone except Ash. "This is a crime area. You'll have to leave," he demanded.

"Tape it off so we'll know where not to go, but we're staying until Betsy's husband comes back," Haley said with authority.

"I can't tape off the entire camp." he grumbled.

"Give me the tape. I'll do it while I'm waiting for Oliver," Haley said.

Ash was becoming irritated. "Don't make me use force," he said, tossing his cuffs in his hands.

"Don't compel me to use my weapon." Haley said, tossing her phone in her hands.

Ash stared at her in a rage.

"Look Ed," Haley said, using his first name. "Her husband is still missing. Is it too much to ask that she be allowed to wait an hour or so to see if he shows up?" Haley put her arm around Betsy's shoulder. "Have a heart."

Gordon defused the situation. "Let us be your eyes and ears up here while your guys search for him. Trust me. We won't do anything to disturb the area. I'm a lawyer. I know the value of a crime scene."

Agent Ash nodded reluctantly, "Here's my number." He handed Gordon a card. "Stay in touch every half hour, so we can coordinate our information. I don't want my guys running all over Colorado looking for him if he shows up here."

He turned toward the Suburban without saying goodbye, "Come on," he said to the two agents observing the situation, "Let's make this place a memory."

# 68

"My clothes are dry," Gordon said. "Sitting near this fire worked."

The three ladies were sitting on a log bench in the shade. "I don't know how you can stand that heat." Marilyn said. "It's getting warm out."

"How long have we been waiting?" Haley said.

Gordon glanced at his watch, "It's been about an hour since the FBI left. Oliver's been gone about two and a half."

A concerned look had overtaken Betsy. She was a strong willed person when it came to her faith in Oliver, but the passing of time and not hearing from him was weakening her resolve. She was staring off into the distance when Gordon broke her train of thought.

"Why don't you call him?"

Gordon's voice snapped Betsy back to the moment. She nodded and picked up her phone. It rang.

She snapped it open and put it to her ear in one motion. "Oliver?"

"Hey Legs" Oliver said. He sounded fatigued.

"Did you get 'em?"

"One down, one to go. Are the cops with you?"

"No," Betsy said. She was feeling better already.

"No?" Oliver was surprised. Other than hearing that Betsy was fine, it was the cops that Oliver needed to speak to. "Where are they?"

"They left, about an hour ago."

"Left?" Oliver was confused. Why would the FBI leave their office? "Where are you?"

"In the camp" Betsy said, "The camp is empty. The FBI rounded up all of the people Gordon was guarding and took them to Fort Collins. It's just Gordon, Marilyn, Haley and me. We're waiting for you so please hurry. I have a bad feeling about this place."

"The reason I called was I was going to ask you to pick me up when I reached the highway. I thought you guys were still in Fort Collins. If you're at the camp I'll start back that way. Maybe you can pick me up on the road out. See if you can find something to eat in that camp and pack some sandwiches, I'm starving."

"Ok honey, but hurry back, lyl." Betsy said and closed her phone. "Gordon, where do they keep the food. Oliver is on his way back and he's starving. I promised to make him lunch."

"Did he get'em?" Gordon asked.

"I think he has one of them. I didn't ask which one." Betsy said standing up. "He said one down one to go." Looking around she said, "Which one is the dinner tent? Where do they keep the food?"

"Come on I'll show you," Gordon said.

He held the door for the ladies as they entered the cafeteria/meeting tent. He was glad everyone was safe and he was wondering if Haley's helicopter could hold five people. He was in a hurry to get back to Jackson.

"What's the holdup?" Gordon said. Marilyn, Haley, and Betsy had stopped just inside the door. He pushed past the ladies expecting to see an opossum or a rodent. Now he stopped dead in his tracks. Standing in the middle of the tent was a very large rat. Jonathan Yokatory pointed a rifle at them.

"Hello people," Yokatory said. "Why don't ya'll just sit down in the corner?" He motioned with the gun.

"How the hell did you get in here?" Gordon barked.

"Same way I got out when you and Clearmountain tried sneaking up on me." Yokatory replied. He half sat on the corner of the table. He was eating some bread and cheese. On the table was a bottle of water and an apple.

They were all sitting on the floor when Betsy said. "What are you going to do now? My husband is still after you."

"Well now lady, I'm not quite sure. I could just wait for him to show up and kill him, or I could take your car and make a run for it."

Other than being very hungry and filthy dirty Yokatory seemed to be very relaxed. He finished his bread and cheese and grabbed the apple. He motioned with the rifle, "Get up, we're going to the bath house. You ladies can watch me take a shower."

The bath house consisted of a row of showers on one wall and three toilet stalls on the other. On the rear wall was a very large sink that could be used for laundry as well as a wash sink. Above it was a cracked mirror.

"Get in there," Yokatory said, pointing the barrel of the rifle to a toilet stall.

"Which one of us," Gordon said.

"All of you," Yokatory replied.

The stall was very small and four people fit as well as they would in a phone booth.

Yokatory wedged a chair against the door so it wouldn't open. He turned the shower on and quickly stripped, leaving his rifle within reach.

The shower had been off for ten minutes when Haley said, "Do you think he's still out there?" She had her back to the wall and her face crunched into Gordon's chest. Betsy was standing on the toilet seat. "I think I can squeeze over the top of the stall."

"No, time is on our side," Gordon whispered. "The longer we wait the better chance Oliver will show up."

"But Yokatory is thinking of waiting around just to kill him," Haley said. Then she realized that wasn't said very well with Betsy here. "I mean to try and get him."

Betsy looked down on Haley from the top of the toilet seat. "That's okay Haley, I understand."

Haley closed her eyes and shook her head, "Sorry."

They heard the chair being pulled away from the door.

"Come on out nice and slow," Yokatory said as he opened the door.

Yokatory was dressed in a golf shirt and jeans. His hair was still wet, but much shorter and his four day growth of beard was gone. He almost looked presentable.

Yokatory put them back in the tent Gordon and Oliver had been held in.

"I think I'll wait just a little while to see if Clearmountain comes back through the tunnel," Yokatory said as he pushed them into the tent. "If he sticks his head up I'll put a bullet in his ear."

"You don't have anyone to stand guard. If you're in the big tent what's stopping us from leaving?" Gordon asked. "I can tear right through this tent."

## THE PAST IS NEVER DEAD

"But I don't think you will," Yokatory said as he grabbed Marilyn's arm and pulled her outside with him. "Because when I come back and check on you and one of you is missing, I'll make this one wish she was dead, before I kill her." He dragged Marilyn with him as he walked back to the cafeteria/meeting tent.

# 69

Oliver reversed his tracks and started back up the ridge. Speaking to Betsy had given him a lift. He had been hard on himself for losing Yokatory and was letting it affect his outlook. He increased his pace. Having a goal and destination always made hiking easier. His new purpose was getting back to the camp and being with friends. The weather had improved and he felt rejuvenated. The birds were singing and all was right with the world. The authorities would find Yokatory. That was their job. His was to protect our national forests.

He stopped abruptly. What was that off to his left? A slick streak of mud that the sun was bouncing off? Something or someone had slipped. Wait, there's a footprint, and another. His heart suddenly felt heavy and his gut just took an invisible blow. Yokatory was heading back to the camp.

Jonathan Yokatory sat at the table near the tunnel corner, eating crackers. He had removed the floor covering because that's the way Oliver had left it. Marilyn sat where he had placed her, at the next table between him and the door.

Marilyn finally broke the silence "Could I have some food for my friends?"

Yokatory stared at the tunnel entrance. He slowly turned his head, gave her a blank look and went back to watching the hole in the corner.

"Why are you after Oliver?" was Marilyn's next attempt at distracting him.

This time Yokatory didn't even look at her. "Shut up," he drawled.

Yokatory heard a noise coming from the tunnel. He moved closer to the rear of the tent, out of the line of vision. The ladder squeaked. Someone was climbing up. He waited breathlessly, a head appeared slowly peeking over the floorboard.

Yokatory could only see the top of the head. A quick glance toward Marilyn showed the shock on her face as she saw the person rising from the hole.

Yokatory fired. Marilyn screamed. Hair flew off the top of the protruding head and then it was gone.

He rushed to the hole and fired again. The muzzle flash exposed a body on the floor of the tunnel. He shined his flashlight down the hole. It wasn't Clearmountain. Although the back of the head was missing, Yokatory recognized the body. It was one of his men that had chased after Oliver and Gordon. He swore as he turned to Marilyn. After a long silence, without taking his eyes off her, Yokatory said. "Clearmountain is responsible for this. He started this whole mess" He ranted. "He's after me. I wanted to let this go years ago. He's the one that came up here stirring up trouble. Trying to ruin my life for the second time." He paused with a cold look at Marilyn and continued fuming. "Seven years ago he had me thrown in jail. I lost my job and everything."

"Everything?" Marilyn said in sheer panic. She was staring at a lunatic.

"Yeah, while I was in jail my wife split and took all my savings." He was stroking the rifle like it was a pet cat.

"Were you innocent?" That was dumb Marilyn thought.

"Yeah, all I did was tell the President I wasn't going to wait for his term in office to end. I was going to remove him myself. They threw me in jail."

"You spoke to the President?"

"Hell no, lady, I sent him a letter," Yokatory grinned. "I even told him the day he was being taken out."

"Why did you want to kill him?" Marilyn thought it was better to keep him talking.

"To save my country," Yokatory said. "He and his fat cats in Washington are ruining this country. And I was fed up, still am."

"That's not the answer," Marilyn said. She was trying to keep him calm.

"It's the only answer and as soon as I get rid of Clearmountain, I'll fix the problem."

"Oliver is a forest ranger now; he doesn't work for the Secret Service." Marilyn offered, trying to quell the tension.

"That's just a cover. He still works for the fat cats in Washington." Yokatory screamed. "If he was just a forest ranger, why did he come up here lying and sneaking around trying to find me?"

"You should ask him. I'm sure it didn't have anything to do with his years in the Secret Service." It was all she could do to keep her voice calm. She wanted to scream for someone to help.

Yokatory turned and stormed over to where Marilyn was sitting. He grabbed her by the throat and squeezed so hard she couldn't breathe. She was thrown backward with the force of his grip causing the chair to go crashing to the floor. He never let go as she landed on her back. He was now kneeling next to her, still with a firm one hand grip, crushing her throat. "I was going to let you live, so you could watch me kill your friend Clearmountain, but now you've upset me by talking too much."

Marilyn's eyes started to bulge out of her head. She was sure she was going to die.

Yokatory dragged her to her feet. "I think I'll let you watch me kill your husband."

He spun her half around and pushed her toward the door with his foot. She fell on her face from the sudden shove. She lay on the floor gasping for breath.

"Get up or die right where you lay," he shouted.

She struggled to her feet and started for the door.

"Slowly," he demanded.

Marilyn stumbled out of the tent with only one thought, 'He's a madman, and I've gotten everyone killed.'

She lurched toward the tent that contained the others. Tears were streaming down her face. What could she do?

A mighty push propelled her into the tent and Gordon caught her before she fell.

Yokatory remained outside the tent. "Well folks I've waited long enough for Clearmountain," he announced in a preachers voice. "Now it's harvest time."

Gordon caught a demonic look in Yokatory's eyes. He was ranting. Gordon pushed Marilyn behind him for protection.

"I'm going to harvest souls for the Lord," he ranted. He looked skyward, "Lord, I'm going to send you some souls. It's up to you whether you keep them or send them to Hell."

"Fire," Gordon screamed.

"You're right," Yokatory screamed, "fire and damnation."

Gordon pointed behind him, "No the tents on fire."

A fire had started and was burning the rear of the cafeteria/meeting tent.

Yokatory turned and saw the tent ablaze. He pointed his gun at Gordon, "Give me your keys," he demanded.

"They're in the car," Haley shouted as she backed away from the tent entrance.

Yokatory knew he had to get out of there fast. The smoke would attract the Forest Rangers. They'd be here in minutes. He ran for the Porsche SUV. He threw his rifle into the front seat and slid in. The keys were in the ignition. As he started to turn the key he unconsciously looked into the rear view mirror.

"Hello Jonathan," Oliver said

Yokatory froze. Clearmountain was in the back seat.

Before Yokatory could react Oliver looped his belt over Jonathan's head and the head rest. He pulled as tight as he could around his neck.

Yokatory's head was pinned to the headrest. He couldn't breath. He tried to reach for the rifle on the seat, but it was too long to point it into the rear seat.

Oliver pulled tighter. Yokatory's feet were trying to climb the dashboard as he tried to relieve the pressure. He tried to turn sideways in the seat. Oliver crashed his Berretta automatic into the side of his head.

Gordon was the first one to see Oliver. He was tying Yokatory's hands behind his back. Yokatory wasn't resisting.

"Oliver," he screamed. And with that, Betsy, Marilyn and Haley came rushing out of the tent.

"See if you can get some water on that fire. I don't want the whole area to go up in flames." Oliver pointed to the flaming tent.

Gordon had already grabbed the exterior hose from the bath house tent and was watering it down. Betsy ran straight for Oliver. He just stood up in time to catch her as she threw herself at him.

"The hell with the fire," she said as she threw her arms around him. "I'm glad you're safe."

"Was there ever any doubt?" He smiled and kissed her.

"Let's go home" Betsy said.

"As soon as we unload this," he said, kicking the prone Yokatory. "The authorities will be here shortly." He pointed to Haley who had already secured a cell phone and was talking to someone.

"I told my pilot to follow the smoke. He said he'd be here in fifteen minutes." Haley said as she snapped the phone shut.

Gordon had the fire under control. "Did you start this?" He said to Oliver.

"Guilty, "Oliver confessed.

Gordon nodded. "I started it to flush out Yokatory, but he left the tent with Marilyn without even noticing it. He was in a rage. I couldn't chance a shot at him without putting Marilyn in harms way. So I hid in the car. I knew once he saw the fire he'd make a run for it. It was nice having him run toward me instead of away from me."

The helicopter settled effortlessly in the field where Oliver and Gordon had their football practice.

Jonathan Yokatory had been tied to a pole in the center of the camp. Oliver was talking to him as the others scurried into the helicopter. He put something on Jonathan's chest and then ran for the chopper.

As Oliver jumped in he said, "Betsy, call Kevin and tell him to meet us at Big Mo's for dinner. I'm buying."

Gordon shouted over the noise the rising helicopter made "What were you doing back there?"

"I left a note for the FBI, pinned to his shirt." Oliver laughed. "It said my name is Jonathan Yokatory. I'm wanted by the FBI for kidnapping and death threats to the President of the United States. Please arrest me."

He looked back and saw three black Suburbans pull into the camp as their helicopter disappeared over the tree tops.

**The End**

The recipe for Roosevelt beans that the Clearmountains and Cundiff have enjoyed was given to me by a Wyoming cowboy named Bob. They were served to me at a chuck wagon cookout and I truly enjoyed them, along with the best cowboy coffee I'd ever tasted.

## Roosevelt Beans

1 lb Hamburger or sausage ½ cup Brown Sugar
½ lb Bacon ½ inch dice 2 tbsp. Cider vinegar
1 Onion ½ inch dice 1 tbsp. Mustard prepared
1 (16oz.) can Pork & beans ½ cup ketchup
1 (12oz.) can Kidney beans Salt and pepper to taste
1 (12oz.) can Lima beans
1 (12oz.) can Butter beans

Fry meats. Drain fat, Sauté onions with meat. Stir in the next ten ingredients. (for thicker product, drain liquid from beans.) Bake at 325 F for 45 min.
Serves 8-12

Although Oliver's favorite dessert was Indian pudding, the pudding Haley served him became his new favorite.

## Cinnamon Bread Pudding

1 (4.6oz) instant vanilla pudding
2 (12oz) cans of evaporated milk
1 lb day-old coffee cake or cinnamon rolls cut into 2" squares
1 cup raisins
½ cup pecans
½ tsp. pumpkin spice
½ tsp almond extract
3qt. casserole dish coated with non-stick spray
1 tbls butter quartered. Place on top

In a large bowl put in all ingredients except the bread squares. Stir and then place 2 inch squares on top and gently push down until thoroughly saturated. Pour into casserole dish place quarter butter on top. Bake @ 350° for 60 minutes or until brown.

This Cinnamon Bread Pudding can be served with a scoop of vanilla ice cream or as Big Mo decided in his restaurant, Whiskey Sauce. There are many hard sauce recipes, here's the one Big Mo uses.

## Whiskey Sauce (hard sauce)

1 cup heavy cream
1/2 tablespoon cornstarch
1 tablespoon water
3 tablespoons sugar
1/4 cup bourbon

Place cream in a small saucepan over medium heat, and bring to a boil. Whisk cornstarch and water together, and add to cream while whisking. Bring to a boil. Whisk and let simmer for a few seconds, taking care not to burn the mixture on the bottom. Remove from heat. Stir in the sugar and the bourbon. Taste to make sure the sauce has a thick consistency, a sufficiently sweet taste, and a good bourbon flavor. Cool to room temperature